Tone Death

D. P. Lewis

**Grosvenor House
Publishing Limited**

This book is published by
Grosvenor House Publishing Ltd
28-30 High Street, Guildford, Surrey, GU1 3EL.
www.grosvenorhousepublishing.co.uk

A CIP record for this book
is available from the British Library

ISBN 978-1-78148-334-3

About The Author

Daniel Lewis was born in 1988 – this hasn't changed from his first novel. 'Tone Death' is his second book in the series - "Albert Murtland Mysteries". His portfolio of writing projects, which includes: situation comedies, pantomimes, and stand-up comedy scripts, still continues to expand. It remains his ambition to develop his writing career, so long as his work continues to be enjoyed by the public. His home is still in Shropshire, and at this very moment, Peter the Cat is purring away on his lap.

Other Books In The Series

— The Movement Of The Mobile

"D. P. Lewis is a highly-skilled author.
This is his eagerly awaited second novel."

Source: D. P. Lewis....

Dedicated To...

Mum

*The road to success is never smooth;
thank you for being part of the journey.*

Foreword

Dear Readers,

Welcome to 'Tone Death'.

I need to say a massive THANK YOU to all of you who have supported me throughout the experience of my first book – 'The Movement Of The Mobile'. The feedback has been incredible, and it has certainly meant a lot to me to see the encouragement from you all, as you purchased, read, and appreciated my words. Special thanks go out to all my friends and colleagues who really did show me overwhelming support. The kind words you all said over your enjoyment of the book, as well as hearing your commentaries, as you progressed through the pages, was quite a unique feeling. I felt privileged to be able to share my work with you, and I appreciate everybody who took the time to rate my book and leave a review on various websites that the book is listed on; these things may seem insignificant but they go a long way, so thank you. Further thanks go out to Melanie, who created posters and went to town on throwing her efforts into promoting it. Phil, of course receives colossal thanks for his time given to proofread, as well as his assistance with the cover designs, and his ongoing support and interest throughout the years (as well as putting up with my inane plans, which I rope him into without even offering him a choice in the matter). The efforts of everyone involved are always appreciated, and will always be remembered.

I received several comments over the proofreding of my first book. I know there were a few mistakes – three, I believe was the final count. It is very difficult to write a book, and then read it several times over and over again, as your eyes are tricked into reading what your mind thinks you should have written. Rest assured that myself, along with my hired team of proofreaders, have endeavoured to do our best on this particular task. When using the word "team", I actually mean my friend Phil; and when using the word "hired" – it's a complete lie…. And no, the more observant ones amongst you can stop acting smug – I purposely spelt proofreading incorrectly at the beginning of this paragraph for added irony. Those of you who didn't notice are undoubtedly going back to check it right now – difficult isn't it? Whereas I strive to achieve perfection, I like to look at it from this point of view: in my first book – yes, I had 3 wrong words, but on the other hand, there were 97,477 that I got right.

Moving away from the book, temporarily. This year has seen me plant a vineyard in one of my fields. All being well, within the next couple of years, it will be producing hundreds of bottles of wine, which, with a good book, surely go together splendidly. Also, the filming of the first series of the sitcom has now been completed. This mainly involved one hectic week where two episodes were filmed, as well as a hilarious moment that occurred while filming at a caravan park – we actually had an audience of eight or nine people from neighbouring caravans that watched us shoot a scene, resulting in a round of applause on completion. Phil took this particular starring role and managed a "one-take-wonder", despite learning his line only two minutes before filming! The sound of laughter gives such a tremendous buzz, no matter on the size of the audience. Great times. Talking of great times – 2014 also saw my sister Michelle get married to her fiancé Rob.I had the honour of giving her away, and she looked truly beautiful on the day. It's always a strange compliment to give someone – "you look beautiful today" – it rather implies that the person in question looks haggard and hideous every other day. This is not the case, and so I will amend my statement by saying my sister looked even more beautiful than normal. Congratulations to both of you – you have my fondest wishes for a long and happy future.

It seems I have developed a small fan base for my own genre of "comurdery". Whereas it is true that I have not reached international stardom or have my paperback in the Number One spot at all the bookstores (yet); it is not actually the fame and fortune that I do it all for. So long that my words provide some happiness, even to just one person, then I believe it to have all been worthwhile.

As always, I would love to hear any comments that you may have. Please feel free to email me: alpaca_dan@hotmail.com. I hope you enjoy this second instalment.

All the best,

Dan

Tone Death

Written by: D. P. Lewis

1

Albert sat in the corner of a fast-food restaurant. He could still smell the cold, greasy odour emitting from the remnants of his unwholesome yet somewhat tasty meal, as he slumped in his plastic seat with his head pressed firmly against the window. His wife Elizabeth would not have been impressed had she still been alive to witness him dining in such an establishment.

The restaurant was heaving with customers seeking a quick fix for their hungry stomachs: several single mothers with their toddlers, claimed various tables and surrounded them with their pushchairs; a group of youths joked around by hurling their chicken nuggets at one another; various businessmen in suits sat alone whilst reading the newspaper, probably deluding themselves that they were at a high-profile business meeting in a New York finance office, and two young parents struggled to keep their children under control as the mother wiped barbeque sauce from around their daughter's mouth while the father repeatedly yelled at their son to stop jumping up and down on the seat.

The rain hammered against the glass, and Albert watched as the forceful trickles tumbled over each other and raced towards the ground. Each droplet represented a tear he had for his departed wife. Never a day went by without thinking about her. He missed her kind, gentle manner; her smile and her laugh; her warmth, and of course the companionship they had shared. The trauma of not being able to bring her killer to justice ate away at him every second of every day. It was ironic to think of all the years he had spent in the police force as a successful Detective Inspector. It had been his living to solve murders, and he had not failed on any case assigned to him. In spite of that, the one case that he would not require payment for his services was the only one that he was not able to bring to a close. A raindrop hit the window and a tear fell down his cheek. He was lonely, but he stayed strong.

Albert had lost himself in an empty daydream. He had been distracted at the sight of a grossly overweight woman, shovelling a bacon and sausage sandwich down her throat as if her life depended on it. If she had been emaciated, then eating as eagerly as she did would probably have been a requirement to carry on living, but once the woman sat down on a chair-and-a-half, it ruled out the argument conclusively. It repulsed him slightly, and wondered if she was aware of the menu's "healthy-eating" option. His thoughts, however, were interrupted when a somewhat timid voice sounded quite close to him:

'Excuse me, Sir. Is this seat taken?' The young, female tones sounded pretty, and his instincts were confirmed as, slightly startled, he turned his head in the direction that it had come from. A young girl, around her late teens or early twenties, stood before him. Her straight blonde hair surrounded her pretty face and hung delicately just below her shoulders.

'No, no, please sit down.' She sat down opposite him.

'I'm sorry if I startled you.'

'Not at all. My mind was elsewhere. It's a popular habit when one gets older.'

'I can find somewhere else to sit if you'd prefer to be alone. There is a space two tables across, next to those boys messing around.'

'I wouldn't hear of it. It's very busy in here today; we can't always have the luxury of one table for each person.' He paused briefly. 'And besides, I would be ashamed with myself if I made you sit with that unruly mob. You're more than welcome here.' She smiled, rather unconvincingly, and stared down at the table as she did so. Albert pondered her expression. It was a look he had seen countless times in the past – the familiar smile that hid a persons' troubles. He stared at her for a short while, as she consumed her meal. She did not rush her food, unlike the famished beast he had witnessed earlier. Instead, she took feeble bites, almost just nibbling away gradually. He observed her actions carefully and it was almost as if she was eating like she wasn't even hungry at all. The girl seemed to notice the presence of his stare, and stopping chewing immediately. She swallowed the small amount of food she had in her mouth before speaking:

'Oh, I'm sorry. Am I eating too loudly?'

'You're in a noisy restaurant and are by far the quietest person here. What makes you ask such a question?'

'I just don't wish to be a nuisance.'

'Rest assured you are not.' He smiled. He gave her his customary kindly smile, which lifted his moustache slightly when his top lip twitched upwards. She took a sip of her drink. 'What's your name, if you don't mind my asking?'

'It's Hannah, Sir. Hannah Krause.' Albert's facial expression turned to one of curiosity.

'That's German is it not?'

'Correct. There's not much that gets passed you is there Sir?'

'And if I'm not mistaken', he chuckled, 'doesn't Krause mean curly-haired?' She smiled; this time it was a more genuine smile.

'Yes it does. Which is precisely why I straighten my hair so much – it's a slight rebellion within me.' Albert nodded.

'Life would be unremittingly tedious if there were nobody to go against the expected from time to time.'

'I agree.' There was silence for a short while before Albert spoke again:

'I have to say; you don't look German.' She put down her drink and looked at him.

'Would you be able to tell me exactly what being German looks like?' Albert stared directly back at her inquisitive gaze. Then, he smiled, his predictable wily smile.

'That is indeed an excellent question. I like your method of thought. I withdraw my statement; it was most infantile.' Hannah was quick to answer:

'It wasn't in the slightest.' She thought for a short while before continuing. 'I suppose it was more simple-minded to some extent, but not infantile. Perhaps you should have said that I don't sound German rather than attacking my appearance.' Albert looked intently into her eyes. Only a few minutes ago, he had forged the impression that she was a weak, young girl. Now, it seemed, she was anything but. The only thing he knew for certain, was however unpretentious she had first appeared, was clearly an act, and she was in fact an expert at concealing her true identity. He managed to hide his own annoyance at being outsmarted by the young girl, and yet remained smiling for one simple reason. Putting his slight anger to one side, he also felt intrigued at her victory over him. She was quite right – his statement had been simple-minded. He admitted defeat:

'I have to say; you don't sound German.' Hannah grinned broadly at Albert's remark. It was the first time he had seen her show her teeth when smiling.

'That's because the German line stopped with my Grandfather. He married an English woman. Their son, who is obviously my Father, studied at an English university, which is where he met my Mother. England is where they set up home, and it was where I was brought up. I can speak

4

German; I'm pretty much fluent to be honest. You see, by making the decision to live in England, my Father was still keen to keep the language within the family, and so I learnt it from a very early age. He would speak in German to me, whereas my Mother would speak in English.' Albert stared at the clearly remarkable girl.

'Fascinating. It's an incredible skill to know more than one language.'

'Can you speak any other languages?'

'My late wife used to tell me I spoke a multitude of languages. English, Double Dutch, garbage, gibberish and rubbish. But sadly, the true answer is no, I only know the one.' Hannah let out a small chuckle.

'It's funny how people meet, don't you think?' Albert nodded. 'Who would have thought that you and I would get on so well by a chance meeting in a fast-food restaurant?'

'Providence certainly plays a large part in all of our lives.' He twirled his moustache, before startling his new friend with a minor outburst. 'I do apologise by the way – my name is Albert.' He held out his hand. Hannah wiped her hands on a napkin, before delicately shaking it.

'So what brings you here then Albert?' She stressed the use of his name, as a sort of joke that she finally knew it. 'You seem too much of a gentlemen, and too well-dressed to be gracing this dump with your presence.'

'I could say the same about you.' He paused. 'Not the part about you being a gentlemen obviously, but I fail to see why a pretty, young girl would be on her own, especially in a place like this.'

'I'm merely passing through. I'm actually on my way to Germany to visit my Grandfather.'

'All by yourself?'

5

'I am very independent. I have found through life that it is not healthy to rely on others. You only end up hurt and disappointed in the end.'

'Those are wise words coming from somebody so young.'

'Age is immaterial when it comes to experiences.' Once again, Albert felt beaten. The petite girl sitting before him spoke as if she was just as old as he was. Yet, compared to her half of their conversation, his input seemed naïve and puerile. What he couldn't fully understand is how she spoke with such wisdom and yet at the same time conveyed the impression of being fragile, lost, and in need of help. She continued: 'I am used to being on my own.'

Several minutes passed, which seemed like half an hour or more. A waitress bustled over with a cart of cleaning utensils, removed a dirty broom and began sweeping old chips from under their table. Albert was unsure whether or not it was a less than subtle hint for them to get out. It took great restraint from the ex-Inspector to hold his tongue when she constantly rubbed over his freshly polished shoes. It wasn't until she pulled out a mop from her cart when Albert decided to say something:

'I hope you aren't going to give my feet the once over with that as well.' The sullen waitress seemed to detect the annoyance in his voice and glowered at him.

'What?'

'You've already covered my shoes with salt and goodness knows what else, by dragging that filthy broom over them. I'd be very grateful to you if you could refrain from washing them in old coffee as well.' He smiled at her. The waitress seemed to take offence to his kind request.

'Who do you think you are?'

'I am merely somebody who would rather the unwanted food be placed in the rubbish bin rather than have it smeared all over his feet. I apologise if this is an unusual concept for you.' The waitress scowled and scuttled away. The only bonus that came from the dispute was it had raised another smile on Hannah's previously saddened face. He carried on his conversation with her, hoping to keep her spirits raised: 'Well I am sure your Grandfather will be pleased you are visiting.' He smiled.

'Possibly. From what I have been told by his housekeeper, he has been taken ill.' Now Albert's smile disappeared from his face.

'I'm sorry to hear that.' He wasn't going to insult her intelligence by remarking he hoped it was nothing serious. Clearly, if he had only contracted a sniffle and a headache, she would not be making the trip all the way to Germany. Although, it seemed as if her Grandfather's illness was almost inconsequential, as she quickly moved the conversation on:

'Do you like classical music?' Albert was rather taken aback with the sudden change of topic. His surprise was evident as he stuttered before answering:

'I do. I find it soothing. It cheers me up when I feel alone.' His answer had rolled off his tongue much more freely than he had expected. He braced himself for any apparent sadness that may be detected in Hannah's eyes. He had forgotten she had said, only a moment ago, that she was used to being on her own. He stared at her thin face, and noticed the look of sorrow in her distant expression. It was like she was mourning a past suffering. He didn't particularly wish to break the silence, but he wasn't sure just how much longer they could sit amidst the awkwardness. He had found her question quite intriguing. It had clearly been something she had specifically wanted to ask; it wasn't a random question plucked from the air to engage somebody in conversation. So, he decided to return the question to her: 'Do you like classical music?' Her answer was almost immediate:

'I grew up with it.'

'That doesn't answer the question.' She ignored him, and instead channelled the conversation in the direction she wished it to go.

'Have you ever heard the symphony, *Geier Leben Für Den Tod*?'

'I'm not familiar with the name of it, no.'

'The English translation is: *Vultures Live For Death*.'

'Well I certainly know of that! It's a very famous piece! In fact, if I'm not mistaken, it was composed in…' Hannah interrupted:

'1984.' Albert squinted his eyes at her.

'Yes, in 1984. How do you know that?'

'It's just like you say – it's a very famous piece.'

'That may be, but that was thirty years ago now. You can't be much older than seventeen or so.'

'I'm nineteen, so thank you for the compliment.'

'It was Symphony Number Eight from the leading composers of the time: Hans Goldmann and Andreas…' He stopped, suddenly. Hannah took over:

'Correct.'

'I didn't say anything.'

'But you're thinking it. And you're correct.' Albert spoke slowly what he had previously begun:

'Hans Goldmann and Andreas…Krause.' Hannah nodded. 'Your Grandfather is the world-famous German composer Andreas Krause?' Hannah kept nodding.

'Richtig.'

'I'm sorry?'

'I apologise, it means correct. Sometimes when I'm talking about him, I automatically speak in German – it's a force of habit, I guess.'

'Listen, I'm sure you have to get going, as you have a long trip ahead of you, but if you could spare another half an hour or so, then I'd be grateful if I could talk with you about him. I've admired his music for many years. There's a small park just on the other side of this building – we could take a quick stroll around there.' Hannah stared briefly at the floor.

'I really should get going.'

'It's fine, honestly. I'm just a silly old man, trying to fill up his day. You get off, and make sure you see your Grandfather gets back to good health. You can give him my best wishes too if you like – just say they're from a big fan.' Hannah stood up and held out her hand.

'It was really nice to meet you. Thank you for letting me dine at your table.' He stood up as he shook her hand and beamed broadly at her.

'The pleasure was all mine.' Quickly, she hurried away. Albert sat back down in his seat. He was alone once more. As swiftly as she had entered his life, she adopted the same speed to leave it. He returned to his former position with his head leaning against the cold glass, watching the rain fall hard. The raindrops still resembled tears, as his memories of Elizabeth returned to his thoughts. It hadn't helped hearing Hannah's age. It was nineteen years ago when his loving wife was taken from him.

The reflection of the scowling waitress appeared in the window, followed by her scratchy voice, which was clearly laden with tar:

'Are you going to order anything else or not?' Albert slowly turned his head around.

'How many meals do people usually eat in one sitting here?'

'There's no need to be rude.' Albert almost choked on his own astonishment. 'Are you ordering anything else?'

'Do most people order things by staring out of the window in silence?'

'There's just no talking to some people. And I bet you won't leave me a tip.' Albert was becoming more and more wound up by the second.

'A tip for what may I ask?'

'My service.'

'Your service my dear, quite frankly leaves a lot to be desired.'

'So you don't want anything else then?' Albert stood up and put on his hat.

'No thank you. If I get peckish later on, then I shall just have a good lick of my boots, as if you remember, you covered them earlier with everybody else's unwanted leftovers.' He picked up his walking cane and tucked it under his arm. 'Good day to you!' He spun around, and saw Hannah standing behind him.

'On second thoughts, I think I can stretch to half an hour.' She smiled at Albert, and he gratefully returned the expression. They began to walk out, however much to both their annoyances, there seemed to be one final exchange with the impolite waitress. She called after them:

'I'll move your tray then shall I?' Albert responded:

'If it's not too much trouble, that would be most kind. Oh, and by the way, there are a few soggy chips left in that cardboard cup. Would you like me to stuff them under my hat and take them away with me? I wouldn't want to inconvenience you into finding someone else to sweep them onto!'

'I hope you don't come again when I'm at work.'

'The feeling is perfectly mutual; I can assure you. And as for your tip, don't try swimming in quicksand. How's that?' He winked, turned, and left with Hannah following closely behind him, leaving the miserable waitress glaring at both man and girl until they were out of sight.

In retrospect, a walk in the park was not the best idea he'd ever had. The rain has ceased, but there was a sharp chill in the air as they ambled along.

'What is it you'd like to know about my Grandfather?' Albert thought for a moment. He knew perfectly well what he wanted to ask, but he didn't want to appear too keen with his questions, as if he had waited his whole life to find out about the famous Andreas Krause. The truth was, he had listened to the music of Goldmann and Krause for many years, and the playing of their records had become more frequent since Elizabeth had passed away. He often sat in his sitting room late into the evening, his cat purring away on his lap, while an array of classical music floated from the speakers.

'Your Grandfather and Hans Goldmann composed a great many famous pieces together. However, Symphony Number Eight was their final combined effort – why was that?' Hannah looked at the ground as she spoke. Her feet splashed through the surface water that clogged up the turf, and she was trying to be careful not to tread in the deeper puddles that had formed.

'After my Grandmother died, my Grandfather was never the same. He effectively turned into a recluse, and still lives like that today, even though it was many years ago.'

'Yes, now you mention it, it wasn't just the last symphony that was composed together; it was the last piece of music that either of them put their name to. Since the release of *Vultures Live For Death*, neither one of them have been heard of.'

'It was because of a feud that started between them after my Grandmother's death. Nobody knows what started it; all we do know is that they were never able to end it. Even their agents couldn't get them into talks; they just wouldn't hear of it. My Grandfather, as I said, has practically lived his life since, in just one room of his house. Herr Goldmann, sorry, Mr. Goldmann, I assume has done the same. He hasn't been heard of either.' Albert's brain started its engine, as typically, various thoughts swamped his mind.

'When did your Grandmother pass away?'

'She died in 1983.'

'But that's a whole year before they released their symphony. They must have worked together amicably enough for that to happen.'

'Not exactly.'

'I don't follow.'

'As far as I know they had worked on *Geier Leben Für Den Tod*, for about seventeen months prior to its release. My Grandmother passed away on the thirtieth of December 1983, and the symphony...' Albert interjected:

'Was released on the second of January 1984.' Hannah stared up at the old man.

'You have followed my Grandfather's career, haven't you?' He looked down at her.

'Indeed I have.' He paused. 'So even though on the surface, it appears that there was a year between your Grandmother's death and the release of the symphony, it was in fact only three days.'

'Richtig.'

'Richtig, indeed.'

They walked in silence for about five minutes until they came to a park bench, where they sat. Albert knew it was not going to be long before Hannah had to leave, and so was a little surprised when she brought the conversation back up again.

'Albert?'

'Yes my dear?'

'I don't believe my Grandmother died of natural causes.'
Albert was shocked. This was such a bold statement from somebody who had never even known the woman.

'Now, what makes you say that?'

'Lots of things just don't add up. My Grandmother died just three days before the release of my Grandfather's most famous symphony. Following that, the successful composing partnership split up and never reunited. Goldmann and Krause had been making music together for the past sixteen years before they separated, and then all of a sudden, they both essentially disappeared from the public eye.'

'It could just all be a coincidence.'

'No. I don't believe that for a second. For a few years now I've been weighing everything up in my head, and my Grandmother's death must have had something to do with it all. It just had to have.' Albert took his monocle from his top pocket, and gave it a quick polish with his handkerchief, before returning it.

'When it comes to investigation, a sleuth must consider every aspect involved with the case. A whim is merely an idea that suggests further investigation may or may not be needed; it is not fact, and it is not proof…'

'I understand that, but…' He held up his finger.

'Let me finish, please.' Hannah kept quiet while he continued. 'I admit, there are a lot of seemingly dubious circumstances that surround her death. Indeed, why would a successful musical partnership not only break up, but also in fact completely disband, after sixteen flourishing years together? Why is their final composition of a much darker disposition than their previous seven symphonies?' Hannah couldn't help herself by adding to the list:

'Why would my Grandfather, who was a media-friendly figure for his entire career, hide away for the remainder of his life? Why does my Grandmother's death seem so coincidentally linked to the composer's separation? And why, after thirty years of silence, has my Grandfather written another symphony?' If he hadn't been hooked before, Albert became instantly intrigued.

'He has?'

'But it's not just any symphony. It's his first ever solo symphony of his career and it's due to be released next month.' She paused to create the desired effect. 'On the anniversary of my Grandmother's death.'

'I must admit that as the tale unfolds, it's all seeming less like coincidence. However, it could just be a mark of respect.'

'I would agree with you. But after researching a little myself, I found that they had been married thirty years before she died. And now, he marks the occasion thirty years after. It just doesn't make sense.'

'I think you need to try to think a bit more rationally; you're getting carried away.'

'You wouldn't say that if you knew the name of his new symphony.'

'And do you have that information to tell me?'

'I do. The name of his only composition in the last thirty years since my Grandmother's death is: *Die Wahrheit Zu Sagen.*'

'And what does that translate to?' Hannah stared at him, directly into his eyes. He noticed how her eyes glistened with fear. It was as if she had waited years to offload all this information and confide in someone about it. He saw both anger and sadness in the whites of her eyes, and he truly felt her pain. To be sure that she felt comfortable with telling him the rest of her story, he decided to ask her the question again: 'Hannah, what does it translate to?' She still stared intently at him, but it wasn't long before she spoke. She spoke boldly, and with great belief behind her voice:

'*Truth Be Told.*'

They spent the last few minutes of their time together in complete silence. Soon enough, Hannah stood up and told him that it was time for her to leave. Quickly, he took some scrap paper from his pocket and scribbled down his telephone number.

'Here. Take this.' He folded it up and handed it to her. 'This is my number. If you need any assistance, then just give me a call.' She took the paper and put it straight in her trouser pocket. She couldn't help a tear escaping from her eye, as it rolled down her pale cheek. She threw her arms around the old Detective.

'Thank you for your kindness! You don't know how much it means to me.' Albert almost had to take her arms from around his neck.

'It's no problem whatsoever. Remember, if you need anything at all – just ring. Have a safe journey.' She smiled at him.

'Goodbye Mr. Murtland.' The young Hannah ran quickly from the park, and Albert watched as she disappeared from view.

He was not a man to ever be completely astounded by a remark or a situation, but as he walked along the path to exit the park and return home, he only had one thing on his mind: he had never told Hannah his last name.

2

Hannah walked along with her small suitcase trundling behind her. The weather was a lot warmer, and drier, than it had been back in England. The River Rhein glistened a deep, sparkling blue as the sun shone down and reflected off it. She had always thought Germany was a beautiful country. Everything was always clean and tidy; they prided themselves in keeping the streets spotless, and adorning the walls, railings and streetlights with hanging baskets filled with an array of colourful flowers. She remembered once, as a young girl, having a ride in a horse and cart through the streets of Heidelberg. The horse pulling them raised its tail to execute its business, but the driver grabbed a net and caught its droppings so that they wouldn't hit the road. That wasn't something you saw everywhere, and it was a typical example of German pride for their country. The people were always friendly, whether you were buying something from a shop, or just passing somebody in the street. They really went to town on special events throughout the year too: the Oktoberfest Beer Festival in Munich, and the famous Frankfurt Christmas Market, where the streets would be decorated in tinsel and bright lights, and stallholders would be selling their novelty candles and decorations, as well as a nice glass of Kirschwein to warm you up. She wasn't a big fan of wine back in England, but the cherry flavour she'd tried in Frankfurt had a rather enjoyable taste. She'd always enjoyed coming on holiday to Germany when she was younger. Her Father used to take her to Daun, where she enjoyed riding a Sommerrodelbahn, which was a summer toboggan run. She still remembered grabbing her black plastic sledge and zooming down the giant stainless steel tubing. She always laughed when she remembered somebody once complained about her for going too fast.

Her Grandfather lived in Rüdesheim, which was a famous winemaking town. Again, as a child, she remembered travelling on the Sesselbahn. At first she had been a bit anxious at being sat in a chair so high up in the air, which only dangled by a hook from a thin wire as it moved along. But as the journey carried on, it was one of the most relaxing experiences she could have hoped for. The views that could be seen were tremendous as it moved calmly up the hills, and when she looked downwards she saw rows and rows of the lush, green grapevines that made up the many vineyards. It truly was a beautiful place.

Hannah was tired from her travelling. She had taken a mid-afternoon flight from Heathrow, and after a slight delay of an hour because of a faulty wing, the passengers had waited for a replacement aircraft to be sorted out for their flight. Eventually, after just over ninety minutes in the air, they had landed in Frankfurt, but she'd still had to get a train to Wiesbaden, and then another one to Rüdesheim. Her eyes felt heavy as she made her way on foot from the train station and into the district of Presberg, where she would arrive at her Grandfather's home. She decided against taking a taxi for the final stint of her trip. She loved walking along the river, and she knew it would only take her a couple of hours to get there. Besides, it was unlikely she would get to see her Grandfather when she arrived. He really didn't see anybody anymore, and she doubted he would make the effort when it was getting late, and especially if he wasn't in the best of health.

Presberg was a very small neighbourhood. It took no time at all to pass through it, and hardly anybody resided there.

But the people that did were friendly, helpful, and seemed to know everybody else very well. Soon enough, she arrived outside the gates of her Grandfather's old-fashioned, majestic house. It was situated slightly back from the rest of the street, with the nearest building to it being the St. Laurentius Parish Church. It had been such a grand house at one time. However, in the last thirty years he had spent nothing on maintaining or renovating it, and it looked increasingly dilapidated as the years passed by.

The house was very imposing, set in its own grounds. It was almost beautifully haunting, as it overlooked the rest of the village, even though it was still sited pretty much in the centre. A small black, metal fence surrounding the building's perimeter. Had the fence been a bit taller, it would have given off a rather unwelcoming impression, but seeing as the house itself was three-storeys tall, it became a delightful feature instead. Two groups of large, verdant trees grew close to the house, one on the left side and one on the right, as well as some pretty little shrubbery bushes that grew on either side of the stone steps that led up to the front door. They blossomed their pale yellow and bright pink flowers all over them, and made the entrance to the property very striking. The colour surrounding the place took the attention off the fact that the house itself needed serious renovation.

Hannah stared up at the house in awe. It did appear somewhat smaller to how she had remembered it, but the last time she had visited, she had been very young and knew it would have looked bigger to her back then. The house had an open porch, which had four wooden posts holding up a balcony for the level above. There were three balconies in total on the second floor, and the house boasted a tiny white railing than ran around each one. Initially, the main colour of the walls had been a pale blue, but now they were faded, almost greying, with cracks appearing in most of the paintwork. Directly above each window was a decorative, white mould made out of plaster and was shaped like royal crown. When Hannah looked up at the third floor, she saw the two small dormer windows on either side of the main one, which extended into another open balcony. She knew her room was behind the small dormer on the left, and wondered if that had remained undecorated over the years. Lastly, the part of the house she loved the best, was a church-like steeple, which extended upwards just off centre to the right of the top open balcony. The steeple turned into a long spike, which held on top of it a striking, golden weathervane on a square base, in the shape of cat catching a mouse. It was only the weathervane that actually looked relatively new, compared to the rest of the building.

As Hannah stood on the steps, trying to build her courage to knock on the door, she wondered why she felt so nervous about going inside. She had been here several times during the first half of her life, but it had certainly been nine or ten years since her last visit. She raised her hand to the metal doorknocker, lifted it up, and then stopped. She heard music. It was a delicate, harmonious sound. She looked around to find its source, although kept the doorknocker firmly in her hand. The music was faint and sounded as if it was coming from around the far side of the house. She felt a shiver travel down her spine, which made her body jolt, as she shuddered her shoulders. She hadn't a clue why it had that effect on her, but she kind of thought the sound had a ghostly feel to it. It must be her Grandfather playing his piano – it was the only thing he did in his room, and by all accounts, according to his housekeeper, he played it hour after hour every day without fail. She smiled at the thought of him still being so active in his passion. After all, he was eighty years old, and surely there would come a time when his fingers were not quite so quick, and he would not be able to perform to the same ability as he had done in the earlier years of his career. Even so, it had to be him playing.

She still felt nervous about entering the house, although she still smiled. She was looking forward to seeing her Grandfather again after so long; that's if he wanted any visitors anyway. True he was unwell, and if he was as bad as she had been told, then she wasn't even sure how much time she would even have left with him. She closed her eyes and shook her head, trying to get rid of the nerves from her mind. Standing on the doorstep for a prolonged period of time was not going to help anyone. She brought the doorknocker down on the door with moderate force and waited to be let inside.

A tall, slender woman with long, dark hair opened the door. She looked up and down at Hannah; her eyes peering above her glasses at she did so.

'You must be Miss. Krause.' The woman's demeanour was not particularly welcoming.

'Yes I am. Pardon me, but where is Miss. Sharp?' The woman didn't seem too happy at this question, and shot back a brusque, surly response:

'Miss. Sharp is no longer here. She left three weeks ago after deciding that the house was too big for her to cope with. I also believe that she had become pregnant.' Hannah was puzzled.

'That doesn't sound like Rebecca. I've been in regular contact with her for years. She said nothing about her leaving, nor about her pregnancy.'

'When was your last correspondence with her?'

'About a month ago.'

'Well I have just told you that she decided to leave three weeks ago. Could it not be possibly that she decided to leave after her last letter to you, and after the disruption of moving, has not had the chance to write yet?'

'I guess so...'

'I am the new housekeeper here. My name is Eleanor Frankwell. Now would you kindly come inside, unless of course you are planning to spend the duration of your visit outside on the front step.' She opened the door wider than it had been, and Hannah picked up her suitcase and entered the house. 'Do I need to show you to your room?'

'I can manage, thank you. I've been several times before. Where is my Grandfather?'

'In his usual room. This is a very strange place, and he is a very strange man. I haven't even seen him since I began my appointment here.'

'That doesn't surprise me. I'm one of his relations, and I've only seen him three or four times in my life. The last one of those was over ten years ago.'

'Well I shall certainly be looking for another job as soon as the opportunity arises. I'm not used to working like this. I'm rattling about in this big house on my own all day long; cooking a few meals for an old man I don't even see. It's not right.'

'He's not a well man.'

'He may not be. But being unwell does not lose you the skill of civility. By all accounts, it doesn't sound like he's got too long left anyway, so when that time comes I shall be out of here in a flash.'

'That's not a nice thing to say Mrs. Frankwell.'

'It's Miss. Frankwell! I'm sorry but if that's the way he chooses to spend his life, if you can even call it that, then in my opinion, he would be better off dead. The only people

I've got for company around here is that idiot gardener, and the milkman that calls from time to time.' Hannah's face finally lit up with a more cheerful expression:

'Is Misty really still here?'

'And who might Misty be?'

'The gardener!'

'If you are referring to Herr Reinwald, then yes he is still employed here. Although judging by the state of the garden, you would assume that he also spends the majority of his life locked away in a room. Why do you call him Misty?'

'Every time I visited, I'd always see him shovelling horse manure onto the flowerbeds. So as the German word for manure is Mist, we just started calling him Misty.'

'As much as I'd love to here many more of your reminiscences, I have work to do. You know where your Grandfather's room is and you know where your room is, so I shall get on with my work. Enjoy your stay.' Without waiting for a response from Hannah, she disappeared upstairs.

Hannah could still hear the music playing. It was a familiar tune, although she was oblivious as to its title. She left her bag in the hallway, and walked along to the room on the other side of the house, where her Grandfather spent the majority of his day. It used to just be his music room, where he would go and practice the various pieces he may be performing at a concert. A fair few years ago, however, he moved his bed inside, and also had an en-suite bathroom fitted. He very rarely left, and even more rarely did he agree to have visitors. Hannah knew something disconcerting must have happened around the time of her Grandmother's death. She was determined to find out what.

The music became louder the nearer she got to the door. In all the years that had passed, the one thing that had never changed was his music. Harmonious as ever with quirky staccatos dotted in here and there, his music was a joy to listen to. Again, the only composition that was ever vastly different from the rest was his last. It had a much more melancholy feel to it, which Hannah thought must have represented his mood at the time it was created. It seemed however, that he would rather play his happier compositions, probably trying to remember the good times in his life, rather than the bad. She smiled, as she leant against the door, just taking in the music that flowed through. She stayed there for a few minutes, until she had picked up enough courage to knock on the door. She knew that ultimately she wanted to see him, but just how much she wasn't sure. She hadn't seen him for a good number of years. He would be a lot older now and would probably look a lot different than the image she had stored of him in her head. Nevertheless, she couldn't put it off any longer, and tapped several times on the door.

The music stopped instantly. Silence ensued for the subsequent seconds, until her Grandfather's familiar, old, velvety voice penetrated the air:

'Gehen Sie weg!' Hannah shouted back through the door:

'Grossvater, ist es mir Hannah! Ihre Enkelin!' The silence resumed. It seemed a long time before he spoke again:

'Es ist spät! Vielleicht morgen!' Quickly, as if she had never even been there, he continued his playing. He appeared to play at a more frantic speed, probably to emphasise the point to her that he did not wish to see anybody. She decided the best thing she could probably do was go to bed and try again in the morning, as he had suggested. She collected her bag from the hallway and ascended the staircase.

Her room had hardly changed at all. It looked at though Eleanor had shaken a duster over it prior to her arrival, but apart from that it had the same carpet, wallpaper, bedding and curtains, even though they had yellowed with age. She was so tired; it had been a long day travelling, and all she wanted to do was get into bed. She removed her top and slid down her jeans, and once in bed, slowly drifted off to sleep to the faint melodies that came from below.

Hannah was still very sleepy when she awoke, but the morning sun that shone through the thin curtains, made it practically impossible to drop back off to sleep. She turned over to lie on her front, and stretched out her arms right under the pillow. She felt something hard; some sort of object, and whatever it was had some paper attached to it. Puzzled, she grabbed it and pulled it into view. It was a thin metal key, which had a small piece of paper wrapped around it and was secured in place by an elastic band. She took off the rubber band and stared at the two items that it had held together. The key didn't look like one for a door or a car, but more like for a tin or a chest. The piece of paper, however, was the part that most intrigued her. It was plain all over, apart from one word scrawled in the centre: 'HANNAH.'

Suddenly, Hannah no longer felt sleepy, as she kicked off the duvet and moved over to the window. She threw back the curtains, and stared again at the piece of paper she held in the hand. She wanted to get a better view in proper daylight to make sure that she wasn't mistaken. The paper was definitely marked with her name, although she had no inspiration as to why, along with the miscellaneous key, it would be under her pillow. It was bizarre enough that Rebecca had made a rather impulsive disappearance, without so much as a sentence about her plans in the letters that they wrote to one another. In addition to that, Hannah now held two items, also added to the mix of obscurity. Of course, she could just be exercising her imagination; afterall, she already believed there to be unsolved issues relating to her Grandmother's death, which she was keen to get to the bottom of. Her primary reason for her visit was naturally to visit her ailing Grandfather before he too passed away, but her ulterior motive was to investigate whatever she could about her Grandmother. She had not been prepared for the shock of finding out Rebecca no longer worked at the house, especially as she had been in the job for over thirty years. This circumstance also meant there was now a stranger amongst them: Eleanor certainly had a strange manner about her, and almost gave out the impression that she resented working there.

Hannah sat down on her bed, and tried to think rationally about everything. It was all too much for just one young mind to cope with. She admitted to herself that she needed help. It needed no further thought as to her next course of action; there was only one thing she could do.

Albert didn't particularly like flying. It wasn't the actual flying he was scared of; it was the crashing part that worried him. But whether he liked travelling by air or not, he never went back on his word if he could help it. Hannah had telephoned him for his help earlier in the day and luckily he had managed to get himself a flight. Admittedly when he had offered his investigative services to her, he had only really meant it as being somebody to run her ideas over with, and perhaps offer some advice on what aspects she should be concentrating on the most. He'd had no intention of travelling to Germany, and yet there he was, collecting his baggage and proceeding through the Passport Control booth in Frankfurt airport. He felt like a cow in a herd of many; being bustled through the gates at the cattle-market, ready to be bought for fattening up by a shrewd farmer who admired the size of his rump.

He didn't particularly like trains either. He hated the thought of hundreds of passengers being crammed together in a confined space, as the train hurtled through the countryside and through tunnels. Everyone who travelled on a train seemed miserable. It dawned on him that the types of people you find on trains don't seem to be found anywhere else – they only ever seem to be on trains. However, he knew that notion was slightly preposterous, as it was probably just the dull experience of rail travel, that turned people unsociable, as all they want to do is quickly get to where they were going, and then get off as fast as they could. Albert couldn't blame them; all he wanted to do was get to Rüdesheim so he could catch a taxi – then he would be able to relax. He stared at the various commuters on board: a smartly dressed businessman in a suit, absorbed himself in a newspaper concerning the stock market; a middle-aged chap sat opposite him tapping away on a laptop, less bothered about his appearance – he was, however, still in a suit, only the top button of his shirt was left undone, and he was missing his tie; a young lad also sat with them, earphones protruding from his ears, as he assumed a sleeping position whilst plugged into his music device.

The train journey, admittedly, was fairly speedy, and he soon found himself on the second train that he had caught from Wiesbaden. He thought he would have trouble at first with the language barrier, but he had purchased a German phrasebook from one of the shops at the airport. It had worked wonders for the first stages of his journey, but had embarrassed himself while getting his last ticket. He had opened the page that listed all the phrases for train journeys, and had started asking for his ticket, when he dropped the book. He hated looking disorganised and in a state, so he quickly picked the book up and turned to the page that he thought he had been on and finished the rest of the sentence. He had walked away from the ticket booth feeling mortified, when it turned out he asked for "a one-way ticket to the nearest toilet, and fast". Nevertheless, he had made it onto the final train and sat peacefully in his seat. It was lovely and quiet until two large African women decided to sit in the section of seats to his right and made a terrible commotion over who was sitting where, and where each one of their bags should be placed. There was nothing worse for him than having nothing to occupy his mind with, and so he found himself drawn to the constant fidgeting of the two women. They were up and down in their seats relentlessly, and if that wasn't annoying enough, one of them kept spraying her feet with some kind of aerosol – goodness knows what that was for. He'd also never before witnessed anybody, let alone two people, be so indecisive about whether or not to put their bags in the overhead rack or leave them on the floor, trapped between their legs. He had a good mind to offer to throw them both out of the window – meaning the bags of course, not the women – but he decided against it, as sometimes he became fed up of being constantly irritated by the rest of the population, and by all accounts the rest of his journey had been on the whole rather pleasant. So, he turned his head to the window, and gazed out at the passing scenery. It didn't take too long for the two women to quieten down, which Albert was silently thankful for.

Albert got out of his taxi in the centre of Presberg. His first impressions of the village were good ones, and he even remarked to himself over how every building possessed its own unique character. It didn't take him long to find the

Krause residence. Hannah's directions were clear, and besides there were not a lot of houses to choose from. As soon as he had walked over to the church, he saw his end destination.

Hannah had seen him walking up to the house from her bedroom window. She had hurried downstairs to greet him, and did so as if he were her long lost friend. It would have been a surprise to anyone witnessing the embrace to discover that they weren't related and had in fact only met just the day before. Albert had pondered their situation and admitted to himself that it was highly irregular, but he was also well aware of certain facts that contributed to the arrangement. Since he had retired from Scotland Yard, he struggled to find things to fill up his days; he also hadn't had a holiday for years; added to that, he knew Hannah was in need of help, and the kind of help that she required was exactly what he was best at. All in all, strange it may be, but the extraordinary predicament had benefits for both of them.

'Albert, thank you so much getting here so quickly!'

'Don't mention it. It seems like we have a lot to focus on doesn't it? Now before we do anything, it is imperative that we safeguard your Grandfather – I have a bad feeling about everything you have told me so far. Something is very, very peculiar, and I fear for Mr. Krause's life.'

'I'm not too worried about him right now. I spoke to him last night, and he sounded pretty much fine – as unsociable as ever!'

'Even so, you say he spends practically all of his time in one room of the house – where is that?'

'His music room; where his piano is. He moved his bed in years ago apparently, and also had a bathroom extended onto it. He locks himself in, and very rarely allows entry to anyone.'

'So how do you know if he's all right or not?'

'Because you can hear him on his piano, pretty much all day long. And if you knock on the door and call through to him, he generally answers you back – even if it's just to tell you to go away.'

'And have you heard him play his piano today?' Hannah froze, and looked up at Albert.

'No', she said trembling, 'I haven't.'

3

Both Hannah and Albert stood outside Andreas' room. Silence filled the air. Not a sound could be heard from within his barricaded quarters. They listened intently, trying to pick up even the slightest sound that could denote signs of life. But there was nothing. Hannah called through the keyhole:

'Grossvater, bist du da?' Still nothing sounded from inside the room. She tried again. 'Ist alles in Ordnung? Ich bin besorgt!'

'What are you saying?' She might as well have been speaking in Hebrew, as far as Albert was concerned, and his phrasebook certainly didn't contain a page dedicated to batty old men locked in a room.

'I've just asked if everything is okay, and told him that I'm worried.'

'Tell him if he doesn't wish to speak, then just play something on the piano so we know he is well.' Hannah gathered the translation together in her head, and shouted it through:

'Wenn du nicht wollst, zu sprechen, Klavier spielen, damit wir wissen, du bist gut!' There was still no sound. Hannah looked up from the door and both her and Albert stared at each other. Neither of them moved for several minutes. Eventually Albert spoke:

'We're going to have to break that door down.'

'It will be bolted from the inside.'

'Even so – we have to get in there.' A voice sounded behind them, which made them both jump:

'There will be no breaking any doors in the house I am in charge of. Hannah, who is this man?' Albert stepped forward and held out his hand:

'My name is Albert Murtland. I am a friend of Hannah's from England.' Eleanor didn't shake his hand. Instead she raised her nose slightly and took a step backwards. She snubbed Albert completely and directed her next question solely to Hannah:

'You did not inform me that you were bringing a prying mob with you. Would you not have thought mentioning it would be courteous to say the least?'

'I'm sorry Miss. Frankwell, I only invited him this morning.' Albert stepped in:

'And I can hardly be described as a mob – I am merely a singular human being.'

'But yet you have not denied that you are here to pry into our business.'

'There is no sound coming from that room. Hannah has told me that Andreas plays his piano throughout the day – does that not worry you?'

'Herr Krause is most likely having an afternoon nap. He is elderly and unwell, and would probably not appreciate being woken up. Now, if you'll excuse me I have duties to attend to.' She turned to Hannah. 'I shall add the preparation of your friend's evening meal to my never-ending list of jobs.' She spun around and quickly disappeared across the hall into the kitchen.

'Isn't she a barrel of laughs?'

'I wouldn't take it personally; I received a similar greeting when I arrived.'

'We still need to get into that room.'

'I know. Perhaps if we wait until…' Hannah was interrupted by the sound of music. The smooth melody of one of Andreas' symphonies sounded softly through the walls. They looked at each other and smiled. 'I guess we overreacted.'

'Maybe we have this time, but don't forget why you asked me to come here.'

'I know.' They began walking away from the room when Eleanor stepped out of the kitchen.

'What did I tell you? Nothing to worry about.'

'You don't mind us caring do you?' Albert asked. Eleanor replied, without the slightest hint of emotion on her face:

'Caring: no; interfering: yes.'

'We're not interfering. Hannah just wants to see her Grandfather.'

'And she will soon, I'm sure.' Just like before, she turned and vanished into the kitchen. Neither of the two remaining houseguests spoke for a while. Instinctively, they moved silently away from the kitchen and went up the stairs. When safely out of earshot in her bedroom, Hannah shut the door behind them. Only then did Albert speak:

'There is something dreadfully strange about that woman.' Hannah just looked at him, unsure whether to agree or disagree. Albert thought she might have at least voiced an opinion on his remark. It was as if there was something she wasn't telling him.

The rest of the evening was pretty quiet. Albert was shown to his room, and he made himself at home, as best as he could. During the evening meal, everybody sat in silence. The only diners, apart from him, were just Hannah and Eleanor. Misty, the gardener, had finished his day's work by the time they ate and so he always returned home. The most peculiar thing that Albert had observed so far, and possibly even in his life, was a giant cat flap fixed to the bottom of the door that led to Andreas' music room. When he'd plucked up the courage to ask Eleanor if he had a feline friend, he became confused to hear that her answer was no. Luckily for him, however, she must have been in an improved mood, when, just before dinner she showed him its use. She carried a hot plate of freshly cooked food from the kitchen, and knelt down beside the door. She rapped on the cat flap with her knuckles and shouted:

'Abendessen!' She turned to Albert. 'That means "dinner".' He nodded to acknowledge her. They waited just a few seconds before the cat flap was pushed outwards. Eleanor positioned the food in front of the newly formed gap, which was taken from her and pulled inside the room, with the cat flap hastily shutting behind it. A small voice sounded from inside the room:

'Vielen Dank.' Eleanor got back up to her feet.

'Don't say a word Mr. Murtland – I find it all just as peculiar as you do.' This was the most pleasant he had ever seen the woman.

After they had eaten, Albert excused himself and went up to bed. If he could, he would rather arise early and go for a brisk walk, rather than stay up late making pointless conversation. He lay down on the hard mattress, and rested his head upon the moderately dusty pillow, and felt his eyes closing. He had a feeling something bad was going to happen – and soon.

He awoke to the tune of one of his favourite Goldmann and Krause symphonies faintly sounding from the music room downstairs. He smiled to himself for two reasons: firstly, it was a rather pleasant awakening, and secondly, at least Andreas was still alive, which showed that his health hadn't failed him yet, and also that nobody with brutal intentions had got to him during the night.

It was a lovely, bright morning. Autumn was his favourite season; he had decided on that a long time ago. The majority of the leaves that had fallen from the tree were a delightful golden-brown colour, and as he walked along, they made a nice, crisp sound as they crunched beneath his feet. The low sunlight really enhanced the colours as well as making the dew on the grass sparkle, with an almost diamond-like effect. The air was fresh; it had just the right amount of that satisfying chill to it that cooled his face with every footstep. He was surprised at just how far back the garden stretched. It was a beautiful, long garden, directly behind the house, which went back a fair way until it ended at a row of trees. Halfway down, on the left, was a small hutch, which Albert noticed contained a group of ferrets, which were eagerly scraping at the surrounding wire, trying to get themselves loose for a mischievous run around. He counted six ferrets in total as he ambled past. The garden narrowed quite considerably towards the end, but there was an understandable reason for it. After the ferret cage was a small stream that forced the grass to become a pathway alongside it. The water flowed towards the trees that sealed the end of the garden. It was quite difficult to get to the trees at the end, as a goat stood on the embankment, tied to a pole, and refused to let him pass for a while. He wondered whom the goat belonged to; it was a rather random pet to have, especially if the six ferrets were added into the equation. Personally, Albert was quite happy with a cat. Eventually, he managed to stumble around the goat, but only by taking a step down nearer the river – an action forced upon him by the insubordinate creature. When he reached the trees at the bottom of the garden, he noticed on closer inspection that they actually acted as an entrance to a small woodland area, where both the stream and the path carried on. Albert decided not to walk any further, but depending on the length of his stay, certainly intended to continue his route on another day. He turned, and made his way back to the house, but felt slightly exasperated on sight of the goat ahead, which was still blocking his path.

The shiny new milk float, embossed on the side with the words "Mohler Molkerei", pulled up outside the Krause residence. The van was bright yellow, and had the traditional open-back, which carried all the blue crates with the milk bottles stacked in. Albert watched as a scruffy-looking chap shuffled around the side of the house to greet the milkman that had hopped out of the driver's seat. He came to the conclusion that the dishevelled individual must be the gardener, whom Hannah had spoken about. He was wearing his trademark shabby green coat, which Hannah maintained he'd had for almost four decades; her evidence being what she can remember herself, as well as seeing some old pictures of when the gardener was much younger. She had enlightened him as to the origins of his nickname Misty, which she called him, however, fortunately she had also told him his actual name – Stefan Reinwald. Albert thought this was a rather posh-sounding name for someone who looked like they had just crawled out of a skip and spent their time working as hired help amongst the worms and the dirt. Nevertheless, perhaps the man had just fallen on hard times, or he supposed it was conceivable that any persons' name was insignificant in relation to anything that happened to them in their life. Afterall, everybody had to do something, whether that was a road sweeper named Cornelius, or a High Court Judge called Bert. Albert chuckled to himself, as he walked steadily along the pathway near to the house, resting the bottom of his cane lightly on the gravel as he went along. Albert had been flicking through his phrasebook briefly whilst in bed, before he had got up for his morning stroll. He shouted over to the two men at the gate:

'Guten Morgen!' Both men looked over at him. The milkman shouted something across to him, which may as well have been Swahili. Albert just smiled and nodded back to him. The term "good morning" was all he had managed to learn, and he had hoped that anybody he said it to would just return the same greeting to him. Stefan didn't speak, but instead waved. Albert had no choice but to walk nearer to them if he wanted to get inside the house. He sincerely wished they spoke nothing else to him, mainly to avoid embarrassment on his part. Luckily, Hannah had come outside to speak to Stefan, as she hadn't seen him since her arrival. She greeted him with a big hug, and he was clearly pleased to see her again. Albert detected he must have been great fun to have around the house when she spent her holidays there as a young child. From what Albert could detect, owing to the odd point towards him as well as the mentioning of his name, Hannah was explaining to Stefan who he was. Stefan had a very broad, stereotypically country-farmer tone to his voice, but obviously with German influence; it really was quite unique. The milkman listened in, perhaps feeling somewhat awkward, as his job was solely to deliver the milk rather than be involved in a very obscure family reunion. He stood there cradling four milk bottles while Hannah and Stefan carried on speaking. At least he could understand the conversation, which was a bonus that Albert didn't have – he didn't even have any milk to hold. The only element that Albert was able to pick up on was, despite the gardener speaking in German, he was clearly not intellectually minded. That wasn't to say he was unintelligent about the things he knew of, but he clearly spoke slowly, and gave off the impression of being quite simple-minded through the manner of his speech. After watching Stefan's lips move for quite some time, Albert diverted his attention back to the milkman and noticed that three of the milk bottles had green tops, and the other had light blue. Obviously somebody in the household preferred a different variety of milk to the others. When the conversation had drawn to a close, Stefan walked over to Albert and shook his hand. He had very rough skin, full of cuts and cracks – probably the typical hands of a good worker. Then, after letting go of Albert's hand, he took the milk off the milkman and carried it inside the house.

'Sorry Albert, Misty doesn't speak a word of English. But I've told him who you are and that you are a good man.'

'That's very kind of you.' Albert smiled. The milkman still stood there. He was practically a young lad, probably late twenties. He was dressed quite smartly, especially seeing as he was doing his milk round. Still, taking pride in ones appearance, was a brilliant value to have, and there was nothing wrong with showing a bit of class whatever the nature of the job. Perhaps Stefan should take down some notes from him. It was soon evident that he'd had enough of keeping silent, however, as it wasn't long before he too joined in by introducing himself:

'Hello. I'm Thomas Mohler.' He held out his hand to Albert, who was rather shocked. 'Don't be alarmed', Thomas smiled, 'I'm only speaking English, same as you.' Albert took his hand, and gladly shook it.

'I do apologise. It just threw me, that's all. Pleased to meet you – I'm Albert Murtland.'

'So I gathered from young Hannah here. What are you doing all the way out here then? It's a long way from home.' Hannah interrupted:

'If you'll excuse me, I'm going to go and see if I can get into the music room – third time lucky!' Albert nodded and Thomas wished her well, so she ran off up the steps and disappeared inside.

'It certainly is a long way from home. One flight, and two train journeys, but I made it. Tell me, you speak English remarkably well – too well for just learning at school. How have you got to be so fluent?'

'My girlfriend is an English teacher in Assmannshausen, so I suppose if she speaks English to me it's like I'm at school all year round.' Albert laughed.

'Indeed! I suppose it would be.'

'I heard Miss. Krause say you're a Police Detective – there's nothing wrong here is there?'

'I used to be a Detective, that is correct. However, I have been retired a while now, so there's no need to worry. I am merely here for a holiday; it's been a good few years since I have been able to get away.'

'Well Rüdesheim am Rhein is the perfect place to come and relax. Have you been on the cable car yet?' He didn't even wait for Albert to answer. 'That's very peaceful and gives out some spectacular views.'

'I'm afraid I actually only arrived yesterday. But I'd certainly like to explore the area as much as I can while I'm here.'

'You should, you should. You want to take a trip down the Drosselgasse – I don't know if you've heard of it, but that's very famous.'

'I can't say I've heard of it.'

'Or if you like your history, there's the statue of Germania at the top of the Niederwald Mountain, or Rheinstein Castle near the town of Trechtingshausen.'

'Well thank you – I'll bear all that in mind.'

'And you're sure there's nothing going on here, what with you being an ex-police officer and everything?'

'I can assure you my visit here is perfectly innocent.'

'I apologise, it's just with Rebecca's disappearance, there's been rumours in the village about her being kidnapped, only it's been covered up just to keep the peace and harmony here. Presberg is a quiet place, and nobody wants any trouble. It would be all over the news if anything like that happened. Nobody here wants their lovely, tranquil village swarming with police investigators, reporters, and meddlesome bystanders. The place would never be the same again.' The man seemed shifty and on edge. He looked as if he was edging closer to his vehicle with every word he spoke.

'Mr. Mohler, just think about it logically for a moment. If anything untoward were occurring here, why would a retired detective from England be called in to investigate? I'm sure Germany has its own police officers – am I wrong?' Thomas thought about it for a few seconds before answering:

'You're right, of course. It's only because this particular house nearly brought this village to its knees many years ago. I wasn't born at the time, but my father has told the story to me many times.'

'And what story might that be?'

'It's the famous composer, Andreas Krause, who lives here, as you know. His wife died in peculiar circumstances. It was eventually ruled as an unfortunate, but natural incident, however, there were rumours flying around about suicide, but also about murder. It ruined Presberg for months, as tourists boycotted the village. Nobody wanted to come here, because let's face it, if a beautiful place such as this could be subject to such hideous accusations, then it just proves that nobody is safe anywhere.' Albert nodded.

'I understand. But like I said, rest assured that I am simply here on vacation.' Thomas took in a big intake of air, and slowly exhaled it. Albert watched his chest deflate, which seemed to have a calming influence on the man.

'I'm sorry.'

'There's no need to be.' The two men stared at each other for a few awkward moments. 'I'd better let you get on with your milk round – I'm guessing you don't want to be delivering sour milk to everyone.'

'That's true! I'll be on my way. Pleased to meet you anyway Mr. Murtland.' He hurried away, and jumped back into his truck. He took a quick, final glance at Albert, before speeding off down the lane. Albert was left in a state of confusion. Thomas Mohler certainly seemed to know a lot, but perhaps he was simply just a concerned citizen.

Stefan was busy digging in the garden. He had a whole row of new plants to put in a long border that surrounded a rockery. In the centre of the rockery was a stone animal of a large frog. It perched itself on top of a large moss-covered rock. Owing to its faded colour, it was clearly an old ornament, but it still fitted in perfectly with the nature of the rest of the garden. The dim gardener dug away merrily; happy in his work, and whistled a dissonant tune as he knelt down to plant the new additions in the flowerbed. As he lowered himself to the ground, he felt a large insect of some kind, like a wasp or a damselfly, shoot passed his ear. It startled him at first, but was used to experiencing that sort of occurrence while working outdoors. Especially during the summer months, he had collided with creatures of the flying world on numerous occasions: moths; bees; butterflies; earwigs, and one occasion when wearing a yellow shirt on an extraordinarily hot day, he had only been outside for around fifteen minutes and found his shirt had turned from yellow to black as hundreds of miniature harvestmen had been attracted to it in an instant. Similarly, there had been many times he had walked through the long grass in various sections of the woodland and been stung by an errant nettle that had been hiding in the overgrowth. He tried to look out for them but they camouflaged themselves so expertly.

He felt an uncomfortable atmosphere as he resumed his work, and turned around to find Eleanor glaring at him from a fair distance away, up near the house. She was standing behind the coal shed, which was an unusual place for a housekeeper to be loitering. She just stood there and stared at him. He felt like he was doing something wrong, and yet he was doing nothing but his daily chores. After a singular, unnerving minute, he decided to continue with his work. He didn't wish to keep looking at her. It was her glare that disturbed him the most. The look on her face had pierced through his skin and touched his very soul, and her eyes appeared dead, which haunted him tremendously. He shook his head to try and forget the image, and brushed away an itch that was niggling him on his ear. His ear hurt him when he touched it, and as he brought his hand down to carry on with the planting, he noticed that his ear was now bleeding. He looked back up to where Eleanor had been standing. She was gone.

Undeterred by the incident, Stefan carried on working. He had finished with all the plants that he'd brought over in his wheelbarrow, and had decorated the circular border with them. Bright colours of fuchsia, yellow, deep red, and light blue now stood out brilliantly, and were a much more pleasant addition than the unmanageable, dull green climbing plant that crept through the dirt. To finish his work on the rockery, he only had to dig in a cherry blossom tree, which would thrive in pretty pink when it bloomed. He picked up his spade and stepped over the flowers he had just planted, being careful not to tread on any of them, and made his way to the centre. The idea was to plant the tree behind the stone frog, which he had decided would look quite charming, especially when the tree was in flower.

He shoved his spade into the ground, and rested his foot on the shoulder of the blade to give it enough pressure to sink in deeply. He began churning up the soil and tipped it all into a pile a short distance away from the hole. He would use it again when the tree was in place, to compact it firmly into the ground. Strangely, the soil moved very easily, which he thought was odd seeing as they'd just had a fairly long stretch of warm, dry weather. He didn't let it bother him too much, however, as he certainly wasn't going to complain about it.

After about ten minutes of digging, he began to notice a strange smell lingering in the air around him. He thought he might have thrust his spade through a sewage pipe, as he was now quite deep, but looking around, he couldn't see any channel that the sewage could possibly run through. Besides, it was an unlikely place for a drainage system to be located. He carried on digging and just hoped that the stench was just passing by. Unfortunately for him, it was quite the contrary. As he kept digging, further and further down towards the Earth's core, the smell became increasingly apparent. It had become much stronger and he knew it would not be going away. About two feet down the smell was rancid, and it clung to the back of his throat. His spade hit a hard section in the soil, which hurt his wrist as it jolted backwards. He was now almost heaving at the odour that came from the wide-open hole. Quickly, the retching gardener dropped to his knees, and scraped his fingers over the hard part he had just hit. The mysterious object was like a hard, dry ball, but with an uneven surface, and seemingly covered in dents and holes. As he uncovered even more of the ground's possession, he knew that the putrid stench was unmistakeably rotting flesh. An army of wriggling maggots squirmed in and out of various cavities, which made him gag even more. He used the end of his sleeve to cover his nose and his mouth, in the vain hope that the smell would not be able to penetrate through his dirty clothing. One hand was now all he had to uncover his unwanted prize. Frantically scraping at it, so that he needn't stay any longer than he had to, he flicked the dirt off, merely so he could confirm beyond any doubt what he feared the most.

Whilst avoiding the maggots and trying his best not to be sick, he scraped his hand across it for the final time. He turned away in horror, and hurriedly threw up on the centre of the rockery. He wiped his vomit away from his mouth with his sleeve and stared back into the hole. The dry, withered face of a corpse stared back at him.

4

The body lay embedded in the soil. The hair had fallen out, although its teeth still remained, albeit looking very brittle. Stefan had raced into the house to tell everybody of his horrific find, and Miss. Frankwell had telephoned for the local constabulary immediately. Three police vehicles had pulled up outside the large house, containing crime scene investigators, as well as many high-ranking officers. A policeman stood guard outside the front door, and other officers manned the rest of the entrances to the building. One even patrolled at the end of the garden just in case anybody had access to the property via the woods.

The presence the police emitted had a frightening effect on the neighbourhood. Many cars drove slowly passed, trying their best to gaze both into the house and around the back. Largely this was an unsuccessful attempt at nosiness, although in some cases it only encouraged drivers to park their vehicles on the side of the road before getting out and wandering over. Around the back of the house, near the rockery, the whole area had been cordoned off, and Stefan was being questioned by a couple of officers near the coal shed. The poor man was still in shock and could barely answer what he was being asked. Hannah stood with him to help steady his nerves, but even her attendance didn't help matters much. Eleanor remained inside the house, not particularly wishing to catch a glimpse of the rotting body that lay buried in the ground. She much preferred to sit outside the music room and make sure that Andreas continued his music. She had been very worried recently about his health, more so than she let on, and didn't want to bother him with the recent events in case it worsened his condition. She knew the police would undoubtedly want to speak to him, in the slim hope that he would be able to shed some light on the matter, but then, and only then, would she allow him to become aware of the incident.

Albert hovered closely on the other side of the red and white barricade tape that segregated the rockery from the rest of the garden. It was essential that the area was preserved; otherwise any evidence that remained on the scene was at risk of being contaminated. The tape read: "POLIZEIABSPERRUNG". He assumed this meant something similar to the familiar "POLICE LINE DO NOT CROSS", which he had seen so many times in his career. He was peering over the tape, when a young policeman walked over.

'Schritt rückwärts bitte.' He was very abrupt in his manner but then again Albert knew he himself would be, and had been, the same. He pointed to himself.

'I am English.' The policeman looked at him, with a suspicious expression, glowering at Albert. He called over one of his team members, which Albert knew by the superior uniform, was a more senior officer. The young constable muttered something to him and was then dismissed to the other side of the secured zone. The older officer walked closer to Albert and towered above him. He clearly spoke some English, even if he was not fluent.

'My colleague told you to step backwards.' His speech was broken and he seemed unsure of whether or not he was using the correct words.

'I apologise. It is a force of habit. Tell me, what does this tape say?' He pointed downwards at the item in question.

'It says: Polizeiabsperrung.' The policeman smiled. Albert detected this was going to be an awkward conversation.

'I meant what does it mean in English?' The officer spoke slowly:

'Police barrier.'

'Thank you.'

'Now step backwards.'

'I am a retired Detective Inspector you know.' The policeman grinned again, this time showing his teeth. In fact, it came across more like a snarl.

'Well I am Sergeant. But I am not retired.'

'Now look, my name is Albert Murtland – I'm very well-known back in England.' The officer bent over and leant nearer; he positioned his face very close to Albert's.

'But you are not in England.' He stood up sharply and straightened his back. 'You are in Germany! And here, you are nobody. Now step backwards.' Albert couldn't really argue with him; he was, of course, completely right. He conceded defeat and went to join Hannah who was just about finished providing her moral support for the distressed gardener.

Hannah sat with Albert in her bedroom; they were both still in shock. Albert was perhaps not quite so taken aback as she was; he was used to such things, although, despite being familiar with the image of dead bodies, the pleasantness of the experience was never enhanced when seeing another one. The nature of the person's death was clear to him, judging by the obvious circumstances surrounding it. Undoubtedly, they had a murder case to deal with. There was hardly a chance that somebody would have died by natural causes and end up being buried in someone else's garden. Similarly, the same could be said for someone who had committed suicide. The deceased would certainly not have been able to bury themselves, and there would almost be no logical reason for anyone else to do so should the nature of death not have been murder.

'I wonder how long it's been there.' These were the first, timid words that Hannah had uttered since their arrival in the bedroom. Albert stared at her. He wasn't sure if he should enter into a conversation about it; afterall, it wasn't a very enjoyable subject. Nevertheless, Hannah carried on: 'Who do you think it was?'

'I really have no idea. But we'll find out – I promise.' He had to offer her a reassuring reply. The trouble was; he had no idea how he was going to be allowed to get involved in the necessary procedures to ascertain the identity of the victim, as well as the cause and the reason for their death.

'It looked horrible.' She paused. 'I remember watching a documentary once about how they used to bury people in Ancient Egypt. The Egyptians used to bury the poor citizens by just digging a hole in the desert and covering them over with sand. I saw the images on the television. They just looked like the scrawny remains of somebody who once existed – all curled up; almost crippled. They were dark brown in colour, and what was left of the skin looked taut and incredibly thin, as you could pretty much clearly see the skeletal frame beneath it. That's what I was reminded of today. It was just horrible.' Albert left what he thought was an appropriate gap before answering. He didn't feel it was a good time for rushed conversation.

'It was sand that preserved the body because it was both hot and dry. It dehydrated the bodies quickly, which essentially mummified them.' Hannah looked up at him. She was partially interested in his elaboration on her story, but she was also thankful that just by listening to him, he was taking her mind off the awful image she had seen. 'When we bury somebody in a coffin, we embalm them, which preserves the body a lot better and it takes years for it to fully decompose into a skeleton.' Hannah pondered what he was saying.

'How long would you say that body had been in the ground?'

'By the look of it – not long. Don't forget that it wouldn't have undergone the embalming process and so the body was not equipped for dealing with its own preservation. With the conditions underground as they are, and without embalming, the rate of decomposition is much faster. Because the hair had fallen out, and yet the teeth were just about still attached, I'd estimate it's been there about a month.' Hannah released some tears, practically uncontrollably.

'As recent as that?' Albert got the impression that she had hoped it had been there for years.

'What does it matter? Unfortunately, I'm afraid these things happen. And whether it was a month ago, ten years ago, or even last week – you won't have known the person. I know that sounds a bit heartless towards the poor person in the ground but I'm just trying to tell you that at least it wasn't someone you knew or cared about.'

'I've just got one horrible thought going through my mind, and I can't get rid of it!'

'Then tell me what it is you are thinking.' Hannah took in a deep breath before she started speaking. She hoped what she had to say wasn't true, but no matter how hard she tried; she couldn't remove the thought from her mind.

'You remember that Rebecca was the old housekeeper before Eleanor don't you?' Albert nodded.

'Well Rebecca and I used to write to each other, and at no point did she ever even suggest that she was thinking of leaving. Added onto that, Miss Frankwell also told me that she had become pregnant, whereas I wasn't even aware she was seeing anybody! As far as I'm concerned, Rebecca has made a sudden disappearance, and I can't figure out any explanation for her departure.' Tears began weeping from her eyes again. 'And now this body has been found in the garden, which you say has been there about a month, and my last contact with her was around the same time!' Albert found her slightly difficult to understand, as she became more and more upset as she went on. 'Miss. Frankwell also said that Rebecca left her job about three week ago and we also have that random piece of paper with my name on it, along with a key that we have no idea what it is for! But the writing on the paper looks a lot like Rebecca's!' Albert put his arm around the distraught girl, and she cuddled into his chest for comfort. Albert agreed that there was something mysterious about the whole situation, but he had been expecting something bad to happen to Andreas; he hadn't concerned himself with the thought that anyone else could be in danger. He decided to reopen the conversation at a different point, rather than upsetting Hannah even more over Rebecca:

'How is your Grandfather today? Have you seen him yet?' Hannah wiped her eyes on her sleeve.

'I've heard him playing, and I saw Miss. Frankwell pass his breakfast through to him so he's okay. I must say I feel rather stupid bringing you all the way out here for nothing.' Albert raised his finger in protest to her apology.

'Instinct, my dear girl, is one of the most powerful senses we possess. Usually, when you go with your gut feeling, you are correct. When you have something bothering you, I find that natural impulses typically offer you the best course of action. You can try to think things through rationally but your subconscious intuition has your answer ready for you the moment you are aware of the problem you face.'

'I don't understand.'

'If you asked me to come out here to assist you then the overriding decision in your mind was that something was wrong. You were right to bring me out here.'

'But I only wanted to find out about my Grandmother, and establish exactly what happened before she died.'

'But you must have known deep down that resurrecting the past would only lead to someone getting hurt, as there would no doubt be other people who would like the events of the past to remain a secret. That's why you requested my presence here.'

'Are you saying that the body in the ground is my fault? And whoever it is, is dead because of me?'

'No, I'm not saying that at all. I'm sure that's completely unrelated. Let's be realistic – it is only you and I that know you wish to find out about your Grandmother. You haven't mentioned it to anyone else have you?'

'No, I promise you're the only person I've told.'

'There you go then. It can't possibly be related to you; it's just an unfortunate incident, that's all.' They sat in silence a while longer before Hannah revived the discussion:

'You know what you said about going by your instincts?' Albert nodded, which was a signal for her to continue. 'You're right; it's true.'

'I know I'm right. Why else would you take the trouble to seek me out back in England?' Hannah looked shocked.

'I didn't seek you out!'

'But you did. You knew my surname before I'd even told you what it was.' Hannah quickly looked down at the floor. 'It's okay; I'm not angry with you. I'd just like to know why.' She stuttered:

'I can't tell you why.'

'You should be honest with me.' She didn't reply. 'Hannah, why did you purposely find me to help you with this?' Eventually she gave him an answer:

'I wanted somebody I knew I could trust.'

'But you don't know me at all, so how do you know you can trust me?' She stopped looking at the floor, and stared into his eyes. He saw her eyes were red and stained from the tears, but they were also wild and alive, hungry for truth; whether that truth is about her Grandmother, or truth that she should be telling him.

'You're here aren't you?' He smiled. 'I went to the police in England and they turned me away. They said they weren't going to waste their time investigating a natural death from thirty years ago just on the whim that it could be murder. So I did some research on policemen that were active in this country around the same time as my Grandmother's death. I figured that by now they would be retired, and may be glad to restore their careers even if it were for just a brief period of time. When I stumbled upon your name, I was looking through past murder cases in the library, and I saw you were very successful. Then, to my surprise, I discovered that you gained another triumph just six months ago with the events at Dewsbury Grange. This came as a great relief to me; finally, I had found the man I had been searching for. Not only were you a prominent figure in crime-solving for many years, but you recently also came out of retirement to solve another string of murders. That's why I tracked you down.' She looked at the floor again. 'I'm sorry.' Albert placed his hand on top of hers.

'There's no need to be sorry. It's quite all right. For the record, Henry Dewsbury was a close friend of mine, and I was at his home celebrating his birthday when the events took place. There was nothing that would have stopped me from getting involved to bring his killers to justice.' Hannah looked dismayed.

'So you didn't come out of retirement?'

'I'm afraid not, no.' His female friend stayed silent. He leant in towards her. 'But that doesn't mean I'm not going to help you.' A single tear fell down her soft cheeks.

'Do you mean it?'

'I promise.'

'Thank you.' She virtually mouthed these words rather than spoke them, but either way she got her gratitude across to him.

'If for no other reason, I don't want to have made that long journey all the way over here for nothing – I don't like flying and I completely loathe trains!' He threw her a comical glower and she even managed to raise a smile at it. 'Do you remember anything at all about your Grandmother's death? I know you weren't even born at the time, but is there anything that was ever said or mentioned to you at any point in your life?' Hannah was a lot more composed now she knew Albert was going to help, and experienced much less difficulty in answering his questions.

'I enquired once about it, but the answer I received was very vague.'

'And who was it that you asked?'

'I asked my Grandfather years ago. I must have only been around seven or eight years old. All he said was she fell down some stairs, and went up to Heaven. At that age, I wasn't exactly going to query his response, and I wouldn't have interrogated him further because as far as I was concerned, it was the truth.'

'That's understandable. Let us not rule out, however, that it is quite possible he could have told you the truth. As we currently know nothing else, unfortunately we must keep accidental death as an option.'

'I understand.'

'But what was it that made you doubt his answer. Something must have happened in your life that made you wonder whether or not his answer was truth, and those thoughts must have carried on to the point where you knew, within yourself, and beyond any doubt, that your Grandmother was in fact murdered.'

'It was quite by chance when I started having suspicions. I think I was thirteen years old at the time. I had just arrived home from school, and let myself into the house. My Father didn't hear me come in because he was too busy arguing with my Stepmother in their bedroom. I stood at the bottom of the stairs and listened in. I know it was wrong of me, but all children hate it when their parents argue, and I just wanted to know what the disagreement was about.'

'What did you hear?'

'I heard Amanda – that's my Stepmother – call my Father a liar. She said she knew he knew the truth about something, and that he should just come clean about it. She called my Grandfather some terrible names, and she didn't see why my family should be struggling for money when he had a vast fortune that he didn't even use.'

'Was Amanda only with your Father for his family's fortune? Was she disappointed that he actually had none of it and had to make his own living?'

'I never thought so, but as I got older it seemed more and more like that. But then again, they seemed very happy, and were married for nine years. They only separated last year.'

'Did anything else get said in this argument?'

'My Father told her to never bring the subject up again. He said the past should stay as the past. Amanda told him that my Grandmother's memory should be honoured and she should never have died the way she did.'

'That certainly is a statement that you're going to remember.'

'Exactly – and it's played on my mind ever since. I know something was untoward; I just need to be able to prove it.'

'What was the reason for their separation?'

'She wanted to come to Germany to visit but my Father wasn't happy about the idea at all. They had another dreadful row and Amanda packed her bags and left.'

'That seems a little drastic.'

'Oh, it didn't happen as quickly as that. It had been ongoing for months. But, I know Amanda felt very strongly, almost as strongly as I do about the whole thing. I think she believed my Grandmother had been murdered too, and I also believe my Father knew she had been, but for some reason the Krause family were forced to keep it a secret.'

'Do you think she ever came to Germany since leaving your Father?'

'I wouldn't know. I guess she might have done, but if their marriage was over, I don't see why she would care about it as much. It obviously bothered her while they were together but now they aren't, it's not exactly her business.'

'Are they divorced?'

'Not yet; why do you ask?'

'Because you've just told to me the reason why she would still care.'

'You mean money?'

'Precisely. If the divorce proceedings have not been finalised, or even started, then if there is any fortune due to your Father from Andreas, Amanda would be entitled to a portion of it.'

'I hadn't thought of that.'

'If she is also aware that he is not in the best of health, then she would know the money was due imminently.'

Hannah thought about it all for a while, but something was confusing her.

'I can't seem to find the link where my Grandmother's death is related to my Father's divorce to Amanda.'

'That's not what I am suggesting. Your Grandmother's death is a completely unrelated incident. However, because of that it obviously had a knock-on effect to the partnership of Goldmann and Krause, and in turn it affected your Grandfather's attitude to life, which impinged on his relationship with his son, and then lastly challenged your Father's marriage to Amanda.'

'I see what you mean. I hadn't thought of it like that.' She paused. 'But then there's the piece of paper with the key. What's that all about?'

'As of yet, that one is also a mystery to me. Can I take another look at them?' Hannah pulled her suitcase out from under her bed. She took from it the two items of interest and handed them to Albert. He took his monocle from his top pocket and placed it in front of his eye. He always inspected objects intently. Even the slightest scratch could indicate a further clue. He looked up at Hannah. 'And you have no idea who put these under your pillow?'

'None whatsoever; they were just there when I woke up.'

'Which means of course that they were placed there before you arrived here.'

'Yes, even I worked that one out! Whoever did it obviously wanted me to find them.' Albert returned to looking at the two objects. The key was made of brass and was inscribed with the lettering "Schlosser Lorenz: Rüdesheimer Schuh & Schlüsseldienst".

'What does this mean?' He handed Hannah the key. She also looked closely at it and translated it for him:

'It is the Lorenz Locksmith: The Rüdesheim Shoe and Key Service.'

'Cobblers.' Hannah was shocked:

'It's true!'

'No, I mean, so it came from a cobblers?' She laughed at him.

'Yes. It did. If we need to go, then it will be easy enough to find.'

'That's handy to know. Right, let's have a look at this paper. This is the most intriguing item out of the two of them.' He picked the paper up and used his monocle once again to try and gather anything he could from it that may help them with their investigation. The paper didn't exactly look old, and it wasn't even crumpled. It was just neatly folded in half, and on one half read the word "HANNAH". 'This is very interesting.' He turned to Hannah. 'This looks like a piece of paper torn from a notepad. Can you see here where your name is written?' Hannah looked at where he was pointing to and nodded to him. 'Can you see any indents around it where the previous paper has been on top of it?' She took the paper from him.

'Yes, I can't make out what it says though.'

'Not yet we can't. But we will. However, something else to note first is how lightly your name has been written.' He turned the paper over. 'The pressure of the pen does not come through on the other side, and the writing is actually relatively faint. Whoever has written this has done so carefully and calmly.' Hannah nodded once again to show she was following his thought process. 'Now compare that to the slight indents we can see around her name – whatever they say, it is quite obvious that they have been written with some force. This indicates that whoever wrote on the notepad, on the page before the one we have here, was probably angry when they did so.'

'I don't follow.' Albert removed his monocle and gave his moustache a quick twirl.

'When somebody is angry and they are writing, they tend to grip the pen tightly and push down hard on the paper. They are riled and applying pressure releases some of their tension. That's how the pen pushes through an indentation to the page beneath, which allows us to try and work out what the contents of the previous page are.'

'So how do we do that?'

'Simple.' He took a pencil from his top pocket and walked over to the windowsill. He leant the paper onto it, and started shading over the indents. Hannah went over to watch and was amazed at how the pencil covered the paper in the grey lead, yet the indents remained white, making them a lot easier to read. He ended up covering the entire page, and when he had finished, Albert held it up for her to see. She began to read what he had uncovered:

'Es ist irgendwo; Ich weiss, es ist. Er ist nicht mehr ein Problem. Ein Teil des Plans abgeschlossen ist. Nur ein zu gehen, dann werde Ich weg sein. Ich werde ihn bezahlen. Johann wird nie wissen.' She clapped her hand against her mouth. 'Oh my God.' Albert stared at her.

'Clearly, you're going to have to tell me what that means.'

'It's not good, I'm afraid.'

'Even so; I need to know.' Hannah read it out to him, saying each word slowly:

'It is somewhere; I know it is. He isn't a problem anymore. One part of the plan is complete. Just one to go, then I will be gone. I'll make him pay. Johann will never know.' Albert thought for a moment.

'Do we know who Johann is?'

'Yes.' She hesitated. 'He's my Father.'

5

It had been difficult for Albert to calm Hannah down. Whether or not they had wanted to find a clue that concerned a close member of her family – made no difference whatsoever. They had done exactly that. Now Johann, Hannah's Father, was implicated in their investigation. Albert considered bringing the letter and the key to the German Police Sergeant's attention, however, he knew that he would be able to make better use of them himself, and so decided against it. He thought perhaps he ought not to become embroiled in the mystery; he certainly didn't want to incriminate himself in any way, and the German officer had seemed to take an instant dislike to him, which would not help matters in any case. They both decided it was best if they conducted their own enquiries; the main reason being, the body found in the garden, whereas most unfortunate and upsetting, was not related to finding out exactly what happened to Hannah's Grandmother. Despite this, they were obviously intrigued as to the identity of the corpse, however they had been told that they would only find out that information if a member of the household were a relation of the victim.

The two sleuths, one expert and one amateur, skipped breakfast and took a taxi down to the centre of Rüdesheim. There were still a few decorations hanging around in the aftermath of Germany's victory in the World Cup. He wasn't a big lover of football, but Albert was always pleased to see a country unite and celebrate together over the achievement of a much sought after trophy; the team had certainly earned it.

Hannah held the key tightly in her hand. They were in search of Schlosser Lorenz. If only they could find out what type of lock their particular key fitted, then they would know what they were looking for. They hoped that the locksmith would be able to also tell them who had purchased the item, although they knew that this was probably highly unlikely. The amount of customers the shop would have greeted through its doors since whenever their key was purchased would be colossal, and the owner surely could not remember every insignificant purchase. Nevertheless, Albert had learnt through the years that if a question is not asked, then an answer could not be obtained. It is much wiser to ask with hope, rather than stay silent with wonder.

Neither of them said much on the way to the town centre. Albert was engrossed in staring out of the window, trying to take in the scenery and various quirky landmarks that they passed. He'd always thought foreign countries excelled themselves with the decoration of their environment; they made it what he described as "pointlessly picturesque". For example, English roundabouts were mainly just covered with overgrown grass, whereas he'd seen some tremendous sculptures during his time, on his various travels through different countries. He remembered travelling through France, just passed Calais, and seeing two figures made of metal on each bridge he drove under. On one bridge they both held tennis rackets, and one had a ball attached to it; on the next bridge the two figures were both mounted on horses. There were several sculptures, which were different every time. He also liked travelling through Portugal, which he'd only done once, but he'd seen a giant snake start on one roundabout, which continued the coils of its body over the next four or five roundabouts. They were all rather pointless, but they were very unique, and it provided some amusement to lighten the mood of the journey. On his current expedition however, while he was busy occupying his mind, Hannah, on the other hand, just stared at the letter, re-reading her Father's name over and over again. She just couldn't believe it. She so desperately wanted it to not be true. Of course, it could be somebody else called Johann, but under the circumstances she knew deep down that wasn't going to be the case. But she was adamant she was going to get to the bottom of it all.

The taxi pulled up near the market street.

'Albert we're looking for number twenty-one.' Albert looked around at the beautiful town. The streets were narrow; the buildings appeared crooked, a lot of them were white with a brown, wooden beam effect; some of them had miniature turrets, which rose upwards into a point, often with a biblical cross on top, and shops had ornate wooden or brass signs hanging from their side walls with their names engraved boldly and invitingly. The town certainly had character and people swarmed everywhere. It was very much alive with shoppers and tourists, and in the distance he could see the cable car moving along with a few people enjoying the view in each carriage.

It wasn't difficult to find number twenty-one. With Albert's typically rotten luck, he usually found that the number he was looking for in relation to anything, usually ran out at the one before. Perhaps it was Hannah's good influence and knowledge of the area that made them find the locksmiths quickly. As they were walking up to the door, an unkempt man bustled out of the door. Hannah recognised his tattered green coat straight away:

'Misty!' The occupied gardener seemed to reluctantly stop.

'Wie fühlst du sich jetzt?' He really didn't seem to want to stop and talk. He mumbled into his coat, rather than speaking directly to her face, like he had previously done so:

'Ja, Ich bin in Ordnung. Ich brauchte nur eine Schlussel Schnitt.'

'Wofür?' He started making his move but did answer her question before leaving:

'Der Kohlenschuppen.'

'Hannah tell him I feel for him over what he went through yesterday.' She translated his kind words and Stefan nodded graciously at Albert, before outstretching his hand to him, which Albert shook. Then, before they could even blink, he had vanished around the corner. Hannah still watched the alleyway where her friend had walked. Albert picked up on her confusion and offered some sensible words:

'Don't forget he has just been through a terrible ordeal. It's amazing he is even out and about.'

'I guess you're right.'

'What did you say to him?'

'I asked him how he was feeling, and he said he was fine, but he just needed a key cut.'

'Did you ask him for where?'

'Yes. He said the coal shed.'

'Well there's nothing unusual about that – we can't read into everything. Let's just go in here and see what we can find out about this key.'

'The only thing was, Misty mentioned something to me yesterday about Eleanor.'

'Which was?'

'He said he caught her acting very strange when he was planting his tree – moments before he uncovered the body in the ground.'

'And what was she doing?'

'Apparently she was just standing there watching him.'

'That's not exactly a major crime; I'm watching you right now but it doesn't mean I've been involved in murder.'

'I'm not explaining it very well. He was kneeling down when something flew passed his ear, which actually made him bleed. When he looked up, Eleanor was hovering around the coal shed just glaring at him. He said it made him feel very uneasy.'

'Did you say around the coal shed?'

'Yes, and when he was being questioned by the police, he noticed that the lock had been broken on it.'

'Who would want to get into a coal shed so desperately? And conversely, why is a coal shed in need of a lock and key?'

'I'm not sure, but one thing I do know is there is a delivery expected any day now so that they have their supply ready for winter.' Albert thought for a moment.

'Right, let's put the coal shed to the back of our minds for the time being, and go in here like we set out to do.' Hannah nodded and they entered the locksmiths.

The bell over the door clinked when they entered. The shop was fairly dark inside due to the small windows that let in minimal light from the narrow alleyway. A thin, wiry man with a neat brown moustache stood behind the counter. Albert actually thought he looked a bit like Hitler, although he thought it better not to divulge his opinion to him. The man, who wore the nametag "Herbert Lorenz", greeted them on entry:

'Guten Morgen.' Albert nodded and congenially tipped his hat towards him. He hoped the action was universal unlike the varying languages throughout the world. Hannah replied in the traditional manner and engaged in a small conversation with him. Albert wondered if she was already asking about the key, however, she still held it in her hand below the counter so he concluded that she hadn't. The shopkeeper then looked up at Albert and directed his next portion of speech to him. 'Your young friend tells me you are from England and do not speak German – is this correct?' He was essentially fluent, and had a more than good enough understanding of Albert's native tongue. It wasn't as if Albert could even criticise anyway; he didn't know any German, and not even his phrasebook stretched to locksmith enquiries.

'That's correct. My name's Albert Murtland; I'm from…' Herbert suddenly livened up with a surprise outburst and interrupted Albert:

'Don't tell me!' Albert stopped speaking at once. Herbert rested his head in his hands and looked temporarily deep in thought. Albert threw a sideward glance to Hannah, which basically communicated to her that he thought the man was barmy. Hannah nodded slowly; it was difficult to think otherwise. Suddenly, Herbert spoke again: 'Kent.' It took Albert a while to realise the word had been directed at him:

'Pardon me?'

'You're from Kent.' Albert was confused.

'Yes. How did you know?'

'I've studied languages and dialects for many years. The different dialects, some even changing within a few miles of each other fascinates me profusely.'

'I didn't think I had a dialect.'

'It was difficult to pick up I admit, but there are certain features to your pronunciation, which encompasses East Anglia and London. They're only very slight, and would go unnoticed to the majority of people. Plus, I noticed that, although no longer a struggle, you strive to leave behind the

63

Kentish dialect, which is being replaced by Estuary English. But, you try to speak as best you can using the Queen's English, with the best Received Pronunciation that you can execute, although not quite being able to ditch the very slight Kentish influence that has been drilled into you from your upbringing.' Hannah had been silent since her first interchange with the remarkable linguist, but could not stay quiet any longer:

'You must have studied languages for some time!'

'I have a Masters Degree in Languages.'

'So why are you stuck in here cutting keys and mending old shoes?'

'I know it's a strange scenario, but it is my Father's business and he is currently indisposed with a broken leg. I have been here for three weeks now just to keep the business going. Hopefully, in another couple of months, he will be fit enough to come back to work, and I can then carry on with my own line of work.'

'Forgive me if my Kentish dialect is too overwhelming for you, but what is your line of work?' Herbert chuckled.

'I am a Professor at Heidelberg University, but I also write textbooks on the study of languages. It's nice to have a break but I will be glad to get back to it. Anyway, enough about me, how can I help you both?'

'Unfortunately, we aren't here to give you any business, we just require some information from you if you happen to know what we want. Hannah, show Mr. Lorenz the key.' Hannah placed the key on the counter. 'What can you tell us about that?' Herbert stared it for a few moments.

'It's a key.' Albert raised his eyebrows.

'We know it's a key! What's it for?' He paused, but quickly added to his question. 'And don't say a lock!' Herbert picked the key up and examined it closely.

'It certainly isn't a traditional key. It isn't for a front door, or anything like that.'

'It is one of yours though isn't it?'

'Most definitely! Yes, it has our mark that we engrave onto all of our products.'

'Are you able to tell us what it is for?'

'That may be difficult. You see, we obviously don't sell keys on their own unless it is a key that somebody wants cutting, just like the gentlemen before you. Keys that have a special design, such as this one, will have been bought with the article that possesses the location of the lock for it.' Albert couldn't help but get slightly frustrated with lack of useful response:

'But you obviously advertise the service of designing and producing these special keys, so you must also have the items for sale that they can be used for.' Herbert looked up at him, seemingly annoyed at Albert's abrupt demeanour.

'Of course we have the items in stock. They are over there in that glass cabinet, and the range of keys are displayed on the counter to the right of them.' He pointed across the room, and both Hannah and Albert went to have a look. 'Customers usually buy those items for reasons such as a small storage for any precious items, or a unique gift for a friend or relative, or even as a keepsake box filled with artefacts or letters that hold fond memories for them. They pick the box that they like and then any design of key of their choosing to go with it.' Hannah looked up from the display.

'So basically the key we've got could be for absolutely any of these boxes?'

'Yes. Is there a particular reason why you are trying to locate the box for this key?' This time, Albert looked up.

'Perhaps, it may be because something is locked inside it, and we need to know what we are searching for so we can open it.' He returned his gaze back to the selection of boxes, utterly astonished at the man's stupidity.

'I meant, I assume it is not your box, otherwise you would know what it looked like.' Albert ignored him and so Hannah stepped in to answer:

'Yes, it is my Grandmother's box and she has passed away. She told me she had received the box as a gift but all she has left is this key. We just wanted to know what we should be looking for.'

'Well, that makes more sense. Yes, I'm afraid it could be any of the boxes in that cabinet. I'm sorry I can't be of more use.' Albert looked up again.

'Well it's going to take us some time to try and find a box that's been hidden away, which has one design out of a possible thirty – I've just counted them.'

'I apologise.'

'It can't be helped; it's not your fault.' Albert paused. 'Now, I know this is a long shot, but out of the keys you can purchase for these boxes, not one of them has the design that our key has. Have you stopped producing that particular design, or is that an extra special, custom-made key?' Herbert moved behind the counter to where the keys were displayed.

'How unusual. As far as I'm concerned, these are the only keys my Father has ever created for sale. I can check the books to see if there was a special order, but he has them at home, so it wouldn't be for a few days.'

'We'd appreciate it if you could. If you have been here for three weeks, I don't suppose you can remember anybody ordering this key?'

'I honestly can't. I certainly haven't made it, so it must have been commissioned with my Father. Like I said, I'll check the books when I next see him. That should be within the next few days. Do you have a time frame that I should be looking for to make it a bit easier for myself?' Albert redirected the question to Hannah:

'What do you reckon Hannah? The last two months?' She thought about it.

'Yes, that's probably a reasonable enough period to start with.'

'If you write down a contact number for me, then I'll get back to you when I've located the order. But I doubt I'll be able to tell you very much I'm afraid. At most, what style the box was, when the order was placed and collected, and how much it cost.'

'Wouldn't he have taken a contact name or telephone number?'

'He may have done; I'll find out when I look. But even if he has, I don't think it would be very professional to give away that information.'

'Well just see what you can do for us; we do appreciate it.' Hannah wrote down the number for her Grandfather's house. She had forgotten to change the settings on her mobile phone so that it would be able to function while she was abroad. She had felt daft when she'd realised, as even Albert had remembered to do it for his old phone.

'Excuse me, Herr Lorenz, but when you telephone, could you say you are a friend of Albert's – we'd like to keep this private from the rest of the household, if you wouldn't mind?'

'Not at all.' Hannah picked up the key from the counter. She had also been mulling something over in her head:

'Also, do you mind me asking how your Father broke his leg? Without meaning to sound rude, he can't be the youngest man, and it's not as if working here is excessively active; I'm assuming he had a fall at home?' Herbert looked at her.

He didn't seem overly bothered about her prying into his family's mishaps.

'I wish he'd fallen over at home. About four weeks ago, the shop was burgled just before he was closing up. Some thug barged in despite the sign saying "Geschlossen", sorry, "Closed", and gave my Father a terrible shove, pushing him over. He hit his head on the corner of the counter, and then if that wasn't enough, they stamped on his leg.'

'Oh my! How awful!'

'The funny thing was, when the police came and inspected the place, they couldn't find anything that had been taken and the money, which he had already bagged up on the counter, was untouched.' Albert twirled his moustache, as he collected his thoughts.

'That's remarkably unusual. It must have been some hooligan who got a sick thrill out of doing it.'

'That's pretty much what the Police Sergeant said at the time. Although, just between us, I didn't like that Sergeant – he seemed shifty, and I'd even go as far to say corrupt.'

'I think I've met the exact same constable. Right, I think we've obtained all the information we can for the time being, don't you Hannah? We shall leave you in peace.'

'I shall be in contact with you soon, I promise.' Hannah thanked him and Albert tipped his hat to him in the same way as he had done so on entry. Feeling slightly dejected, as they had both hoped to have more answers, they left the shop.

Andreas warily opened the music room door. Stefan had knocked, and had called through to tell him that he was outside with a cup of tea for them both. Even though Andreas enjoyed seeing Stefan; in fact it was only him he didn't mind chatting to occasionally, he was still very vigilant in allowing access to anybody, in case there were any other people that were nearby hoping to glance in and pry. Stefan scuttled in quickly; his large ragged coat trailing behind him. Despite being in poor health, Andreas gave it his best shot at trying to shut out a fly that seemed intent on following Stefan into the music room. It wasn't much of a battle, as Andreas soon conceded when the fly whizzed passed him. He closed the door and bolted it tightly.

The music room was remarkable. It had three windows, all on the opposite wall to the door. They were all locked securely, with exterior safety blinds pulled downwards. No natural light entered the room, which left the ceiling light burning brightly all day long, no matter how light it was outside. To the left of the entrance, a double bed was shoved up against the far wall. He never made it when he arose each morning. Instead, he thought of sleep more as an inconvenience between bouts of piano playing rather than as a necessity that everybody has in their lives. In the centre of the room was a small coffee table, where he sat with his minimal guests to drink their tea. Only two chairs were placed around it: one for Andreas, and one for whichever chosen guest was lucky enough to have access to his living quarters at any particular time. Stefan placed the tray of drinks down on the table, and sat in his seat. He knew that the visitor's chair was the one that faced the bed. Andreas had made it quite clear on everyone's first visit that his chair was always the one that faced the piano.

His piano was his pride and joy, and had been for decades. It stood proudly, on the other side of the room opposite the bed, and it was the same piano where he had composed all his symphonies with his musical partner Hans Goldmann. The Steinway Model B grand piano looked beautiful in mahogany and was made in 1917 during Steinway's golden era. Andreas had taken great care of it over the years, since he had purchased it, and had since paid for it to be magnificently restored. He'd had a new soundboard and bridges put in, along with a new pin block and tuning pins. The highest quality custom made bass strings were installed, plus new damper felts and Renner wippens. New hammers, shanks, and flanges had all been included in the restoration, as well as the refurbishment of the original ivory key tops. There was no expense spared for his most prized possession, or in actual fact his only true possession, and it still gave out its powerful sound, full of richness and warmth, exactly like it would have done when the first note on it was ever played, nearly a century ago. To the side of the piano was a small box, which contained several dusters and some polish. Every night after he had ceased playing for the day, he went through his customary routine of after-playing care. The piano came to life when Andreas played it, and it carried on sparkling when it was allowed to rest.

Stefan spoke with Andreas for about an hour each time. He had been employed as gardener at the Krause residence for a great number of years, and had become good friends with Andreas. Despite being a wealthy, famous man, Andreas was by no means snobbish. The status meant nothing to him; he had always played the piano because he had enjoyed it. He had started out his working career very early in life, labouring for his father as a steeplejack. They did a roaring trade, and were never out of work. Old churches and cathedrals always needed renovation, and they made a great deal of money. His parents had always been musical, which is why he had grown to love it as equally as they did. His mother had played the flute, and his father played the saxophone, but also dabbled from time to time on a harmonica. When Andreas was six, they bought him his very first piano. It was also a Steinway, but it was an eighty-five note upright, made in the 1880s. From that point onwards, he craved nothing more but to create beautiful music from its very rich tone and smooth touch. His talent spiralled from playing in his parent's lounge, to performing a small concert at a village hall, to being approached by a musical agent and selling out full theatres of sixteen-hundred people or more; everyone of them appreciative of being given the opportunity to hear him play.

How different his life was now. He had never confided in Stefan, or any of his guests, about his wife's death, and any other circumstances that had pushed him into becoming a recluse. Apart from a dark secret in his past, he was happy just spending the rest of his days playing his piano. He didn't particularly get lonely, but sometimes it was nice for him to see an old friend, such as Stefan. "Old friend" was exactly the right terminology for Stefan. He too, was an elderly man, who refused to retire. Andreas saw the similarities between them constantly. Whereas Andreas essentially kept himself as a loner, there were certain people he wished to see once in a while, and although Stefan didn't shut himself off from the outside world, he still only kept his job because it was the only bit of social life he experienced. Each day that Stefan's heart kept pumping, his eyesight and hearing faded further away.

The two elderly men sat with each other every so often, enjoying their conversation and the company, but both men wondered at the back of their minds, when their last days would be.

6

Hannah and Albert arrived back at the house. They entered the front door just in time to see Stefan leaving Andreas' room and they heard the door get bolted once it had closed. Hannah thought it was greatly unfair how he agreed to let the gardener visit but not his own granddaughter. Albert was of the same opinion, but he didn't really feel it was his place to pass comment, and he certainly didn't want to judge the great man whom he had admired for many years. Stefan sloped off back into the garden. It wasn't long before they heard the familiar sound of masterpieces being played from behind the door. Hannah ran up to the door and started slapping it with her hand.

'Grossvater! Grossvater!' The reply came quick and sharp:

'Gehen Sie weg!' With tears in her eyes, she glanced quickly at Albert before racing up the stairs. He heard her slam her door, and knew she would not come out for a long while. He understood her hurt and sadness. Any moment is precious with any cherished person, but when those moments are known to be lessening and running out, they become much more valuable. Time is something that couldn't be bought, and Hannah felt her time with him was almost up. Albert made his way into the kitchen and found Eleanor making some tea.

'Would you like a cup Mr. Murtland?' He pulled a chair out from under the table.

'That would be wonderful; thank you.' They stayed in silence until the tea was almost made. She picked up a bottle of milk with a green top from out of the fridge door and poured some into both cups. She pushed Albert's along the table towards him. Albert stared at the milk bottles as she put it back in the fridge. 'Is there any reason for the different milks?'

'Of course – the one with the light blue top is for Herr Krause. It is better for his health.'

'I thought the blue top was whole milk?'

'It is in England yes, but not in Germany. It is the other way around here. Green is the whole milk, and light blue is skimmed.'

'Why can't everything be universal? It's just unnecessary confusion if you ask me.'

'Don't ask me; I'm not a milkmaid – I just make the tea.' Albert raised one side of his lips into a small smirk.

'I apologise.' They both took a sip of their drinks. 'What do you think of Andreas Krause?'

'I believe him to be an extraordinary musician.'

'He is very talented to say the least. But I was enquiring more as to his current personality and peculiar living habits.'

'His current situation is not exactly recent Mr. Murtland, but rather it has become the norm. You see, as far as I know, he has lived like this for the best part of thirty years.'

'Surely his health has been affected by being cooped up in the same room for so long, with no natural light getting to him?'

'The windows on the side of the house where he is, cannot be seen into by anybody, as they are not easily accessible. This is because the house is built so close to the neighbouring hedge. Therefore, he can open them whenever he chooses without any fear or prying eyes. As for his health, I admit that the lack of sunlight does probably speed up his deterioration, however, he takes Vitamin D tablets every day to try and make up for it.'

'It's not exactly the same thing.'

'You try telling him that.' She brought her cup up to her mouth to take another drink; Albert copied her action, feeling almost compelled to do so.

'Hannah is upset because she isn't able to see him.'

'That girl should never have come here.' Hastily, she continued: 'It was only ever going to be upsetting for her.'

'How would you know that?'

'Because of how he acts; he cares for nobody but himself. He'd be quite happy to die alone in that room.'

'Is that what you think will happen?'

'What I think is of no consequence; it's what might happen, which is what you need to focus on.'

'Never a truer word said, Miss. Frankwell.' They both took their tea again, simultaneously.

'I don't suppose you have heard anything about the body that Stefan found in the garden?'

'I'm afraid I wasn't even allowed near the police tape, let alone entitled to ask to be informed of the person's identity.'

'It's such a dreadful business. You just can't imagine something like that happening so close to you.' She paused. 'If you ask me, that filthy gardener probably had something to do with it.'

'What makes you say that?'

'Well you only have to look at him; I mean, he's practically a vagrant. And those sorts of people are always dubious and involved in shady shenanigans.'

'By all accounts, he seems like a very pleasant chap.'

'And I suppose that information has come from that girl? To the best of my knowledge, she has only ever met him once or twice – you can't possibly know somebody inside and out after such short periods of times. And we mustn't forget that her brief encounters with him, were spread several years apart when she was very young.'

'I do understand your concerns, but I also believe in instincts and first impressions.'

'Well if you wish to live your life taking people at face value than by all means don't let me stop you.'

'I could say the same things to you, couldn't I?'

'How do you mean?'

'I have only met you once or twice, and each time has only been for a few minutes. Should I just label you as guilty now?'

'Don't be ridiculous! You only have to look at the way in which I dress to see I'm not a secret lunatic! That gardener is very uneducated, and quite possibly deranged. He grunts when he's looking at me, and I feel like he's undressing me with his eyes.'

'I don't believe his eyesight to be all that good.' Eleanor was becoming irritated:

'That is not the point and you know it! Who knows what depraved activities he gets up to in that coal shed – he's always going in and out.'

'Well now you come to mention it,' he paused, 'you don't think that he's…' Eleanor leant forward, intrigued.

'Yes?'

'You don't think that he's…' Eleanor forward even more and loudly whispered:

'I don't think that he's what?' Albert leant in closely.

'Getting coal?' She jumped up.

'No I do not think he's getting coal! If you aren't going to take this seriously then really I do not see any point in discussing the matter! I am trying to help Mr. Murtland, and yet you seem intent on making constant jokes, which are not amusing in the slightest!'

'What I don't find amusing Miss. Frankwell, is that you were hanging around the coal shed yourself, rather suspiciously I might add, moments before the body was found. And I have to say you looked rather nervous at seeing Stefan digging around the area where the body was found. Do you have an explanation for this?'

'I suppose he told you that did he? Did he also tell you that I'd caught him lingering outside my bathroom, probably hoping to catch a glimpse of me?' Albert hesitated, and so she carried on with her claim. 'I can see that he omitted that part of the story. I wasn't nervous – I was furious!'

'Well I shall certainly be asking him about that.'

'That man is a menace; it's no wonder that the housekeeper before me left – he probably did the same things to her.'

'Incidentally, while you've mentioned that. Why is it that Andreas only seems to hire English housekeepers, when he can't speak a word of the language?'

'I have no idea. Perhaps he doesn't want people he can talk to because he'd rather not converse with anybody! But I can't ask him about it because I never see him.'

'It just seems strange that the old housekeeper was English, and you are of course also English.'

'Everything about this house is strange. The old house-keeper, the gardener, Andreas himself, his granddaughter – the whole house is quite frankly barmy! I shall be glad when I'm able to leave.'

'What's keeping you here?'

'I'm an agency worker, and so do not get to choose where I am sent. Besides, the money is more than sufficient for the nature of the jobs that I have to carry out.'

'Do you think anything underhand is going on here?'

'Not particularly. The body found in the garden is most unfortunate, but I do not believe it has anything to do with anyone here. It was probably an accidental death and somebody just panicked and buried it wherever they thought was the least likely place it would be found. Apart from that, nobody here is in danger.' Albert smiled, and took one last gulp of his tea. He stood up and clapped his feet together, as if he was a young soldier standing to attention for his commanding officer.

'Thank you for your time, Miss. Frankwell.' He left the room, leaving her to enjoy her own company.

Stefan and Hannah were back walking through Rüdesheim. He had gone up to see her when he realised she felt upset about her grandfather's manner. She looked up to the kindly gardener and she knew it wasn't his fault. She didn't even blame Andreas; she understood it must have been a horrendous incident for him to change his life so drastically. She just wished she could be closer to him. Her relationship with her father was not the intimate father-daughter relationship she had seen in films, and she had never known her mother as she had died during childbirth. A lot of the time she felt alone, and even in the house of her oldest blood relative, it was no different. Stefan had offered her the option of accompanying him back into the town to collect a pair of steel-toecap boots he had left at the cobblers that same morning. She agreed to go because she had not had much chance to see her green-fingered friend since her arrival, and the weather was too nice to waste it crying in her bedroom over a matter that, although upsetting, she could do nothing about.

It was lovely walking along the Rhein. The water gave a delicate splashing sound as the soft ripples travelled with the current and came into contact with the riverbanks. A small boat sailed past, filled with joyful tourists. Some were waving, and everybody seemed to be genuinely having a lovely time. She had been taken on the river cruise a couple of times when she was younger, and she remembered feeling exactly how the passengers looked. They crossed the road and headed into the alleyway where they had both been only a few hours ago. The milk wagon of Mohler Molkerei trundled past, and Thomas gave a little toot of the horn as he went on his way. He had a woman in the passenger seat with him, who was young and pretty. She was dark-skinned and looked as if she was of oriental origin. Both Hannah and Stefan raised their hands to him, but it was unlikely that he had seen by the time they did so, or at least he shouldn't have seen if he had been keeping his eyes on the road like a cautious driver ought to. Hannah asked Stefan if he knew whom the woman was, and Stefan informed her it was Thomas' partner. They stared after the milk wagon for a short while before deciding to go inside the locksmiths.

Herbert raised his head as they entered the shop, and gave Hannah a welcoming smile. Hannah stayed near the door while Stefan collected his boots. She didn't really want to enter into a conversation about what they were speaking about earlier with Albert, because it was to be kept secret, for the time being at least. She also hoped he would not shout something out to her. It would be fine if he spoke to her in English because Stefan would not be able to understand, however, seeing as the shopkeeper was a German national, she didn't think it would be the language he naturally chose to use. He seemed too preoccupied with Stefan to speak to her anyway, and besides, with him being a Professor at a university, she hoped he retained a certain amount of common sense to not broadcast a sensitive matter. Stefan moved away from the counter holding a carrier bag with his mended boots in. Hannah opened the door ready for them to leave, but then Herbert Lorenz spoke:

'Sagen Sie Ihrem Freund die Bücher sind tatsächlich hier. Ich werde ihn später mit der Informationen rufen.' Hannah froze. Stefan had spun around, and she didn't know how to reply. Even Herbert now looked confused. Perhaps he had remembered incorrectly; if her friend from earlier had only spoken English, it was possible that she didn't speak German either. Afterall, he was sure she had only said "good morning" out of politeness, and that phrase was easy to pick up. But then on second thoughts, he remembered they'd had a short conversation. He spoke again, this time in English, just to be sure. 'Tell your friend the books are actually here. I will ring him later with the information.' Stefan still stared at him, and then he fixed his gaze on Hannah.

'Thank you,' she mumbled, and then hastily left. Stefan followed, unsure of what was taking place.

It was driving Albert insane not being able to find out any information about the body in the garden. He had tried speaking again to the German Sergeant but he received very little in the way of cooperation. What also baffled him was the way the cold atmosphere of the house, complete with a feeling of gloom, seemed to suggest that a death was imminent. However, when thinking of the actual facts that he possessed to confirm this, there was nothing that indicated towards it. He wondered if Hannah's certainty regarding her Grandmother, which only spurred thoughts about Andreas' poor health and supposed looming demise, had carried him away. Eleanor was also acting in a rather unusual manner, although he reminded himself of the fact that he didn't know her in the slightest, and so could just not be used to her peculiar demeanour. When he reassessed the finding of the corpse under the rockery, his mind worked over time. After his long career at Scotland Yard, he was expertly used to conjuring up different explanations for various situations. A contestant for the identity would have been

Hannah's Grandmother, but the burial was much too recent. Admittedly, if the body had been embalmed it would have protected the condition of the deceased for a good while longer, but he just couldn't believe that the culprit would have been bothered about preserving the body, when they had dumped it in a spot they had hoped it would never be found. The only other people he knew of that could almost be described as missing, were: Rebecca Sharp, the former housekeeper, and Amanda Krause, Hannah's ex-stepmother. But, he just couldn't fathom any reasonable explanation as to why. He felt he needed to delve into Andreas' past to be able to come up with any answers that might feasibly shed some light onto the matters in hand. The thing that still haunted his mind, however, was why Hannah specifically picked him to assist her, and why the one man at the centre of it all, had still not been seen.

There was not really any gardening work that Stefan could get on with. He wasn't overly enthusiastic at getting back to work, but even if he had wanted to, the police still occupied the area. It had been a shock for him to find the body, as it would have been for anyone, but he was a good, conscientious worker down to his bones, and it tortured him not being able to be outside, maintaining the beauty of the place. He didn't want to take any time off work and stay at home; he'd rather wait around at the house so he could dash out as soon as the police vacated the property. He just didn't know how long it would take. Therefore, he decided to nip into the town again; not for anything in particular, just for a peaceful stroll where he could gather his thoughts. He didn't particularly have a specific direction where he was going to walk; he just decided to go wherever his feet would take him. Soon enough, he came across the cable car and watched it carrying large numbers of tourists for a calm, pleasant journey over the vineyards. It had been years since he had travelled on it, and as he stared at the carriages trundling along, he thought there was probably no better time than now to take a relaxing ride on it. He paid his money, and waited for the carriage to scoop him off his feet. He pulled down the safety bar, and off he went, rising higher and higher, with his feet just dangling in the air.

The air was cool, and felt fresh around his face. It refreshingly nipped the tops of his ears, as he had taken his woolly hat off to enjoy the chilly feel. He looked down at the vineyards below. He admired the multiple picturesque rows of vines that flourished with their fruit. The fruit had probably all been picked by now, ready to go into the winemaking process. He knew of some vineyards that timed the picking of their grapes so precisely, literally to a specified minute, because they had calculated the optimum moment in time to achieve the highest quality wine from their crop. He had always thought that if he hadn't stayed employed by Andreas, he would have probably sought out a job at a vineyard. He wasn't a big drinker, but he did enjoy a fruity glass of Riesling from time to time. There had also been many times when he had tried to persuade his boss to allow him a little allotment at the end of the garden. He'd had high hopes of planting a small vineyard of his own, of about fifty vines or so, just to see if he could make them work. Sadly, his enthusiasm was not shared and so it never happened, but he was generally a simple man of simple pleasures and remained contented in life nonetheless.

He reached the top where there was a restaurant and a small shop. He wasn't bothered about stopping off for refreshments or a souvenir and so he stayed in his carriage as it spun around for the return journey. The mechanism never stopped. If people wanted to get off, they had to quickly raise their safety bar themselves and leap off. Similarly, when getting onto a carriage, there were some pictures of feet painted onto the launch pad; people stood on them and jumped on the moving carriage as the wire swung it at them to travel back towards the ground. As he sat in his seat, quietly enjoying the exquisite views around and beneath him, he was surprised to see two people in a carriage opposite him, going up towards the restaurant. One of them had a very familiar face.

Eleanor hadn't seen him because she was too busy cuddling up to her male companion. They were kissing and laughing, and it looked to Stefan as if they were enjoying a first date, or at least a very early stage in their relationship. He had always considered her to be a bit of a martinet, as he was yet to see a softer side of her personality. Also, after her peculiar actions of her extensive stony expression directed towards him, he had become quite apprehensive of her. There was certainly more to her than met the eye, but he did find some comfort in the fact that she obviously did have a warmer quality, even if the only person that ever saw it was the lucky man in the carriage with her. At one point, he thought he recognised her companion, but he couldn't place his face quickly enough, and by the time he had plucked up the courage to stare again without making it obvious, their carriages had passed and all he could see were the backs of their heads.

After his ride on the Sesselbahn was complete, he continued to walk around the town. He bought himself an ice cream, and sat on a bench with it, staring at the river. Perhaps he was getting too old to keep working; it certainly was nice to spend his time in this manner. But the more he thought about it, he knew he would quickly tire of the retired lifestyle, and it also saddened him to think that if he were to quit his job, he would feel very alone; nobody would have any need for him, and he would have nobody to spend any time with. Getting older was certainly not nice for him, and he concluded to himself, that he would very much prefer to die either working in the garden, or in his sleep after a hard day's work. He sat for a few more minutes watching the boat return home from its last cruise of the day. Stefan had one more stop off to make before the shops all shut, and so he got to his feet and wandered, for the third time, in the direction of the locksmiths.

Herbert Lorenz sat in his swivel chair in the back of his father's key cutting and shoe repair shop. He picked up the receiver on the retro-style telephone and turned the numbered wheel several times to dial the number he had been given to reach Albert on. It may take longer to make a call, but there was something satisfying about hearing the tender clicks as the dial whirred back to its starting position. He had the book on his lap, which contained the orders, and it was open on the page that held the information Albert sought. He listened to the phone ringing for a few seconds, before the voice of a young girl sounded on the other end.

'Hallo.' Herbert had an inclining' it was Hannah, and so spoke English to her. Afterall, she had asked him to pretend to be a friend of Albert's.

'Hello. I hope you can understand me; this is Herbert Lorenz calling from Schlosser Lorenz: Rüdesheimer Schuh & Schlüsseldienst. I'd like to speak with Albert if I may.'

'Hello Mr. Lorenz – thank you for getting back to us so quickly. I'll just go and get him.' Herbert waited while Hannah put the phone down on the table and went to find the ageing detective. He didn't take much finding; he was

8 3

only in the next room munching on a sandwich. In fact, he had been closer to a phone than she was, but of course he would never have answered it. Albert hurried over to the phone, and Hannah waited by his side while he spoke to the locksmith.

'Herbert – what have you got for me?'

'I think I've got the information you wanted. The box you are looking for is in the shape of a cuboid. It was specially made for a one-off customer order. We sell similar ones to it in the shop, which you probably saw when you were here. The one you are looking for is modelled on one of the standard designs, but is just bigger; about twice the size.' With his back to the shop door, Herbert hadn't noticed a shadowy figure entering the premises.

'How big are we talking?'

'It's about fourteen inches in length, about a four-inch width, and four-inch depth.'

'What colour?'

'Completely black. It's strange because as they are made of metal, we usually suggest that the main sides of the boxes are in full colour, but then offer the edges with a silver effect. They are much more decorative like that.'

'But the customers wanted it black all over?'

'That what it says here.'

'So the key belongs to a large all-black rectangular box?'

'That's quite correct.'

'So tell me about the person who ordered it; did you find any information?'

'Well that's actually very intriguing. It says here that the customer refused to give a name.' The figure lurked in the darkness, as they crept closer to the informant.

'Does it say if they were male or female?'

'I'll read out everything it says: "Customer refused to give name or contact details. Said they would collect item in a few days. Filthy green coat.'

'Filthy green coat?'

'Yes, and earlier today I met the gardener that works up at Herr Krause's home, where you are staying. He's been in a few times today with various bits for me to do: a new key, boot repair, but the last time he was in, I noticed something very strange about him.' The intruder reached just a few steps away from Herbert. They passed the workbench and picked up the cobbling hammer that lay idle on the side.

'Which was?'

'He had such a distinctive accent to me of the East Low German Pomeranian dialect; I knew instantly he must originally come from north-eastern Germany, somewhere like Rostock. But when he came in earlier for yet another key to be cut, I don't know how, but I must have made a mistake because I could have sworn he was from West Germany. He was sniffing a lot though; I certainly hope I don't catch his cold. The main thing, however, that I must tell you is, disregarding the language differences, the gardener must have…' A lot of crackling sounded on the phone line.

'Hello? Hello? Herbert?' Albert slammed the phone down. 'Great. He's gone. The line must have died.'

The phone at Schlosser Lorenz dangled by its cord, as the commotion was over. An unfamiliar hand reached over and ripped the cord out of the phone. Herbert lay on the floor, with his cobbling hammer smashed into his skull. Blood trickled down his neck, as he slouched on the floor, with his eyes staring at the ceiling. The door to the shop swayed in the breeze, as his killer fled through the streets. It wasn't the phone line that had died; it was Herbert.

Police swarmed the scene. Unfortunately, it was sadly ironic that had the locksmith taken the advice of the family profession and locked his door, his death probably could have been avoided. It hadn't been until the following morning when his body was found. Herbert Lorenz was not married, nor was he in a relationship, and therefore nobody knew his whereabouts. If he did have a closeness with anybody who was expecting him home, they would more than likely have telephoned the shop trying to locate him, and would have heard an irregular tone on their receiver. It was in fact the shop's first customer of the day who had stumbled across him, much to their horror.

Albert and Hannah had joined the upheaval in the town. The authorities were anxious to question members of the Krause residence regarding Herbert's death, as they had found the phone hanging beside him and so had traced his last call. Albert confirmed he had been in conversation with him, and had written for the police, a detailed report about the strange circumstances concerning the end of their phone call. The surly German Sergeant, who retained his grudge against Albert, glowered at him throughout the proceedings, which had to be in the presence of a translator. While Albert was being interviewed, Hannah had managed to eavesdrop on a group of constables talking about the crime scene. She learnt that a small hunting dart had been found behind the counter in the shop, which by all accounts they believed to have been dropped by the killer when they made their exit. She made a mental note to tell Albert of her finding later on. There were no signs that the dart, which were often poisoned and fired from a blowpipe, was used in connection with the killing. It seemed that whoever had attacked him, obviously knew the layout of the shop, and was aware that a suitable weapon would be readily available to them to carry out their terrible deed. Regrettably, after his questioning had drawn to a close, Albert was denied the opportunity to look at the book that Herbert had been reading from. He wasn't exactly sure how much help it would have been, but it would have been nice to put his mind at rest and take a look for himself. His presence was not required, and certainly not wanted, at the scene, and so he and Hannah had no choice but to return to the house.

As they walked up the stone steps to the front door, they both heard Andreas softly playing his piano. It seemed that the one person they had been worried about, was the one who seemed the most safe. Hannah, however, had decided that she would not wait any longer to see her grandfather. Part of the reason she had made the effort to visit was because she had been worried about him. She at least wished to see him once more before his health failed him altogether, as by then it would be too late. She planned to demand seeing him on the following day. It had been an unpleasant and tiring experience being in the midst of a murder investigation, and she also felt rather guilty that Herbert's death undoubtedly had something to do with her and Albert's enquiry. He certainly didn't deserve to die.

She joined Albert in the lounge, which was a room that had once been very impressive. The same wallpaper that had been pasted to the walls many years ago, now hung off with a dull yellow tint. A large space, where Andreas' grand piano once stood, remained in the corner of the room. It was such a shame that her grandfather had lost interest in everything to do with life, everything, except playing his piano. Albert sat on the settee, with his head hanging loosely over the back of his seat. He wasn't in the mood for conversation. He had now fully switched into his old investigative mode, and his mind had automatically reverted to churning the facts over and over inside his head. Hannah didn't speak, but just sat down beside him and switched on the television. She flicked through several channels; until momentarily she felt her heart practically stop beating, as she came to a programme that provoked profound interest.

A newsreader had appeared on the screen with the headline "FEHLT" written at the bottom. The woman reading the report, read from her sheet of paper:

'Eine Frau aus Presberg, in der Nähe von Rüdesheim am Rhein, hat nach nicht für fast einen Monat gesehen berichtet fehlende.' Hannah grabbed the remote and turned on the subtitles to English as quick as she could.

'Albert – read what's on the television! It says a woman from Presberg has been reported missing!' A picture of the missing woman appeared on the screen. Albert almost choked as he struggled to sit upright in his seat. He studied the television carefully, trying to take in each word quickly, as the words on the screen changed in time with the newsreader. He read out the subtitles to fully absorb the news:

'Rebecca Sharp, forty-seven, was last seen by family on July 23rd, and has not been seen since. We are aware that she handed in her notice at her place of work, and has since left the home of the famous composer Andreas Krause, where she was employed as housekeeper for almost thirty years. Her parents, who live in Düsseldorf, have stated that it was usual for their daughter not to be in regular contact, although she usually telephoned every fortnight. Once three weeks had passed, they became fearful that something was wrong and reported her missing. They hope that she is safe and well, and that she gets in contact with them as soon as possible. If you have any information regarding the disappearance of this woman, please contact the number listed above.' Quickly, as if the news was now old and insignificant, the newsreader leapt straight into another story. Hannah muted the sound on the television and looked at Albert.

'I told you something was wrong with her swift departure.'

'I didn't disbelieve you. There's something very strange going on here, and I trust you are correct when you say it stems from your Grandmother's death all those years ago.'

'So what are we going to do?' Albert thought for a while.

'The only person who connects everything together is your Grandfather, Andreas Krause.'

'Do you think he may have had something to do with my Grandmother's death?'

'Almost certainly. We need to find out exactly what happened.'

'How are we going to do that?'

'I think the best option we have is you trying to get in to see him – don't take no for an answer. While you're doing that, I'll go to the library in the village and see if I can dig anything up there.'

'Okay. I'm also guessing that Mr. Lorenz's death is also connected.'

'Unfortunately, I would assume that to be the case. Murder is a terrible business, as you know. But, when secrets begin to unravel, the culprit will do whatever it takes so that their identity remains hidden. If they've killed once, then they are undoubtedly capable of killing again. I'm afraid that Mr. Lorenz, helpful as he was trying to be, probably faced the terrified wrath of the person whom we seek.'

'And what about what he tried to tell you about Misty? Could he really be involved?'

'I wouldn't like to say at this stage. Do you know where he was last night?' Hannah looked at the floor.

'I have no idea.'

'Don't be too downhearted about it yet. Don't forget, he was not able to carry out his duties in the garden and so there was no point in him being here. Also, he doesn't live here and so he could quite simply have gone home; he has no reason to come here today.'

'But if I know Misty, he'll be dying to get back to work and so would probably be hanging about the place in case there was a slight opportunity that he was able to go back into the garden.' Albert placed his hand on her shoulder, and smiled down at the disconcerted girl.

'Let's forget about Stefan for now, and focus on finding out a bit more about Andreas.' She smiled half-heartedly and nodded to him.

'When shall I try?' Albert smiled again.

'No time like the present.' She paused momentarily, and then sloped off towards the door of the lounge. She turned around to ask Albert a question:

'If I do manage to get him to let me in, where will you be?'

'I'll be wherever you want me to be. I can wait in here, or outside the room, or I can go to the library; it's your choice.' She thought about it for a few seconds before answering:

'You may as well go to the library and see what you can find. I'll be okay, so there's no point you wasting your time by just waiting around for me. I'll come to the library when I'm done.'

'Or if I finish first, then I'll come back in here.'

'Deal.' Slightly less feebly, she managed to smile once more, and then disappeared from view. After thirty seconds or so, he heard her knock upon the music room door and start her German spiel, which no doubt translated to various pleading phrases to try to coax him into letting her in. Albert turned back to the television, where something else caught his eye. The female newsreader was still on screen reading her latest headline. He grabbed the remote control and raised the volume just slightly so that he could only just hear it, but so there was no chance that Hannah would be able to listen in from where she was standing. Almost instantly, however, he muted the sound again, forgetting he would not even be able to understand what the reporter was saying. Instead, he mumbled the subtitles under his breath, and was astonished at what he was reading:

'A man from Rüdesheim was found dead this morning. Herbert Lorenz, a University Professor at Heidelberg University, was found bludgeoned to death by a hammer, in his father's shop, Schlosser Lorenz. Seemingly an unprovoked attack, police have already arrested a man in connection with the murder.' Albert's suspicions rose alarmingly inside him. In just a few moments, Stefan's picture would be on the television, and with Hannah being so fond of him, he knew when he broke the news to her, her spirit would be crushed. He carried on reading: 'This man was seen fleeing the street where the murder took place, and was found by police acting agitated and distressed. Educated at a university in England, the man has been identified as Johann Krause, son of the famous composer Andreas Krause.' Albert spoke aloud: 'Johann Krause! That's Hannah's father!' Suddenly, events had darkened enormously.

Hannah waited patiently outside her grandfather's room. He was clearly ignoring her, as she could hear him playing. However, she was determined not to get angry in case her mood made him retreat even further. She was content enough to play the waiting game for now, although, she was not prepared to wait longer than that day. However she managed to accomplish it, she was adamant she was seeing him within the next few hours. She continued to knock softly on the door in the hope that he would eventually concede and allow her to enter. She was surprised to see that the door remained intact; due to the frequent taps it must receive, she would have thought part of it would have worn away. At various intervals, she also carried on shouting out to him; hopeful that each shout out would be the final one she would have to voice. It must be very distracting for him when trying to play his music, to have somebody on the outside, making a racket, but she was no longer concerned with his selfish needs. All she required was a short meeting to ask him some questions, and then if he so wished, from then on she would leave him alone.

Constantly hammering at his door became tiresome rather quickly. Albert had waved to her in support, as he headed out of the door to conduct his business at the library. She saw he had his phrasebook clasped in his hand, and couldn't help chuckling silently, just imagining was sort of irritable predicament he was likely going to get himself into. She called out again to her grandfather:

'Grossvater, liess mich in!' The usual harsh reply was batted back to her instantly:

'Gehen Sie weg!' Her determination was still unwavering. She was going to get in to see him no matter what.

'Nein. Ich bin nicht überall.'

'Du bist mir zu stören. Ich will nicht die Besucher.' She couldn't care less that she was disturbing him, and the fact that he didn't want visitors was, quite frankly, immaterial to her. She thought momentarily, and then called out the one thing that she hoped might force him to grant her the permission she wanted:

'Ich möchte über Oma wissen.' There was silence for a long period of time. Even the piano had ceased its music. The silence that seemed to seep under the bottom of the door was like the feeling of death that circled through a cemetery at night. Even the very mention of her grandmother had turned the air cold. She waited for what seemed like a prolonged period of time. Still no sound emerged from behind the door. She brought her hand up the door once more and felt the smooth wood brush over her skin. Pulling back her hand to knock she gulped heavily, as her patience now suffered in the hands of the infuriating situation. Suddenly, she heard a bolt slide backwards and click into place. The door pushed itself a few millimetres away from her as the pressure of being held against its frame lessened. A few moments later, the door handle was gradually pulled downwards, and the door slowly swung slightly ajar. Hannah still waited. Now she was trembling with anticipation. Surely nobody else could feel this when visiting a grandparent. All she heard after the door handle had creaked back up to its natural position were soft footsteps on the carpet, moving away from the door. They finished with the soft exhalation of the cushioned piano stool, as she heard her famous grandfather sit back down. She felt nervous, still stood outside the door, but she knew she had to go in. It was what she had been waiting for, for a long time now. The little hairs on her arms were standing vertically, and even taking a deep breath did not help to calm her down. She plucked up the courage to push the door open, mainly because she had to. Trembling all the way, she entered the room and closed the door behind her. His manner was very terse, as his first gruff command sounded:

'Schraubst du es.' She turned away from him and bolted the door. He was strangely paranoid about anybody gaining access to his room. Hannah had never wanted to see somebody so badly as she did him, but now she was there, she prayed for the minute she could leave. She felt very uneasy around the man; the man who had barely hugged her as a small child, despite seeing her once or twice many years ago. She thought perhaps he had only agreed to see her when her father had first took her to Germany, because she was afterall his new grandchild and he could hardly refuse. When she was younger, his disinterested demeanour would not have come across to her, as her childlike, innocent naivety would not have picked up on it. But now he appeared detached and cold-hearted, which, when she thought about it, she couldn't remember him being any different. He spoke again, another instruction: 'Sitzen.' She obeyed. She couldn't be disobedient, afterall this may be the only chance she got at gaining access to him, and she certainly didn't wish to upset him and cut it overly short without finding out the answers she wanted. So, she slowly shuffled over to him, and sat on one of the chairs by the coffee table. This meant he now had his back to her, and they sat in silence for several minutes. The awkwardness that strangled the atmosphere strengthened its grip with every second that went by.

As she glanced around the room, she noticed an old gramophone at the bottom of his bed. Several records were untidily dumped in a heap around it, and from what she could ascertain from where she sat, they looked like old records from when his partnership with Hans Goldmann was at its strongest in their heyday. When she turned around to look at her grandfather again, their eyes met as he had also turned and was watching her. He was almost glaring at her, as if her very presence was such a disastrous intrusion on his life. She felt like he would prefer her to sit there with her eyes closed so she could not snoop at him or at anything in his room. His eyes were not filled with love. The whites of his eyes were dull, and his pupils were jet black. His hair, which once was shoulder length, curly and golden when he was a lively performer at theatres across the country, was now straggly, dark grey, and mostly gone. He wore a suit, which looked as if he had bought it twenty years previously, and the shoulder pads on it were smothered in dandruff. His nails were overgrown and were an unsightly colour of dark brown and yellow. She wondered if they impaired his ability to play the piano in any way; it certainly didn't sound like it when he was heard throughout the day. The one thing she did notice was his skin was not as pale as she had expected it to be. Being inside for such a long period of time, she would have thought his appearance to be pallid and quite sickly, but he looked healthy enough under the circumstances; obviously his vitamin pills were of the highest quality.

'Was willst du?' His voice was still gruff, but this time Hannah detected a very slightly more amenable tone. Although, in answer to his question, she wasn't quite sure what she wanted. She didn't know whether to just dive straight into questions about her grandmother, or whether she should ask some general questions out of common courtesy first. It seemed to her, however, that he was not interested in small talk, as he had not bothered to even ask how she was, what she was doing with her life, or anything similar. If she was honest with herself, it felt like they had never met. The constant pondering over his question, and weighing up in her mind about the best way to answer, clearly irritated him. He gave the impression as if he wished she would ask her questions and then leave at the earliest opportunity. Therefore, with that in mind, she decided to ask exactly what she had wanted to know for years. Inside she was fearful, but her voice was intrepid:

'War meine Oma ermordet?' If his face had not shown enough anger already, it certainly showed it now. He became incensed with rage. On reflection, perhaps asking him if her grandmother had been murdered, was not the best ice-breaker to their conversation, but it was his own fault for being the champion time-waster that he was. He tried to keep his facial expression to one of neutral, but she could tell just how livid he was. He had turned away after she had asked him, but he had now turned back with his reply:

'Was für eine seltsame Frage.' She disagreed with him. It wasn't an odd question at all, especially after everything that surrounded her death was most peculiar. 'Warum denkst du das?' Of course, she knew why she thought it, but she was unsure whether she should divulge all her thoughts about it to him.

'Weil es keinen Sinn macht, und Ich will die Wahrheit wissen.' She paused. 'Bitte hilf mir.' She didn't know why she added the last bit. Fair enough, she had admitted to him that her death just didn't make sense, and it was already obvious that she wanted to know the truth, without needing to tell him so, but why she had asked him to help her, was just as much a mystery to her as it was to him. He didn't even want to see anybody, let alone help someone he hardly knew find out the truth about something that had clearly affected him for a large portion of his life. She went on to tell him that she wasn't going to leave until she had her answers. He looked worried, almost threatened, by the stance that Hannah was making. He closed his eyes and turned away again. After cracking his knuckles, he proceeded to play a tune on the piano, which sounded rather light-hearted in comparison to the intense conversation they were having.

He played for several minutes. His hands were bouncing up and down on the keys using the full length of the keyboard;

his feet were changing pedals all the time, sometimes softening the tune that the instrument gave out, and sometimes making it louder with a lingering echo. It wasn't the best tune she'd ever heard him play. Suddenly, he stopped and crashed his hands down on the keys. Hannah was startled. She didn't know what to say. She just sat in her seat in silence, awaiting his next move.

Suddenly Andreas stood up. He edged sideways out from in between the stool and the piano, and went over to his bed. He knelt down beside it and pulled out from under it a small black box. It seemed to be a struggle for him, but he got to his feet and made his way back over towards Hannah. He sat on the other chair by the coffee table next to her. It was the closest she had been to him for such a long time, and she actually felt rather privileged that he dared to sit so near to her instead of snubbing her for his piano stool. He placed the box on the table and looked directly into her eyes.

'Dies sollst du mit den Antworten, die du suchst werden.' She couldn't believe what she was hearing. The box in front of her looked like the one that Herbert Lorenz had described to Albert. On top of that, Andreas had just told her that it should provide her with the answers she was looking for. She had only just stopped trembling and shaking from being so nervous when entering the room, and now she had resumed the movements.

'Danke schön!' He nodded at her in acceptance of her thanks to him. Hannah was so happy. Of course, she had no idea what the box contained but it was certainly colossal progress on her investigation. She stood up to leave, and picked up the box. All of a sudden, just as she was about to take a step away, he shot out his hand and grabbed her arm tightly. His grip was strong for an old man and it hurt her, but she did not move. Instead, she just looked at him, and stared into his cold, black eyes. She wanted to look away, but something stopped her from doing so. His gaze was lifeless, as if his very soul had been removed. She noticed just how much his face had wrinkled over the years, and how skeletal he had become. Hannah felt genuinely frightened, as he continued to hold her. He opened his mouth and she saw his black teeth clamped together as he snarled. He spoke slowly, and with a power that fully embraced her attention. His voice had changed, but she was forced to listen to every rasping word he said:

'Holen Gerechtigkeit für deine Oma.' Then, once he had finished, his hand went limp, fell off her arm, and crashed down onto the table. Quickly, she moved away and hurried with the box towards the door. She unbolted it and pulled down on the handle, which opened it slightly. Something within her made her look back at the dishevelled man. She saw someone who was living, but was not alive. He had clearly died a long time ago, but the despondent, miserable part of his soul, kept his body going. He was slumped over the table, seemingly oblivious to what had happened.

'Danke noch einmal. Bis bald Grossvater.' He kept staring down at the table and did not look up. He just mumbled something, which was barely audible:

'Auf Wiedersehen Hannah.' She took one final glance at him, and then hurriedly escaped, closing the door behind her.

His last line had puzzled her. Why would he say goodbye? It wasn't exactly what he said, but more with the expression he had used to say it. Was he fearful of his own imminent demise? She didn't know, but she could do nothing more than store it at the back of her mind. The line that now haunted her, however, had been his penultimate sentence. That had shocked her the most and it also eradicated any doubts she may have had: "Holen Gerechtigkeit für deine Oma". A chill travelled down her spine. He knew. He had always known. She needed to see Albert, but she just couldn't bring herself to move away from the door. It was frightening to think just how tragic her grandfather's life had become. She slid down the door and slumped on the floor, while she attempted to put her many thoughts into a logical order. She also thought that perhaps she should go back in to see him. They hadn't particularly spoke, and she had come out again within a matter of minutes. She stood up and was about to knock, but decided against it, when she heard the cold, steel bolt delicately slide into its place on the other side of the door. He had sat on the truth so for so long, so why only now, had he told her to get justice for her grandma.

8

It was late at night. Hannah hadn't bothered trekking down to the library to meet Albert. She had felt disturbed from her meeting with her grandfather. A meeting that she had craved for so long, and now she almost wished it had never happened. She sat on her bed with the black box he had given her, resting on her lap. She didn't want to open it, as she felt fearful for what she might find. All she wanted to do was to sit upstairs, alone and in silence until Albert returned, and then they would go into the new discovery together. She just couldn't seem to shake Andreas' haunting words from her mind. Why had he told her to get justice for her grandma? She knew, of course, that her grandma needed justice – she had come to that conclusion herself years ago. But, she was greatly puzzled as to why he had told her. He had kept the secret of her suspicious death for half of his life, and only now had he spoken out, and that was to her, his granddaughter who he barely knew. Everything else also spun around in her mind: the piece of paper under her pillow with 'HANNAH' written on it; the key that was there too, although now she at least had the box that it was for; the indent of the previous sheet of paper that showed a peculiar selection of words, which also implicated her father in some way; the mysterious disappearance of the old housekeeper; the body found buried in the garden; Misty's strange behaviour, and the murder of Herbert Lorenz. All these things plagued her mind. There was clearly a lot more going on than it had first seemed. She shuddered at the thought of what she had plunged herself into. At least she had Albert with her. He was such a kind, helpful man, and she knew he was not going to let her down. She turned to look at the clock. It had just passed closing time for the village shops, which included the library. Thankfully, she knew she wouldn't have much longer to wait for him to return, and so she stayed sitting on her bed just staring at the black box in front of her.

Within half an hour, Albert had returned. He walked calmly through the door carrying a bundle of papers that he had printed out at the library.

'I sincerely hope I never have to go back there! I might happen to be foreign to that librarian, but she was talking to me as if I just landed on the planet! Just because I'm not German, it does not mean I am deaf and dumb – there's no need to shout and talk as slowly as a sloth scratching it's own backside!' He was about to continue with his rant, until he noticed Hannah quietly perched on the end of her bed. She hadn't even looked up at him. She also looked quite forlorn, and he detected that something was wrong. He closed the door behind him and walked across the short distance to the bed. He sat beside her. 'What's wrong? Did you see your grandfather?' She nodded, although she didn't appear very convincing in her reply. Albert saw the box that was balanced on her legs. 'What's in the box?'

'My grandfather gave it to me. Do you recognise it?' He picked it up and turned it around, examining it closely.

'Is this the one that we are looking for?' She nodded again, this time more strongly.

'I think so.' Albert put it back on her knees.

'Have you opened it?' This time she shook her head.

'No.' She paused. 'I was waiting for you.' He took in a deep breath and then exhaled it gently.

'Well again, there's no time like the present. Do you have the key?'

'I'll get it.' She handed the box back to Albert, and got off the bed. She started rummaging in the suitcase for the key, however, when she returned, Albert had already been looking at the box a little more closely.

'Let me have the key for a moment.' Hannah gave it to him. He looked at the key and then again at the box. Finally, after just a few seconds, he handed both items back to his young assistant. He smiled. 'You can open it.' Hannah looked slightly confused but took the two objects from him nonetheless. She positioned the box on her legs once more, and held the key in her right hand, ready to push it into its lock. Then she stopped. She turned the box around, and looked at it again. Getting slightly frustrated, she looked at all six sides of the box, before putting it back down. She looked up at Albert.

'There's no keyhole.' He grinned. It wasn't exactly a triumphant expression, as it meant they were back to square one, but nevertheless the box was still a clue of some sort, otherwise Andreas would not have given it to her. 'I'm afraid that's not the box we are searching for.' Hannah looked incredibly dejected at the revelation. 'Don't be disheartened. If this box didn't mean something, then he would not have entrusted you with it.'

'I suppose.'

'Did he say anything of importance when he gave it to you? Or indeed at any time during the duration of your visit?'

'I wasn't there long. I'm not even sure if I want to see him again. I needed to see him once, but he scared me. It was creepy, and the whole experience gave me shivers. I didn't even see him as my grandfather anymore.' She paused, becoming emotional as she spoke. 'He was just a shell; a hollow carcass that lives on. The only emotion he has is pain. There was no love in his eyes; no warmth in his heart, and no trust in his soul. It was as if I was talking to the remains of a great man from long ago. I felt nothing, and neither did he. It was chilling.'

'I'm sorry.' Albert put his arm around her. He wasn't the best person to provide comfort. In some ways he knew how Andreas must feel. The void that was created within his soul when Elizabeth had been taken from him was an agony that not many people could truly understand. However, Hannah was still young, and so as her elder, he felt it his duty to try and provide the consolation that she required.

'In answer to your question though, he came alive when he spoke one specific sentence to me, which undeniably meant everything to him.'

'And what was it that he told you?' She hesitated.

'He handed me this box, and he told me to get justice for my grandma.' Albert removed his hand from around her.

'That certainly is a revelation. He obviously feels strongly about avenging her death.'

'But is it that? Or is it guilt? For all we know, he could be responsible. Is he even ill? He looked frail, but wouldn't anybody look unwell after being cooped up for so long?'

'Do you think he killed her?'

'In all honesty, I don't know what to think. But I reckon we should open this box, and uncover exactly what he thinks will be useful to us.'

'Then open it. I've seen these kinds of boxes before. Just push in the two small sides of the box together, and the lid should flip up.' Hannah did as he had described, and the top panel of the box popped up. Both Albert and Hannah peered in to have a look at its contents. The inside of the box was as preserved as the exterior. It was lined with beautiful purple velvet, which was delicate and soft to touch. The box contained just two items: a diary and a wristwatch.

The diary was chocolate-brown and made from suede. It was held together by a strap of the same material, which penetrated through it, tied up in two knots on the reverse. Hannah flipped through the pages, not reading anything that was written in it. It was just one of her habits when presented with a new book. The pages were an incredibly pale yellow colour, and virtually looked like old parchment. All in all, she thought the diary was quite exquisite. On the front of the diary, in faint gold lettering, was the inscription "1980 – 1985".

'Albert, it looks like a five-year diary.' She showed him the front of it. He took a glance.

'And it covers the year of 1983, which we already know to be the year your grandmother died.' He turned his attention back to the wristwatch. He had picked it up almost instantly after the box had been opened. It was most definitely a ladies' watch. The raw metal of the delicate strap predominantly showed over the original gold colouring, which indicated that the watch had seen some wear in its lifetime. The main part of the device was rather hefty. It had very square features, and was beautifully rusty, which would have been a vast contrast to its appearance when it was originally made. The only numbers it had on its face were twelve and six, the rest were substituted for raised lines or dots, which circled around the dainty hands. The little crown that altered the time was in the shape of a small seashell, and similarly above and below the face were two more shells, which attached the strap to the main component. Albert pondered the rationality of a nautical theme but disregarded it as quickly as he had thought of it. As he stared through the glass, which bore minimal scratches, he noticed the brand logo name of Junghans – it was clearly a very exclusive watch and whoever has been given the pleasure of wearing it was indeed very privileged. What struck Albert the most, however, was a small diamond that had been set in the lower part of the case under the number six. The diamond was noticeably a lot newer than the watch itself as it retained more shine and gleam, which sparkled sharply, just like the timepiece would have once done. Albert wasn't an authority on old watches, although he was fairly certain that it was post-war; however, he had no idea when the diamond would have been added. 'Have you ever seen any pictures of your grandmother?'

'Only one, but that was a long time ago. All I remember is her curly blonde hair, which fell just below her ears. She was thin and looked tall, although she was sitting on a wall wearing a long skirt and a white cardigan. That's all I can tell you.'

'Don't worry about it. It's not as if any information about her would be much help, not after all this time.'

'I wasn't allowed to ask anything about her, especially not to my grandfather, and so I just found it safest if I never spoke about her to anybody. Not even my father.'

'Do you know her name?'

'Yes. Her name was Imelda.'

'What a beautiful name.'

'Where do we go from here?'

'May I suggest we have a look in the diary? That might give us a clue of where we should be looking. I'd quite like to get this watch checked out too; just to see how old it is and why it should be such a valuable keepsake to be kept in this hidden box.'

'There's a jewellery shop in Rüdesheim that should be able to look into that for you. I see loads of watches in their display window every time I walk past.'

'I would say that's a job for tomorrow. Let's look in that diary.'

The two intrigued investigators sat side by side on the bed, flicking through the pages in the old diary. The vast majority of them were empty, which disheartened them both with every turn. Even on the date that Imelda died, there was no entry written in. Hannah was ready to give up. She had just turned through nearly three years of blank pages and had hoped to uncover something by that point, in particular around the time leading up to her grandmother's death. It was shattering to keep finding nothing, not even a single word was recorded inside. Albert was a lot more patient. He had lived through many years and lots of circumstances of disappointment in his line of work. He had learnt to deal with setbacks and defeat like they were nothing. Over the years he had taught himself to expect the worst, which meant anything else would be a bonus. He urged her to carry on turning the pages, backing up his argument by assuring her that Andreas would not have handed over the diary to her if it were not related to her search. She was overwhelmingly downhearted but eventually she conceded and turned over another page. Here, they stared at the first entry made into the journal that was supposed to chronicle her grandfather's life for a five-year period. The page for December 31st 1983 displayed a short paragraph that both Albert and Hannah prayed and hoped would give them the knowledge they needed to get to the bottom of it all. Hannah slowly read out the passage:

'Es tut mir leid Imelda. Dieser Kummer war es nicht wert. Ich werde meine Affäre zu beenden. Deine Gedächtnis darf nicht verblassen. Du warst mein Fels – keener der anderen. Die Hände der Zeit wird mich immer verfolgen. Es ist nichts mehr, als ich verdiene. Unsere Trennung ist meine Schuld. Ich kann nicht glauben, was ich getan habe. Ich habe meine Frau umgebracht.' Albert sat in silence.

There was not a single word he had understood. He looked at Hannah who just stared at the page.

'Of course, you're going to have to translate that for me.' Hannah looked up at him. She had practically forgotten that he was there. It took her a few moments to reinstate her mental presence, but once she had done so, she obliged and read the diary entry out again, at the same pace only this time in English.

'I am sorry Imelda. This heartache was not worth it. I will end my affair. Your memory must not fade. You were my rock – none of the others. The hands of time will haunt me forever. It is nothing more than I deserve. Our parting is my fault. I can't believe what I have done. I have killed my wife.' Now they were both silent. Albert pondered each part of the passage. He was used to churning information over and over in his mind. He voiced an obvious thought:

'It would seem that Andreas was not exactly faithful to Imelda.'

'But it looks as though he cheated on her time and time again. When he says that she was his rock, he follows it up with "none of the others". Just how many times did he betray her?'

'Countless, is the implication.'

'He has also admitted to killing her.'

'Indeed he has. I have to say it puts a very dark spin on my admiration for him. For years I have admired his work and considered him to be a truly remarkable man, but now even I feel hollow. I am someone who has never met him, whereas you are his blood relative. I cannot even begin to try and understand the way you must be feeling right now.'

'I don't know how I feel myself. I don't know if I even feel anything towards him. I do not love him, as I don't particularly know him. But I don't feel hate for him because I never knew the woman who he killed. I just feel vacant.'

'What do you want to do now?'

'To be honest, I think I'd like to go home.'

'Are you sure?'

'Why should I stay now? I have my answer. I knew my grandmother was murdered and it's now been confirmed.'

'Don't you want to ask him about it?'

'What for?'

'Because you've come all this way to find this information out. Don't you want to know why she died? Or how?'

'What use is that to me?' Albert hesitated before he spoke.

'Something just doesn't lie right. What's going on here is not just about Imelda. Her death started it all off all those years ago, but it seems as if the body in the garden and the death of Herbert Lorenz are also connected with it.'

'I don't see how they can be. I've got the facts that I came here for and now it's time for me to go. You are more than welcome to stay if you think there are any further mysteries to sink your teeth into but I am finished here, and I never want to come back.'

'What about your grandfather's funeral? I mean, when he dies, are you going to come back for that?'

'I don't think so. He means nothing to me. Going to somebody's funeral is to show them respect. I don't respect him. You can't respect someone you don't know. Besides, the only thing I know about him is the fact that he killed my grandmother.'

'I think you're being a little hasty.'

'Perhaps. But I guess that's for me to live with.'

'I really don't think you should go.'

'I've made up my mind. There's nothing here for me. I want to forget it all and go back to England. Tomorrow,

I'll be booking the soonest flight back home and I'm going to do my best to forget everything German.' Hannah got up and handed the diary to Albert. He still held the watch loosely in his hand. 'Thank you for your help Albert. If you wish to be on the same flight then just let me know.' She smiled at him, turned, and slowly walked towards the bedroom door. Albert was in two minds about divulging some more information to her. She was just about to pass through the doorframe when she heard his voice behind her.

'Your father was arrested today in connection with Herbert Lorenz's murder.' She stopped. She froze. Then slowly, she turned around.

'Is that supposed to be a joke?' Albert's face was stern.

'I do not joke about matters such as that.' Hannah walked back over to the bed.

'I'm sorry; I know you wouldn't. It was just so unexpected.' She paused. 'When did you find that out?'

'This morning, just before you went in to see Andreas. I didn't want to tell you because you were nervous enough, and I didn't think it would be a good move for you to have that stuck on your mind while you were trying to probe him for information.'

'You did the right thing. Why was my father here anyway? I thought he was in England.'

'I'm afraid I don't know anything further. That is all I know; it was on the news more or less straight after the headline about Rebecca's disappearance.'

'I wonder why he has been arrested. There must be something incriminating otherwise they wouldn't waste their time would they?'

'Perhaps he was just around at the time. It could be anything. Has he ever been in trouble with the police before?'

'Not that I'm aware of. I know he doesn't drive anymore but I'm not exactly sure why. He used to years ago, but I've never known him to. I've always grown up knowing Amanda to drive us all around.' Albert made a noise that suggested he was contemplating what she had said.

'I don't think that will be relevant. Perhaps you should go down to the police station and try to find out what's going on. Hopefully, it will have just been circumstantial evidence, which made it seem like he was linked to the death. I shouldn't worry too much about it until you get there.'

'I guess you're right. What are you going to do?'

'I'm going to attempt something that I fear is going to be practically impossible.'

'Which is?'

'I'm going to try and see Andreas. There's more to all this than meets the eye; I just know there is – and I want to find out what it is.'

'How are you going to tackle the language barrier?'

'I was hoping if I told you the questions I wanted to ask him, you might write them down in German. I can try and say them to him correctly, or he can read them himself and write his answers down for you to translate afterwards.' Hannah nodded.

'Do you really think there is more to all this then it appears?'

'In my experience, nothing is ever as it first seems. I believe we've only just barely scratched the surface.'

'He told me to get justice for my grandmother. Why would he say that if he killed her?'

'At the moment I haven't a clue. But just consider the fact that you asking me that very question, proves that there is more for us to uncover. If he killed her, there is no justice to be got. If he didn't kill her, then justice can be got.'

'But we know he killed her – he has confessed to it.'

'He has indeed. But we don't know the circumstances. I can't lie to you and say this is going to be easy because it's not. It's going to be extremely difficult, emotional, confusing, and hurtful. But if you want the final truth, you're going to have to stick at it.'

'He killed her.'

'I know.'

'Then what else is there to find out?' Albert stood up and moved over to where Hannah stood. He placed his hand on her shoulder and squeezed it softly.

'Hannah, have you ever heard the phrase of never judging a book by its cover?' She nodded. 'Well you should never judge any of the pages it contains either.'

Hannah had written the list of questions that Albert had dictated to her. They waited outside the music room while Albert built up the courage to request entry. The familiar sound of the grand piano could be heard distinctly from the other side of the room. He wasn't usually a nervous man, but to him, despite the circumstances, it was like meeting a high-profile celebrity.

'Do you want me to stay while you're in there? That's if he allows you in anyway.'

'No, go and find out about your father. Or you could make yourself useful by doing some more research at the library if you like? You might be able to pick up on a lot of things I've missed because I didn't understand them.'

'I don't mind waiting – I doubt you'll be in very long anyway. I wasn't.' Albert chuckled.

'Yes, but I won't leave until I have all the answers I want; no matter how much he protests. I can be very stubborn when I have to be.'

'I don't disagree with you!' A few moments of silence passed by. 'What's the best way to get in then? Do you want me to pretend I want to go in and when he unlocks the door you can just enter instead?'

'I doubt he'd take too kindly to that. Probably best to just be honest with him from the start. I don't want him thinking that my visit is underhand otherwise he might clam up even further and I'll get nothing out of him.'

'Would you like me to shout for you?'

'Now that's a good idea seeing as I haven't got a clue what I would be shouting!' Hannah stepped up to the door and knocked loudly upon it.

'Grossvater, es jemanden gibt, würde ich mag dich zu treffen.' The music that sounded from within the room stopped, as soon as she had finished speaking. Hannah looked at Albert, who shrugged his shoulders in reply. He had no idea what went through the composer's mind.

'What did you say?'

'I told him there is somebody I'd like him to meet.'

'Do you think you should tell him who I am?'

'I'm not sure. Would you want an ex-policeman snooping around; especially when there are strange occurrences going on?'

'I guess not. But surely anything is worth a try; I mean, I'm not in the room yet am I?' She lowered her eyebrows slightly, possibly in mild annoyance; Albert was unsure. Nevertheless, however she felt, she sprouted out another string of unfathomable German words. This time, she used great force in her voice. The eruption quite startled Albert who actually clutched his heart, as he shuddered at her outburst.

'Grossvater, es ist ein elend, eigenartig und störrische Alte, so wie du bist. Beantwortst du die Tür jetzt!' She turned to Albert. 'Well if that doesn't get him to let you in, I don't know what will! I'll see you later.' Without a second glance, she left, leaving Albert standing outside the room all on his own. He leant against the wall and looked down at the carpet, shuffling his feet from side to side. The music didn't restart but he heard no other noises from within the room either. He would not be able to call anything else out to Andreas, as he would not understand him. Feeling defeated he pushed himself away from the wall and walked away. Several steps from the door, and just about to mount the staircase, he heard the sound of the bolt sliding backwards and clicking against the metal panel behind it. Albert swung around, wondering if he had heard correctly. But there were no misgivings over the quality of his ears, unless his eyes also deceived him. He watched as the door handle lowered and the door creaked open, slightly ajar.

9

Andreas stood at the window looking out, away from the room. Albert sat, feeling rather uneasy, in one of the chairs by the coffee table. He wondered what pleasure the famous composer got by staring out of the window when he had the blinds down and firmly shut. No light entered the room and similarly it was not possible to see out of them. It felt like a long while that went by but then again what was either of them meant to say? Whatever one man said, was likely not to be understood by the other, and Albert began wondering what the purpose of his visit actually was. He looked down at the floor – something which seemed to be forming as a habit when around Andreas. He noticed the piece of paper in his hand that contained the questions written down by Hannah. That was the reason for his visit. The language barrier didn't matter because he simply required Andreas to write his answers down on the other side. All he needed to do was attract his attention in some way. He didn't much fancy creeping up behind him and tapping his shoulder for fear of scaring the poor man to death. It wasn't even a more favourable option to pretend to obviously cough in the hope that he would turn around. The last time he had attempted that particular strategy had resulted in him irritating his throat something chronic, which led to a very unpleasant bout of coughing, making him look like a complete fool. His next idea took him to looking around the room. He saw the two cups on the table he was sat at and even picked one of them up, seriously contemplating hurling it at the man. That would certainly attract his attention; either that or kill him, which was actually the overriding factor in putting it back down on the coaster. He decided to leave it to Andreas to make the first move. Instead he got to his feet and walked over near the bed to look at the pile of records that lay on the floor beside it. The record at the top of the stack was a vinyl of one of Goldmann and Krause's releases from 1968. The cover showed a picture of them both. Andreas was sitting at the piano with his hands folded together in his lap, and Hans stood beside him, leaning against his musical friend. Andreas smiled broadly, while Hans acted as a sophisticated clown, bearing a cheeky grin and holding a giant cigar. They looked so happy, and it was still surprising to think it had all, at some stage, gone so wrong. Albert placed the record back where he had found it and sighed deeply as he had exhausted all his ideas of either occupying himself or gaining Andreas' attention. He turned back to look at Andreas and almost fell onto the bed; he was standing right beside him. The two men stared at each other for a few intense seconds, before Andreas lifted his thin arm, pointed his bony finger at Albert and beckoned him to follow. Halfway across the room, he then pointed back at the chair where Albert had previously been sat. Albert followed the man's instruction and obediently sat down. Andreas carried on to the piano where he placed himself on the stool, shuffling around on it briefly until he had found the most comfortable position. He turned his head slightly towards Albert and pulled on one of his own ears, indicating that his guest should listen. Albert felt quite excited – was this really going to be a private performance? The man whose musical talents he had admired for decades was going to execute his exceptional talents for a singular audience; he was honoured. Andreas started playing.

Twenty-five minutes passed by. Truthfully, it only felt to Albert like a couple. The smooth melody of the composition relaxed him and its slightly quirky rhythm in parts made him smile and cheered him up immensely. The piece Andreas was playing was the one Albert had been looking at from the pile by the bed. He wished he had looked at them all, in the futile hope that the musical genius would have performed the entire collection for him.

A feeling of admiration soared through the whole of Albert's body, which promptly reduced itself to minor sadness once the great musician had hit the final note. The note lingered on for thirty seconds or more, with a reverberation that seemed to channel across the floor and absorb itself into every item of furniture. It even travelled up Albert's legs; the music was powerful, as he had always known, but to experience it so personally was an experience he never thought would have ever happened, and he certainly was never going to forget it. He applauded with such energy for the performance Andreas had given, although he knew the sound of his claps was worthless compared to the recital he had been treated to – but it was all he could offer.

Andreas stayed at the piano for ages, just staring at the music stand. There was no music on it, however, as he had memorised every note for every piece of music. His ailing health clearly did not affect his memory. Unfortunately, despite both men appreciating the last half an hour, the awkward silence had resumed and the same problem of who would be first to attempt a conversation returned in full force. It was Andreas who moved from the piano stool to sit in the chair next to Albert. He gazed at Albert, and the old detective picked up precisely on the haunting look that Andreas' eyes possessed. The musician looked down at Albert's hands and saw the piece of paper gripped tightly in his palm. A few seconds went by, but slowly he outstretched his arm and opened his own hand, encouraging Albert to pass it to him. Albert obliged and surrendered his ownership of the paper. The frail composer unfolded it and began to read. Albert watched his eager eyes flick over the words. He saw the pupils move left and right, and subsequently downwards, as he neared the bottom of the page. When he had finished, he kept the position of his head where it was but moved his eyes to look up at Albert. His posture made him look crazy. He had the sort of look that you would expect from somebody who cuts peoples' limbs off for the sheer fun of it. Leisurely, he put the paper down on the table, and rested the tip of one skeletal finger on top of it. Bit by bit, he pushed it back across towards Albert. Albert watched as the paper moved, and when he looked back up at Andreas, he saw that the old man was smiling. It was a terrible smile. His black teeth looked like pieces of worn down coal in a fire grate. But the fire was in his eyes. Quite frankly he looked like a lunatic, but Albert knew it was the look of a sinister presence that smothered a contender for its deathly grasp. It was Albert himself, however that could have easily dropped dead when out of the blue, Andreas spoke to him:

'Do you know what a crescendo is?' He still smiled. Albert was unsure whether he was supposed to look menacing, or whether it was his natural smile that he just could not help. His heart had skipped a beat. It was enough of a shock to hear him speak, let alone to listen to English words escape from his lips. Albert didn't exactly know what to say, but cobbled together an answer, out of politeness if nothing else:

'Is it an increase of sound?'

'It is a gradual increase in loudness in a piece of music.'

'Thank you for letting me know.'

'Or it is a progressive increase in intensity. Were you relaxed when you listened to me play?'

'I was very relaxed.'

'Since talking to me, have you become more and more intense?' Albert felt uneasy. He was unsure where the line of questioning was going.

'Yes.'

'Then you have just experienced a crescendo of your feelings. Point proven.'

'There was no point to prove; I wasn't arguing with you.'

'Even so.' Albert left it a few moments before resuming the conversation:

'I was not aware you could speak English.' Andreas stayed silent. Albert opened his eyes wider and stared at him, trying to provoke a reply. He didn't receive one. 'Hello?'

'Hello.'

'I asked you a question.'

'No you didn't. You stated a fact. It was not a question; it required no response.'

'A response would have been courteous.'

'So would the respect of a person's privacy.' Albert opened his mouth to retaliate, but abruptly reconsidered. Afterall he was right. He rephrased his fact into a question:

'I was not aware you could speak English, have you done so for long?'

'A short while.' Albert wished he had a stone he could siphon some blood out of. This conversation was even more difficult now they were both speaking English than when he thought they would not be able to understand each other. Thankfully, Andreas added to his answer. 'I have achieved a lot of things in my life; many of which I have kept secret. I have chosen to live my life a certain way, for reasons that I wish to keep to myself. During the time I have spent mainly on my own, I decided to learn a different language. I chose English because my son married an Englishwoman.

Therefore, should the occasion have ever arisen, I would have been able to converse with her perfectly. At least talking to you, my efforts in learning the language have not been wasted.'

'I still would have thought people would have known you spoke English. Everybody thinks you only speak German.'

'Nobody ever asked if I spoke English. I see no need to tell them. It would just be useless information for them.'

'Have you ever thought about opening yourself up and being more approachable? You might find you enjoy it.'

'Have you ever thought about minding your own business?' Normally, Albert would retaliate to the extreme over such a remark, but somehow he again felt that the man was right. Albert was the intruder and so Andreas was perfectly entitled to voice his opinions in the comfort of his own home, in spite of how Albert intercepted them. He had never before experienced such a battle of wits; especially with someone whom he had thought the attempt at a conversation would have been a severe strain. Therefore, he decided to stay silent and leave it to Andreas to speak again if he so wished. It wasn't long before he did, and his voice had become softer. Perhaps even he regretted being so brusque towards his visitor. 'What is it you would like to know?'

'You have already read the list of questions I brought in.'

'But I am sure there are more you would like to ask seeing as now you are more comfortable with conversing in your own language.'

'I'll get straight to the point. I have admired your work for many years; what happened in 1983 that changed your life forever?' Andreas looked incensed and filled with rage. 'If you're going to erupt in anger, then at least have the decency to do so through the use of a crescendo – that way it will not be such a shock to me, as I will be able to sense it coming.' The anger dropped away from the composer, as quickly as it had appeared. He liked the way Albert had manipulated his own words and used it against him. The air was calm once more.

'That's a big question.'

'Then I expect a big answer.'

'I'm afraid I cannot give it to you.'

'Why not?'

'It is best forgotten. It is too hurtful to speak about.'

'If it is best forgotten then why did you give Hannah that box telling her to get justice for Imelda?' Andreas shouted:

'Don't use that name!' Albert stayed silent. 'I'm sorry. Her name should be used; I just haven't heard it in a while.'

'There's no need to apologise.'

'What is your name?'

'My name is Albert Murtland.'

'Are you married, Albert?'

'I used to be.'

'She left you did she?'

'You could say that, yes.'

'She had an affair then; women are all the same.'

'No, she didn't have an affair.'

'You said she left you.'

'She did, but unwillingly. She was taken from me.'

'Another man forced her from you? I don't understand.'

'Why are you obsessed with other men leading wives astray? My wife Elizabeth was killed in a hit-and-run accident nineteen years ago. So you see, she left me. But it was not her fault.'

'You can understand to some extent how I feel then?'

'Not exactly. I understand your loss. But not how you feel.' There was a long pause until Albert spoke again. He had to speak because it didn't look like Andreas was going to. 'You have a very distraught granddaughter staying at your house. She is worried about you, and she is adamant to know the truth about her grandmother, which to be honest, I think she deserves to know. Do the decent thing. By all accounts, as I'm sure you know, you do not have long left in this life – a matter of weeks I believe. Go to your death knowing you have told the truth and can put everyone else's minds at peace after you have gone. It's the least you could do.' Andreas stared at him. He still said nothing but he did pick up the piece of paper that Albert had brought in with him.

'You want to know how Imelda died – I killed her.'

'Why?'

'Because…' A knock sounded on the door. A gruff voice came from behind it:

'Es ist Stefan mit Tassen Tee.' Andreas whispered to Albert:

'It's Stefan. He's brought some tea. I'll have to let him in.' He walked across the room to the door and pulled back the bolt. Then, he retreated back to his seat. Stefan, looking scruffy as ever in his revolting green coat, entered the room carrying a tray. Albert was pleased to see that the kindly, old gardener had returned. Stefan had to look twice at Albert; he obviously hadn't expected anybody else to be in the room with Andreas. This was understandable owing to Andreas' strict visiting guidelines – two people in the room at once must have been an astonishing prospect for everybody. Albert nodded at Stefan but received no response. The gardener hobbled over to the coffee table and put down the tray of drinks. He arched his back and spoke quietly to Andreas:

'Es gibt nur zwei Getränke. Ich wollte nicht wissen, dass du Unternehmen hatst.'

'Möchtest du noch eine Tasse zu bekommen?' Albert was trying to decipher the interchange between them. He knew a couple of words, after being around various German nationals for the last few days. He knew "zwei" meant "two", and he guessed "Getränke" meant "drinks". So he assumed that Stefan had explained there were only two drinks, probably because he didn't know Andreas would have company. He waited for Stefan's answer to Andreas' question.

'Nein, ich kommen später zurück.' After that, Stefan stood back upright, glanced at Albert for a final time and trudged back across the room to leave. He walked slowly, just like a decrepit old man should. Albert carried on their conversation without even waiting for Stefan to completely leave. He figured that as he knew for sure Stefan didn't speak a word of English, he was safe to continue.

'So you were about to tell me how you killed Imelda.' Stefan closed the door behind him on his way out. He was in a world of his own. Andreas poured some milk into his tea. His eyes still followed Stefan, but they soon turned back to look at Albert.

'I was about to tell you, you are right. But the time for that has passed. It is getting late and you have outstayed your welcome here. All I am going to tell you is that despite this grand house, or rather former grand house, I am in fact penniless. I have minimal funds with which I pay my staff, but I haven't even got a spare eight Euros for a pot of paint for the front door. If you wish to find out what happened to Imelda, then that's all the information you will need to accomplish it.'

'But I thought you were going to tell me.'

'Well you thought wrong didn't you? You caught me at a moment of weakness, which will not happen again. Now, I am very thirsty at the moment – thirsty enough for two cups of tea. Therefore, you may leave. However, I will allow you to return tomorrow at the same time. I can put up with you for a short amount of time because we are alike.'

'I beg to differ; I'm nothing like you.'

'That's where you are wrong. Du bist ein elend, eigenartig und störrische Alte. Do you remember that?'

'I think so. It's what Hannah shouted to you before you let me in.'

'Correct. It means you are a miserable, peculiar and stubborn old man. Just like me. It was the only reason I let you in; I wanted to see if it was true.'

'I just want to know one thing...'

'There are lots of things that I want to know, but sadly we do not get to know them all. You can go now.' Albert stared at him, disbelieving that the meeting had come to such a sudden end. There were no further words from Andreas that suggested otherwise and so he had no choice but to stand up and walk away from the man who had earned his tremendous admiration over the years, but which now diminished by the second. He reached the door and pulled down on the handle. He was just about to leave when Andreas said one last thing:

'For a lot of things we wish to know in life, people usually find they are waiting in vain.' Albert stared at him, unsure of what to say. So he chose not to say anything, opened the door and left. When he was outside the room, he closed the door behind him. He saw Eleanor quickly dart out of view as he looked up. She disappeared from sight around the corner and he only saw the strap of her apron, as his eyes became more focused from turning around from the music room door. Albert thought she had been acting strange and distant for a short while now, and he had hardly seen anything of her recently. She had always seemed to keep herself to herself but had been increasingly secretive over the last twenty-four hours. A few seconds after she had vanished, clearly not wishing to be seen, Albert heard the click of the bolt behind him, which was fast becoming one of the only sounds that suggested the composer was still alive.

The following morning, Albert got out of bed and hurriedly dressed himself in his suit trousers and a shirt. His first intention was to knock on Hannah's door and let her know about her grandfather being surprisingly bilingual. She must have gone straight to bed when she had got in, as he had not seen anything of her over the course of the night. She had not turned up for dinner and neither was she present during any of the hours that followed, right up until Albert was ready to retire to his bedroom for a peaceful night's sleep. As much as he was in a rush to see her and ask her a barrage of questions, he could never exit his bedroom without first being properly dressed. There was no shame in being a gentleman right down to the very core.

Albert edged across the landing and stood outside Hannah's room. The time on his pocket watch had told him that it was at a decent enough hour but seeing as he was clueless as to the time that the rest of the household rose from their sleep, he tried to stay as quiet as he possibly could anyway. Incidentally, he was intrigued to find that the old watch they had found in Andreas' black box also confirmed the same time as his own pocket watch. It was obvious that the wristwatch manufactured by Junghans was the height of German technology for that era of watch making. Even looking fairly battered, it hadn't faltered on its timekeeping one bit.

He knocked gently on the door. Sounds of movement came from within the room and so he waited patiently for the door to be answered. The door soon opened, but seeing as it was Hannah's room, he had not expected anyone other than his young female companion to answer his knock. A man in his early-fifties opened the door. He was dressed, if that was the best adjective, in just some black underpants. He had short black hair, which matched his incredibly hairy chest, as well as overgrown stubble stuck on his cheeks and around his chin. Albert also noticed a very visible scar above the man's left eye. It looked like an old wound, but it was still quite evident, as it stretched from the centre of his eyebrow, horizontally through to the middle of his temple. He had a thick, coarse voice and a crotchety demeanour to match. He coughed before he spoke, clearing the morning phlegm from his lungs:

'Who are you?' Albert was astounded by the blasé attitude of the practically naked man. By no means did he wish to act like her father, but he would certainly be having strong words with her when he could. She shouldn't be out all night and then bringing strange men back to her room in any case, let alone when peculiar things were happening, as well as their own investigation.

'I, my good man, am a gentleman, which is more than can be said for you. I suggest you get dressed at once, clear off and never return.' The man stood up straight and towered over Albert. It was at this point that Albert realised he was in his seventies and perhaps picking a quarrel with an athletic-looking younger man was not the greatest idea he'd ever had.

'I suppose you're going to make me.'

'Not as such, no. I think we both know that would never happen.'

'Then what's your problem?'

'My problem is people like you who just think they can go out and pull a girl, take them home and just use them without a second thought. I doubt you would even call her and the age gap is just ridiculous!'

'She's quite adult enough to decide whether she wants to offer me a bed for the night. But you are right, I don't there's any need for me to call her, so no, I don't think I'll bother.'

'How can you be so callous?'

'It comes naturally from life experiences. Everyone is out for what they can get. What are you knocking on her door for anyway? You dirty old man.'

'How dare you! I can assure you my intentions are honourable, as they always are to any female that I meet.'

'Then why have you come knocking her up?' Albert looked at him, coldly.

'I hope for your sake that was an unfortunate phrasing mistake.'

'Look, why don't you ask her yourself what we've been getting up to? And then if you still don't like what you hear, I'll leave – how about that?'

'Well where is she?'

'Making breakfast I think. She went downstairs about ten minutes ago.' Albert shook his head in disgust.

'And you're even getting her to make the breakfast. You abhorrent individual. I suggest you put some clothes on and come downstairs at once. Good morning to you.'

'Now wait a minute…'

'I said good morning to you!' Albert turned and swiftly descended the stairs, glaring at the man with every step downwards until he could no longer see him over the banister.

Albert marched into the kitchen and found Hannah buttering some toast.

'I want a word with you, young lady.'

'Oh good morning Albert, do you fancy something to eat?'

'Not right now, no.' He paused. 'Actually that toast looks good.' He shook his head to try and regain his focus on the matter in hand. 'But first, what is the meaning of you bringing strange men back for the night? Have you no self respect?' Hannah put down the knife on the worktop.

'You've seen him them; I was hoping you wouldn't.'

'I bet you were. Look, I know things are difficult at the moment, but seeking solace in the arms of a lout is not the answer.'

'I've done no such thing!'

'Hannah, I may be old, but I haven't lost my memory quite yet. Young lust is a very powerful emotion. But you have to try and control it and make sure it takes place with the correct person, at a proper time and location.'

'I don't need this lecture from you; thank you very much. You're acting like my father!'

'Well I don't mean to.'

'Good! Because you're not!'

'That's right,' sounded a deep voice behind them, 'I am.' The man from upstairs appeared in the doorway of the kitchen. He outstretched his hand to Albert. 'Johann Krause, pleased to meet you.'

10

Shortly after the misunderstanding that had transpired between them, all three people started to get along. Being a typical teenage girl, Hannah was still not overly impressed with Albert's miniature outburst regarding her sexual antics. Johann, on the other hand, thanked Albert for looking out for his daughter. He told him it was comforting to know that in his absence there was someone he could trust to make sure Hannah was in safe hands. It turned out, fairly obviously, that Hannah had bypassed the library and taken Albert's suggestion to go to the police station to see if there was anything she could find out about her father's arrest. He had been released for the time being, as they had no condemning evidence that warranted a charge against him. Seeing as he had nowhere to go, she had offered him the floor of her bedroom until he could get fixed up in a more permanent dwelling. As it was Albert's fault that he had rushed Johann downstairs, the new household member had returned upstairs for a shower, leaving him alone to talk with Hannah.

'So why has he come to Germany? He doesn't look like he's on a holiday as such.'

'He's here for the same reason as me. Well, not the bit about my grandmother's death. I mean; he wanted to be here during the final moments of his father's life. He too had been contacted and told that his health was on the decline, and so felt he should be the doting son and make an appearance.'

'But what about his arrest? He comes over to Germany for a visit to see his ill father and ends up getting arrested for the murder of a local shopkeeper; that doesn't add up at all.'

'Apparently he was the first person who found him. He had got a late flight, and had landed just after midnight.

By the time he had reached Rüdesheim, it was the very early hours of the morning. He saw a light shining brightly from one of the shops; obviously the locksmiths, and went over to see if everything was all right. He was the one who found Herbert Lorenz's body.'

'Then why didn't he report it there and then?'

'That's what I asked him. He said he knows what the German police are like, and especially in this day and age where you are now unfortunately guilty until proven innocent. After he had knelt down to check if Herbert was still alive, he had got his blood over his hands and the shirt he was wearing. He said he tried to use the telephone to call the police but the cord had been cut. After that he knew whatever time he phoned the police would look suspicious as it wasn't going to be immediate, and so he panicked and ran out.' Albert looked confused.

'At what point did he think running out would be the best option for him?'

'Don't ask me; it wasn't my idea. He said he wanted to change his clothes as quick as he could, and then he was going to contact the police and act like he had just found the body.'

'That's ridiculous. So how did he end up getting arrested anyway?'

'A policeman saw him getting changed using the clothes he had in his suitcase. He was in an alleyway, a few streets away from the shop. Before, he could even mention about the body, he had been whisked away for indecent exposure in a public place. Unfortunately that meant somebody else had to go through the trauma of finding Herbert's body, as it wasn't until they got my father back to the police station when he was able to tell them.'

'Do you believe his story?'

'Why wouldn't I?'

'Don't you think it doesn't add up?'

'I think it's peculiar, yes, but it does add up.' Quickly, Albert put his finger to his lips, as a signal to Hannah to stop talking. He had heard somebody coming, and it certainly wasn't a conversation he wanted just anybody to listen in on. It was Eleanor who wandered into the kitchen.

'Good morning everybody.' Both Albert and Hannah said their respective greetings to her. 'Hannah, please tell me who on earth that rough looking man is. He looks like a vagrant. I'm quite sure he has nothing to do with Andreas or Albert, and he certainly has no connection to me. So unless Stefan has a twin brother that we know nothing about, that only leaves you. Would you care to explain why you have brought a tramp here without asking the permission of me, the housekeeper?'

'Eleanor, he doesn't look that bad.'

'I must say though Hannah, I'm afraid I agree with Miss. Frankwell. I don't particularly judge a person's character on their appearance, but I would have thought that the son of a famous composer would have had a little more style and be more image conscious than he is. Although, he isn't exactly a tramp; I think that's going a little too far.'

'You're not telling me that's Johann! What a disappointment; I was expecting a handsome, charming man, when I eventually had the pleasure of meeting him.' She went over to the kettle and started pouring in some water from the tap. Suddenly, she stopped and turned around to face the others. 'Hang on a minute; he was arrested for murder yesterday – what is he doing here?'

'I was cleared of all charges.' Johann had entered the room, looking cleaner but still somewhat scruffy in the tight t-shirt and torn jeans he had put on. 'All charges apart from indecent exposure anyway. Fancy a look?' He moved his hands to the zip on the front of his jeans, with a broad smile on his face. He became ruggedly handsome when he showed his cheeky grin. Eleanor, however, looked disgusted.

'You can keep that in your trousers thank you very much Mr. Krause. I fail to believe that anybody wishes to see it; especially so early in a morning, and certainly not before breakfast!' Everybody smiled. It was always fun to get Eleanor's back up.

The clock struck eleven and Albert watched from the lounge as Stefan trundled outside to collect the milk from Thomas, who had just pulled up outside the house. They were having a long chat, and both seemed to be enjoying the sunshine. The sky was a beautiful pale blue, with the odd cloud dotted around, and the sun shone brightly and lit up the ground and everything on it. Albert had suspected it would be a nice day. The previous night he had witnessed the clouds turn a burning orange colour, set against the deep blue night sky. An old saying he had grown up with, which he always remembered was: "Red sky at night, shepherd's delight; red sky in the morning; shepherd's warning". He wondered if it meant the shepherd's did not have to move their flock of sheep into shelter if they could tell by observing the sky what sort of weather the following day was going to give them.

He didn't want to make it too obvious that he was watching them, and so he just peered around the curtains. Thomas had already handed over the milk, which Stefan had balanced on the wall while they continued their conversation. Albert thought that if he didn't hurry and get it inside, it would likely turn sour quickly in the heat that they were experiencing. Suddenly, he was startled by a loud cough, followed by a prying tone of voice.

'Is there something particularly interesting out there Mr. Murtland?' Albert stammered slightly, as he turned around to see Eleanor standing in the doorway holding a feather duster.

'No, not really; I'm just enjoying watching the weather.'

'Might I suggest that you enjoy it outside; you'll be able to top up your tan a lot easier actually being under the rays rather than being cooped up in here like a withered chicken.'

'I'm not sure I completely appreciate the comparison to a withered chicken, but I take your point.' He smiled, tipped his head slightly towards her, and then turned back to the window. He heard her footsteps get fainter as she walked away. He carried on watching the gardener and the milkman exchange their pleasantries. From where he was stood, their discussion looked quite lively. Strangely, however, when he heard the front door open, which must have been Eleanor, going out to dust the windowsills or some other similar task, both men looked up in the direction of the door, then simultaneously turned to the window Albert was standing at. Albert quickly darted behind the curtain. He only waited there a moment, but when he had looked back, both men had gone. Thomas was just getting into his milk float, and in fairness did throw Albert a quick wave, but Stefan was nowhere to be seen. It wasn't the most unusual of circumstances, however, because he thought the gardener was potty anyway. Besides, Stefan reappeared a few seconds later to collect the milk that he had placed on the wall. Albert just couldn't help wondering why the two men had been so startled at the sight of Eleanor. Had she said something to them, or did they just not wish to see her? It was something else he now had to find out.

He decided to move away from the window and went into the kitchen to get some tea. He had nobody to enjoy a cup with but seeing as the fresh milk had just arrived, he thought of no objections why he couldn't partake. Hannah had gone with Johann down to the library to try and find out anything that they could about the money troubles that Andreas had spoke about. It was nice; especially now he was retired, to have a keen helper such as Hannah. Obviously, it was for her benefit to find out everything she could, but she was so dedicated to helping him, he was actually quite touched. Even with them gone, he was quite capable of drinking on his own and besides, he wanted to try and get a glimpse at Stefan. He was acting very detached, but he probably just felt lost without having his proper job to do. It must be difficult to not really have anybody in your life; it was a feeling that Albert knew only too well.

Albert passed Andreas' room on his way to the kitchen. No music emitted from the crack under the door, but he could quite possibly still be asleep or even just staring out of the window into the opaque blind, despite that being a peculiar habit. It was still several hours before his allotted visit would take place. He felt quite honoured that he had been allowed to return, and it was not even Albert's suggestion; it came from the famous Mr. Krause himself. When he reached the kitchen, he could hear Eleanor muttering to herself. She had quickly re-entered the house to make the tea for everybody. She had mentioned something the day before about the personal hygiene of the gardener whom she detested, and was not keen to let him anywhere near the porcelain. He remembered she used the phrase "grubby little hands" when describing him. Whatever she was saying, she was saying it in German, and even though he had no hope of understanding her rant, he could tell by the hurried, unfriendly tone of voice, that she was yet again feeling irritated at something, or rather someone, as Albert found out when he walked in.

Stefan was sitting at the table holding his head in his hands, desperately trying to drown out the constant whingeing coming from Eleanor. It mustn't be very nice to come to his place of work and have another member of staff repeatedly moaning and nagging at him. Stefan looked up at Albert as he entered, and then quickly looked back at the table. A tray was in front of him with two cups on and Eleanor was just finishing filling the two cups up, complaining about something or other while doing so. Stefan even raised his head to look at her, but after a furious glare, he expertly imitated the action again that he had done after clapping his eyes on Albert. He obviously had plenty of practice at it. Eleanor poured milk into two milk jugs, which were also on the tray. She filled one with the light-blue top, and the other with green. It didn't surprise Albert one bit to see her fill up the whole milk for Stefan; he got the impression she didn't particularly care about the status of his health, but it was her duty to treat Andreas to the best of her ability. The tea tray was ready. Stefan stood up and extended his arms to take it. Albert noticed he had put on a pair of mittens, which still didn't look overly clean, however, it was the thought that counted – he was probably trying to relieve himself of some of Eleanor's complaints. The old gardener didn't look at anybody when he was on his way out. He balanced the tray on one hand, and as he passed Albert, the ex-detective held out his hand just like Stefan had done to him on the previous occasions they had met. Stefan, however, perhaps found the tray unsteady and so instead of shaking Albert's hand, changed to carrying the tray with both of his. After Stefan had left, Albert shut the door behind him.

'I assume you were giving him another hard time?'

'Give me a good reason why I shouldn't.' She picked up a disinfectant spray bottle and began squirting the substance on the seat where Stefan had been and also on the table where his arms had been resting.

'I think you're going a bit over the top. Don't forget Mr. Krause has employed him here for years, personally; whereas, you are an agency worker, and have been sent here only recently because someone was required for the job.' Eleanor stopped spraying.

'Mr. Murtland; it is of no consequence how long a person has been here or whom they were hired by. My job is to keep a clean home, whether that is on my first day or my last. Herr Reinwald hinders my efforts simply by being present. His place is in the garden, and he can be as filthy as he likes out there, just as long as he doesn't bring it in here.' She paused while she put the bottle down, and picked up a cloth to wipe the surfaces with. 'And I hope he doesn't think that just by putting on a pair of dirty gloves, he can excuse himself from maintaining an acceptable level of personal hygiene, because I can assure you it does not.' Albert tried to get a word in while she took to scrubbing the table, but he failed and instead had to listen to more of her gripes. Never before, had he felt more like Stefan Reinwald. 'I mean it's that dreadful coat – goodness knows what it's riddled with. It's needs burning; that's what it needs.' She started shaking her cloth at Albert. 'Do you know, he even brought a ferret into the dining room last week – a ferret Mr. Murtland, into the dining room! Who does that?' Albert shrugged his shoulders. He had the feeling that whatever his response would be was going to be wrong, or at least provoke further outbursts, and he deemed it a good decision to just remain silent. 'And don't even get me started on the time he came into the kitchen wearing his wellington boots; covered in chicken manure. I had to tell him off for that, and when he took them off, his big toe was sticking out of a large hole in one of his socks. I mean, really!' Quick as a flash, Albert picked up his tea.

'Thanks for the tea!' He turned to leave.

'Is that all you can say? What about Herr Reinwald; do you have no comments about him?'

'Miss. Frankwell, he is friendly enough, and I am sure you would miss him if he wasn't around anymore. The likelihood is that after the awful find in the garden, and with Mr. Krause's failing health, Mr. Reinwald will probably not have a job anymore. Why don't you try and get on with him until he has to leave?'

'If he respects the house rules then I haven't got a problem with him; really I haven't. Well apart from he seems very keen to develop into a peeping tom! But even with that aside, he doubles my workload – I have to clean the house, and then clean up after him too!' Albert stood under the doorframe, ready to make a hasty exit.

'Like I said, you'll miss him when he's gone.'

'I doubt that, Mr. Murtland, I doubt that very much indeed.' Albert raised his cup to her, as another silent way of thanks, and quickly scurried out of sight before she could say another word. He left her polishing the table, while continuing to mutter under her breath.

Several hours later and the music coming from the room sounded just like normal. Albert, as a rare occasion, sat and listened to it. He didn't have to sit directly outside the door; instead he sat in the lounge with his head back against the armchair. He closed his eyes to have "forty-winks" – an expression his own grandfather used to say to him, especially after a hearty meal. He always maintained that he wasn't asleep, but was just having "forty-winks". Albert had believed him time and time again, being a young boy, until eventually he heard snoring coming from his grandfather's nostrils. Albert, however, was adamant not to drop off. Even though he was resting, he was still working. There were lots of avenues that he had to think about, which he needed to order into a sequence of importance before deciding which was the best course of action to take next in the investigation. He failed to see how Andreas' minimal information about becoming fundamentally destitute, as well as hinting that Albert would most likely just be waiting in vain for his answers.

He sat there for quite some time with his eyelids gently closed. Andreas was certainly on top form with his playing. Perhaps because he knew his life was drawing to a close, he had decided to play with an enthusiastic vigour for the remainder of his days. His notes were a lot sharper, and from what Albert could ascertain, his efforts were faultless. He didn't seem to stop between pieces. Perhaps he would have ten or twenty seconds just to relax after finishing each stretch of music, but it was certainly no more than that before he plunged straight into the next one. Albert definitely still admired the man, but only for his music abilities like he always had done. He didn't condone anything else he had achieved in his life, and by all accounts, it didn't seem like he had accomplished anything else to be proud of.

A bit longer went by and when Albert looked at the clock, he saw it was time for his appointed visiting opportunity. He rose to his feet and made his way to Andreas' living quarters. The music still projected out from behind the door. Nevertheless, Albert was not going to miss his slot and so he knocked upon the door. There was no response from within. Albert knocked again. Still nothing. The music did seem a lot louder than it had done before. Andreas was really going at it. The symphony that was playing was *Vultures Live For Death*. Albert recognised it from his own collection of Goldmann and Krause that he had back at home in England. He was unsure of the German translation; he could never recall them. A heavy knock was what Albert next placed upon the door, followed by hammering with his fist, and then by slapping the palm of his hand repeatedly on the large wooden panels that held the door together. There was no response, and the piano playing was unaffected.

'What is all the noise down here?' Eleanor had come charging down the stairs. Albert spun around.

'Andreas won't let me in.'

'Herr Krause hardly lets anybody in Mr. Murtland.'

'No, you don't understand, I'm booked in to see him; I have an appointment.'

'This isn't a doctor's surgery. And if it was, I do not expect that you start charging down the door because your general practitioner is a few minutes late seeing you for your slot.'

'I think this is slightly different under the circumstances, don't you? My general practitioner does not segregate himself from the rest of the world and neither does he live in isolation away from all human contact. He would be a very shoddy doctor if he did, wouldn't he?'

'Don't you take that tone with me? Don't forget I am the housekeeper here and you are to abide by my rules while you are gracing us with your undoubtedly worthy presence.' Albert made a face at her, which pretty much indicated his own disgust at her attitude.

'If you have nothing helpful to say then I suggest you go away! With a face like that I'm surprised your cornflakes don't try and crawl out of the bowl! I am making a lot of noise because I am trying to attract his attention, as I believe something is amiss. For someone who shies away from seeing everybody, I found it very unusual that he invited me back again. He wouldn't have done that if he didn't mean it. The time for that second visit has now arrived, and he is not letting me in. Couple that with the overpowering volume of the music he is playing, which would probably drown out my knocking, and I think you'll agree that there is something strange about it all. Now if you'll excuse me.' Albert turned back to the door and started beating at it once again, as well as calling out Andreas' name. It wasn't long before he was shoved out of the way by the impolite housekeeper. 'Do you mind?'

'I have a key. You want help don't you?' She began fumbling about on a large ring of keys, which she had pulled from the large front pocket on her apron.

'I didn't know you had a key. I didn't think anybody had a key to this room.'

'I had one cut. There was no way I was going to take a job for someone who spends his life locked away in a room. If I ever needed access, I was making sure I could get it. And as you say, now seems to be the time for access so unless you have any further objections, I'm going to use it.' Albert stood back.

'Be my guest.' She pushed the key into the lock and turned it. To their surprise they could easily push open the door. It had not been bolted from the inside. They slowly creaked open the door, and even at this horrendous intrusion, an intrusion that Andreas would have loathed, he carried on playing his piano. Something was not right. Eleanor swung the door wide open, and both her and Albert saw Andreas sitting at his piano. The music was fast and loud. Had Andreas really not noticed them entering? The two concerned intruders felt like they had to creep in. They didn't wish to startle him. He was not looking in the direction of the door because he would naturally presume that he had clicked the bolt into place. Therefore, if he was so engrossed in his music, they needed to make their presence known without finishing him off with a heart attack.

They edged nearer and nearer to him. Albert closed the door behind them so that nobody else could see what was happening. They managed to get right up to the beautiful grand piano, and Andreas had still not seen them. Eleanor moved around to the front of the piano, which is where she noticed that for the lively music erupting from the keys, the composer was actually very, very still. She let out a horrified scream. Albert dashed around to where she was stood. It was there that they in fact saw Andreas in his true state, hunched over the piano with a large knife sticking out of his back. Blood had trickled from his body and stained the ivory keys. Albert looked around the room. The pile of records at the end of the bed had been disturbed, and tucked away in the corner of the room was the record player that belted out his music.

Andreas had been murdered. Stabbed to death in his own room, in a room where he was pretty much the only person ever in it. He chose who came in; he told them when to leave. And yet he had been murdered. There was to be no encore. He had lived his final crescendo, and embarked upon his final rest.

11

The evening did not provide the best atmosphere. Not that any other evening was a bursting barrel of fun, but at least they hadn't held the taste of death in the air. Of course, it had a similar ambience to the night that the body was dug up in the garden, but the feeling tonight was different. Albert had felt relatively close to Andreas. He had played a considerable part in his musical interests, and he was a big name for the world to lose. When the news of the found body had reached them, everybody turned to shock, whereas Andreas' death plunged them into sadness. It was a shame that a man who had once been so famous had been reduced to the life of a loner, and ultimately met his end with a knife in his back. The police had been to investigate the crime scene, and the authorities had removed the body for further analysis. The impudent German Sergeant had led the proceedings, and had taken great delight in ignoring Albert throughout. However, Albert had discovered through talking to Eleanor that the officer had requested a meeting with Johann once he had returned from the village with Hannah. It would seem that he had some news regarding his father, and needed to consult with him as soon as possible. Albert had no idea where the father and daughter duo were. They had gone to the library and he thought they would have returned over an hour ago. Perhaps they had found something out in their research, which needed exploring further. He had no idea how Hannah would take the news. It meant that any more questions she had for Andreas would no longer get answers. This would make it a lot more difficult to find out about her grandmother. As it was, they only had a few partial scraps of information to aid them, and they were yet to get any luck with their investigation so far. Without Andreas, they were restricted to their own ingenuity and it wasn't looking promising they would even encroach upon the answers they sought.

Albert sat in the lounge by himself. Stefan was nowhere to be seen; he certainly kept his distance while he was temporarily out of work. Eleanor had taken some tablets for a migraine and had retired early to her bedroom. Albert was determined to wait up for Hannah. The chances were she had no idea of the terrible event that had taken place, and he would rather she heard it from him than from anyone else, especially since all other people would just be busybodies prying for information they could reel off to their other equally nosey acquaintances at a later date.

The clock struck midnight, and Albert sat in the dark listening to the repetitive ticking of the swinging pendulum. He didn't find it eerie; he was used to the moroseness of such circumstances. In a weird way, he felt at home in the gloomy, chilling setting, as it was a sensation that he had been subjected too for a large part of his life. It was almost where he belonged; it was what he knew best. He turned his attention back to the steady tick of the pendulum. He had once seen a metronome simulate the same motion on a film he'd watched. The speed of the metronome could be either increased or decreased depending on the tempo of the piece that was being played, and helped the performer keep time with the music. Even in the film, the metronome had symbolised death. The constant flick of the thin metal pendulum had represented the pianist's heartbeat. When the musician had breathed his last breath, the metronome came to a standstill. He remembered he had felt very moved by the effectiveness of the scene, and the memory brought him back to thinking about the all too real demise of his own favourite musical mastermind.

It was gone half past one when Albert finally heard the door open. He had been struggling to stay awake, but had been determined to do so. The light flicked on, and Hannah was surprised to see her old friend still up and out of bed.

'Albert, what are you still doing up?' Albert turned to look at her.

'Just thinking. Is Johann with you?'

'Yes, he's just here taking his shoes off.'

'Would you both like to come and keep me company for a few minutes?' Hannah turned around and looked out of the doorway, presumably at her father to get his answer to the question. He must have nodded, as before long they were both sitting on the settee in front of the retired detective. Johann was first to speak:

'We've found out something that could relate to my father's financial situation.' Hannah interrupted:

'Yes, we have. But we're going to have to ask him about it.' Albert's face fell. If he had looked any more crestfallen, he feared his chin would be scraping across the scratched parquet flooring.

'I'm afraid you won't be able to do that.'

'Albert, don't be silly – I meant in the morning!' He stared deeply into her eyes.

'Unfortunately, that's not going to make a lot of difference.'

'I don't understand.'

'I'm afraid it is my sad duty to inform that your grandfather,' he turned to Johann, 'and of course your father, is no longer with us.' Johann spoke:

'You mean he's died.'

'I'm afraid so. Unfortunately he was killed this afternoon.'

'So his health finally got the better of him?'

1 4 3

'Not exactly.' Albert could see Hannah's brain working overtime. She piped up:

'You said he was killed. I know his health could have killed him, but that wasn't what you meant was it?' Albert shook his head.

'It seems Andreas Krause has been murdered.' Tears filled Hannah's eyes. Clearly affected by the terrible news, she couldn't hold them in and they dripped down her cheek like a faulty tap that never fully switches off. Johann didn't seem as distraught over the death of his father, which Albert duly noted before storing the observation in the back of his mind. Surely the loss of a parent would provoke some streak of sadness, but on the other hand, grief affected different people in a variety of ways. Suddenly Hannah got up from her seat. She mumbled something that was largely inaudible, and quickly walked out of the room. The two men heard her ascend the staircase, and following that her door shut loudly behind her. An awkward silence filled the space in Hannah's absence. Albert had never really been alone with Johann.

'How are you feeling? The news must surely have been hard to hear.' It looked as if Johann thought about his answer. Usually questions such as that provoked an instinctive response.

'It's difficult to know what I feel.'

'What do you mean?'

'How can I feel anything for a man I haven't seen in years? He was somebody who shut people out so much that eventually the people around him just stopped caring because they were no longer able to get close.'

'Did it look like Hannah stopped caring?'

'Hannah is young. She is naïve to the situation.'

'From what I know of her, she is a very intelligent young girl.'

144

'With all due respect, you do not know her as well as I do.' Albert sat up in his chair. However, despite being ready to retaliate at full throttle, he reconsidered his actions and plunged back into his seat. If he was honest, Johann was correct. How could he possibly know Hannah better than her own father?

'I have become very close to your daughter; in a respectable manner, I hasten to add.'

'I know. I also know that she sought you out to help her find out the things she feels she ought to know.'

'And what things might they be?'

'You know what I'm referring to. My mother.'

'What about your mother?'

'Stop acting the fool. You know my mother died in mysterious circumstances.'

'On the contrary, I know nothing. I know nothing for I was not there. I am here to find out.' Johann seemed very much awake for the time of night that it was, or rather the time of morning. The clock had struck two, and he wasn't relenting on the conversation.

'When we were at the library today, we were scrolling through old articles of my father's life and found out he and Hans Goldmann had invested a lot of money together in a mining corporation.'

'Is that so? Did you happen to find out when that was?'

'We did. It was…' Albert held up his hand, which silenced Johann mid-sentence.

'Let me guess: 1983.' Johann nodded. 'I thought so. There's something about that year that put Andreas' whole life into turmoil. What was the mining corporation called?'

'The name was "Die Diamant-Garten", which translates to "The Diamond Garden". Albert repositioned himself upright in his chair. He was shocked at what he was hearing.

1 4 5

'They invested in a diamond mine?'

'Surprising isn't it?'

'Ridiculous is another word for it. Those sorts of investments are pretty risky now, let alone over thirty years ago. Surely, they would have had no idea at what they were getting involved in?'

'You're right when you say it was risky. The diamond mine had one small find in the first few months of 1983, but after that they had nothing. The mine was sealed up in the November, and the company became officially bankrupt in the December of the same year.'

'How much did they lose?'

'Near enough nine million Marks.' Albert looked perplexed for a short while before remembering that the currency would have been Deutschmarks before the country switched to the Euro several years ago.

'Forgive me, how much would that have been in English pounds?' Johann let out a large exhalation of air while he tried to work out the exchange in his head.

'At the time, I would say it would have been over three-and-a-half million, but I can't be sure.'

'Whatever it was, it would certainly have been a substantial amount of money. Naturally, I assume this is where Andreas lost his fortune?'

'Unquestionably.'

'I wonder…' Albert took from his pocket the old watch he had found with Hannah in the box Andreas had given her. 'Have you ever seen this before?' He handed it to Johann who took it and examined it closely.

'This belonged to my mother. Where did you get it?'

'Believe me, I haven't been looting the house. Your father gave it to Hannah on their last, well actually their only meeting.'

'I thought this had got lost.'

'It would seem not. What do you notice about it that's different, or unusual?' Johann gave it another brief glance, probably out of courtesy more than anything else.

'I don't know what I am supposed to be looking for.'

'Anything you would consider to be unusual about it, something out of place, or something that doesn't belong there.' Johann continued to look at the watch. He handed it back to Albert.

'That's not the original strap.' This threw Albert; he hadn't expected that as a response.

'How do you know?'

'You can clearly see the marks on the metal casing around its face. That indicates the age of the watch. If you look at the brown leather strap, it is like new, or at least substantially less worn than the rest of it. It's obvious that my mother had seen through a few replacement straps during her life, or rather she has changed it once as a minimum.' Albert hadn't noticed that particular detail. He wasn't sure whether it was a significant find or not, but it was indeed something he hadn't seen, and was willing to store it inside his head on the off chance he needed to recall the information at a later date. Of course, he wasn't going to let on that he hadn't been aware of it, and so he carried on the conversation without even so much as blinking.

'That's true. But what I was in fact referring to was the diamond that has been embedded into the case. That looks a lot newer than the watch itself.' Johann held out his hand to take the watch again. Albert passed it to him and waited as the famous composer's son inspected the item once again.

'You're right. Do you think this is a diamond from the company my father invested in?'

'I would say so. And he chose to add it to his wife's watch. If nothing else, it shows that he loved her dearly.'

'Do you think he killed her?' Albert stared at him, directly into his eyes. He saw the trepidation that swarmed them, as they lit up in the moonlight.

'No.' Johann let out of a sigh of relief. His facial expression showed slight respite from something that he too had evidently feared for a long time. 'Of course, I cannot guarantee that to you at this point in time, but I will do my best to find out just who exactly was responsible, if anybody at all.' Johann held out his hand to shake Albert's.

'I don't know who you are, or how you managed to end up here – but I'm glad you are. This has been a shadow in my family for decades. The family has pretty much been torn apart by the fear that my mother was murdered. Hopefully now, we can put the suspicions to sleep, for good.' He got up. 'Talking of sleep, we'd better get some ourselves. It won't be long before morning is upon us.'

'It was nice to talk to you. I'll see you in the morning, and we'll see what tomorrow brings us shall we?' Johann threw him a slight nod before leaving the room. Albert heard him go up the stairs, not as quickly as Hannah had, but the mood was different now. Hannah had stormed off feeling angry and hurt, whereas Johann had left filled with optimism, no matter how feeble his hope and expectations were. His footsteps were those of contemplation, a desire for the truth, and the anticipation that he might get it.

Albert stayed sitting in the dark room. He hadn't thought it a good idea to mention the entry in Andreas' diary, admitting to killing Imelda. Perhaps he should have done, but somehow he didn't believe what he had read. He poured himself a small measure of whisky, and dragged his chair nearer to the window. The moon shone brightly. It was big and full, and as he looked out at the sleepy parish of Presberg, Albert half-expected a werewolf to be pacing around the streets. The village looked eerie in the soft, shadowy light. The Church of St. Laurentius lit up to an almost medieval effect, as it loomed in all its glory over the rest of the buildings around it. It had a magnificent steeple on it, and Albert stared up at the large cross, positioned at the very top. It was beautifully sinister, and appeared evil in the moonlight.

Albert now had several questions in his mind; more queries that required answers. Why would Andreas have invested such a large some of money in a German mining corporation? The Germans weren't exactly known for their expertise in that particular field. In relation to that question, why did they become bankrupt so rapidly, and was the loss of his fortune the reason that his marriage presumably broke down? Did Imelda take her own life because she couldn't cope with the trauma of becoming desolate, and felt that it had brought a vast amount of shame upon her? Additionally, it was in Albert's nature to trust nobody, especially under these circumstances, therefore why had Johann only suddenly decided to make an appearance now? He has had plenty of years to get in touch with his father, but had chosen not to do so. All these people, Hannah included, are all swarming around considerably more in the knowledge that he was soon to die. Suddenly, he remembered his favourite Goldmann and Krause symphony: *Geier Leben Für Den Tod*, or rather, *Vultures Live For Death*. It was only now that Albert realised just how true that title was.

As he carried on looking outside, struggling to find the effort within him to prise himself out of his chair and climb the stairs to bed, he did see a figure lurking amongst the shadows. It wasn't a werewolf, as he had joked about in his own thoughts earlier; it certainly didn't look like a lycanthrope anyway. Without a shadow of a doubt, it was a fully-fledged human being. The pale light made it difficult to see details clearly, and the colours that would usually show up brilliantly in the daytime were also hard to distinguish. One thing was for certain, however, he would recognise that old green coat anywhere.

Morning came around quicker than normal. Albert had never made it to bed, and had been woken up in his chair by Hannah, who had shaken him. At first, she had thought he'd passed away in his sleep, as firstly it was unusual for him not to make it upstairs to bed, and secondly he was very proper and liked getting in his pyjamas rather than spending the night in his day clothes. He'd actually nearly suffered a heart attack, and in hindsight shaking the old man awake was probably not the best course of action she could have taken.

'I was worried about you.'

'I was only asleep.'

'I thought you were dead though.'

'Well that's just charming. I may be old but there's a few years left in me yet! I had no idea I looked so much like a corpse!' Hannah smiled, which was an unexpected sight for Albert's eyes. He'd wondered if he was even going to see her for a while, after she had disappeared so quickly last night. She was prone to hiding away when trying to deal with her sadness. 'How are you feeling today?' She twitched one side of her mouth quickly in the direction of her left ear and repositioned it back to normal.

'Not too bad considering.' She didn't sound very convincing.

'Are you happy enough to carry on with our purpose for being here?'

'I think so. Sadly, it's a death that won't really affect a lot of people. He only has himself to blame. I know my father won't be too cut up about it either because he was shut out just as much as I was. We were the only family he had; there is nobody else.'

'What about the staff?'

'Well you can forget Eleanor can't you; she never clapped eyes on him! But Misty on the other hand, he'll be devastated. They were pretty much like family to each other.'

'Where is Stefan now?'

'I have no idea. He's become very surreptitious recently. Have you seen him lately?' Albert shook his head.

'No, I haven't.' He moved quickly on. 'I've heard about the mining investment.'

'I guess my father told you.' Albert nodded. 'What do you think about it?'

'Clearly it's the reason why he lost the vast majority of his money, and it was obviously quite a scandal at the time. But I can tell you one thing for sure.'

'What?'

'I had a lot of time to think last night. Andreas did not kill Imelda.'

'How can you know that?'

'Because it just doesn't make sense; and with situations such as these, everything has to make sense in the end.'

'Are you absolutely sure?'

'Completely. He didn't kill her; never mind what we found in his diary. But I tell you something else, we're going to find out exactly who did.' Hannah threw her arms around him.

'Thank you Mr. Murtland! I was hoping it wouldn't be him!' Footsteps moved away from the door. Hannah hadn't heard them, but Albert had. Somebody had listened in to the conversation. 'Do you promise Albert?'

'I'm afraid I never make promises I can't keep.' Hannah's face dropped instantly, until Albert leant in closer to her. 'Hannah, I promise Andreas is not a murderer, and I promise we'll bring Imelda's killer to justice.' Hannah forced another hug upon him, accompanied by a small kiss on his cheek.

'Thank you! Thank you!'

'Calm down! We still have a lot of work to do. Johann entered the room.

'Are we celebrating?' Albert answered hastily, before Hannah could even contemplate an answer.

'Not as such; we've just agreed to get to the bottom of everything that seems to be going on here.' He looked neutral with his expression, and carried on the conversation only this time it was directed specifically at his daughter.

'Hannah, two policemen are outside to see us. They want to talk to us about your grandfather.'

'Can Albert come with us?'

'I'm not sure darling, I'll have to check.' He left, and they heard a brief exchange take place in the hallway. Johann soon returned. 'The German Sergeant has reluctantly agreed, providing Albert stays silent.' Albert made a face of annoyance, which Johann seemed to detect. 'I'm just repeating the message Albert. If it was up to me, you could speak for us; I don't like that Sergeant either, he's a nasty piece of work.' Before long, the two officers who had been waiting in the hall, entered the lounge and sat down on the sofa ready to speak with the two family members, as well as the inquisitive retired detective. It was their favourite irritable officer who chose to speak first:

'Wir brauchen, um mit Ihnen über Herr Andreas Krause zu sprechen. Wir verstehen, er ist Ihre Beziehung. Ihr Vater,' he nodded at Johann, 'und deine Grossvater.' He nodded at Hannah. 'Wir sind führend bei der Untersuchung seines Todes. Könnten Sie mir sagen, sowohl…' Hannah interrupted him:

'Please talk to us in English. Not all of us present speak German.' She was abrupt in her request, which the German officer did not appreciate. He curled his top lip and couldn't resist letting out a little snort. Similarly, Albert then couldn't resist posing with a haughty stature, as if a minor victory had just occurred. The Sergeant restarted his speech, with a curt, angry tone to his voice:

'I shall start again. We need to talk to you about Herr Andreas Krause. We understand he is your father and your grandfather.' He omitted the nods this time around. 'We are leading the investigation into his death. Could you both tell me when the last time was that you saw him?' Johann looked uncomfortable in his seat. He didn't give the most natural response, although Albert was the only person to pick up on his uneasiness.

'I haven't seen my father for a number of years.' He scratched the back of his head. 'Probably six, I've lost count. He was a difficult man to try and be around.' The officer who hadn't yet spoken scribbled some words down in a small notepad. His colleague resumed the conversation.

'And what about you, Frauline Krause, when was the last time you saw your grandfather?' Hannah was a lot more natural with her answer.

'I saw him the day before yesterday. Not for long, but I did see him.' The officer who sat there scribbling, looked up at the Sergeant, who returned the glance with considerable perplexity. Albert chirped in with his own response.

'And I saw him yesterday. I believe I was the last person to see him; apart from his murderer, naturally.' The constable shot him an evil glare.

'I told you to say nothing if you are to be present here.'

'You need all the details and so I am saving you time in asking. I know how it all works, don't forget.' The Sergeant seemed to have developed a slight twitch above his left eye.

'Do you think we are stupid?' Now it was Albert's turn to look confused, along with Hannah and her father. 'What are you trying to hide from us?' Albert couldn't help himself:

'Why don't you try explaining yourself? You've lost us completely.'

'I said at the beginning, we have come here to talk about Andreas Krause. Why are you wasting our time with such nonsense? The responses you are giving to us are wrong.' Albert stood up:

'I assure you they are not.' The German Sergeant stood up, and towered above Albert, which always made him feel inferior whenever anybody did it, although he didn't ever let it show. He always felt like the little man fighting for what was right.

'If you do not cooperate with me, I shall have you all arrested.'

'Oh, that's very consoling. I can see why you aren't with the Family Liaison Department. If you have us unjustly arrested, I shall have you reported to your Chief of Police. We are telling you exactly what we know.'

'Then, you English worm, you know nothing, which is what I suspected of you all along.' Soon enough, Hannah erupted with shouts that made Johann almost fall off his seat:

'My grandfather has been stabbed and you are telling us we know nothing! I'm not delirious – I saw him two days ago. He was as fit and well as could be expected, so don't you dare say we're lying because we're not!' The policeman raised his arms to calm down the chaos, and pushed his hands downwards, indicating them to sit.

'Perhaps I should explain myself. This is something I thought you already knew.' He paused and took a deep breath before looking at the three keen listeners in front of him, eager to hear the information he was about to divulge. 'We have come here today in relation to the body that was found buried in your garden.' He paused again. 'That was the body of Andreas Krause.'

12

Nobody knew what to say. It was unbelievable to think that the decaying corpse had been that of the great musician. There must have been some mistake. Perhaps Andreas had a brother, who would naturally have had similar DNA, hence confusing the identification. Hannah could just not believe the revelation. If her grandfather had been buried in the ground, then who on earth was the impostor who had been locked away in the music room. Albert was also sceptical about what the German Sergeant has relayed to them. The only thing that made any sense was the presence of the record player in the room. If it had been a phoney residing in there all this time, then by merely putting a record on it would give off the impression that Andreas was playing his music. And when Albert had heard him play the piano right in front of him, he could probably have just pressed play on the gramophone before he simulated playing the music at the piano. Whoever was in that room, quite simply, could have been anybody. But why would they have chosen to spend part of their own life hidden away from the world – that surely, was not any life at all. Also, what had they accomplished by doing so? They too had ended up dead. Albert knew there was a lot more to this case now than he had first thought. It was an intricate state of affairs, undoubtedly pieced together by one mastermind: but who?

Johann had fled the house almost immediately after the shock disclosure. It seemed to have hit him hard. Perhaps it was because he felt guilty for not seeing his father for such a long period of time, and now he would never get the chance. The thing that was likely to be on everybody's mind was the undignified circumstances in which such a high-profile celebrity should meet his end. He had lived a glorified life, and was celebrated for his work nationwide. Yet, after all that, he found himself murdered, buried in the ground, and left to rot.

The identity of the pretender, who had occupied Andreas' room, was yet to be revealed. Albert knew it would be a while before they received the information, and that was if the police would even bother allowing him to have it. Logically, Albert's first thought was simple: whoever the man in the music room was, surely must be Andreas' killer. If he managed to find that information, he would be able to solve the case. However, he had already thought that this was no longer possible, otherwise that person would have ensured their own safety; unless of course, somebody else rumbled what they were up to and decided to put a stop to it themselves. But who could that have been? It could have been anybody. At first, when everybody, for obvious reasons, believed him to be Andreas, they all knew that he only let people in that he wanted to see – friends and family mainly; people he knew he could trust. The only exception had been Albert himself, and he of course knew he wasn't responsible for the man's death. Therefore, why should the impostor make the effort to permit Hannah to visit him, when he knew that he could be rumbled at any point? Similarly, if his intentions were fraudulent, why had he agreed to see Albert, and then offer a second meeting to him? Of course, Albert now knew that he had no intention of the subsequent meeting actually taking place. But then saying that, surely the man would not have known he was going to be stabbed.

Everything was just so confusing. There were so many questions, so many paths that needed investigating, and yet

Albert didn't have the slightest clue where to begin. He had been sitting in the kitchen with a cup of tea, mulling over every thought. His head was frazzled but he couldn't stop it, even if he had wanted to. After deciding to go upstairs to see Hannah, he pushed his chair backwards and walked out of the kitchen. He passed the room, the room that was on the forefront of everyone's mind. It was closed, as it predominantly had been for a number of years, except this time it had the police tape sealing it off from the rest of the world. It was incredibly sad to think of all the events that had taken place. The strange part about it all was the tremendous, incredible sadness that was felt for the unknown man in the music room, simply because he had been thought of as Andreas by everybody. The body in the ground, which was the legitimate Andreas Krause, was indeed thought about, but received no sadness at all; simply because nobody had known it was him. It was very difficult to generate instant feelings just because the circumstances had changed. The main thing to bear in mind, however, was the grief that was felt for the passing of Andreas, whichever body he happened to be. He looked at the boarded up room one last time, and then ascended the stairs to find Hannah.

The young teen was quietly sobbing in her room, which in all honesty, was where Albert had expected to find her. He knocked on the door and waited for her to answer. She said nothing, but knowing she was in there, he opened the door ajar, and softly said her name.

'Come in.' He could barely understand her, as her lips fought through the tears that had fallen down her cheeks. Albert waited a further few seconds, then went inside and shut the door behind him.

He sat down beside her and desperately tried to work out what to say that would be comforting or helpful in some way. At is happened, Hannah spoke first:

'You probably think I'm crying because I'm upset.' She paused. 'I'm not. I'm actually less upset than I was before. I'm upset because I'm confused. I only came out here to find out about my grandmother's death, and now some stranger has been found dead in the garden, the man who was in the locksmiths has been killed, and my grandfather has been stabbed. Although now, it turns out that my grandfather was the stranger in the garden, and the man in the music room we have no idea who he was! What is going on here?'

'I'm afraid I don't know. I know exactly what you are saying, but your guess is as good as mine. There's something very peculiar happening.'

'Is it all connected to my grandmother?'

'Possibly. It would certainly make sense if it were anyway. But there's just so much going on, it's difficult to know where to even start.'

'We have to find out Albert, we just have to.'

'I've promised to you before that we'll bring all this to an end and find out exactly what we need to bring it to a close. I stand by that promise. It's going to be tough, and I'm not saying you aren't allowed to grieve, or feel hurt and sadness, but you have to stay focussed if you want us to succeed.'

'It was just a shock to me that's all; you know, what the policeman said.'

'That's understandable. It was a shock to me too, believe me.'

'But I promise to you that I'll stay focussed. I owe it to my grandmother.' Albert smiled.

'Now all we have to do is decide what needs our attention the most.'

'We need to find out who the man was who pretended to be my grandfather.'

'Agreed. The only problem with that is we haven't the capabilities to accomplish such a thing. I'm afraid our hands are tied on that particular avenue, and we must wait and hope that the police will divulge the information to us.'

'I'm not sure I agree with the identification. That Sergeant seems to have an irregular persona for the professional role he has.'

'If you're suggesting he might have something to do with it all, then I have to disagree with you. He may have shoddy skills when it comes to being personable but I sympathise with him in that respect. I would not like me interfering with his work, and I have acted in the same manner countless times during my career. Nevertheless, I am not one to rule something out just because I happen to disagree with it on hearing it initially, so I will store your point on the backburner of my mind.'

'But how can the man in the room have been anyone but my grandfather? We all went in to see him!'

'We did, but I've had time to reflect on that. You see, when you've been doing this line of work for as long as I have, your mind becomes trained in scrutinising every detail there is. True, we have all seen him, but in reality, none of us have.'

'What do you mean?'

'When did you say the last time you saw him was? I mean before this current visit to Germany.'

'About ten years ago.'

'So it would be true enough to say you cannot remember a good enough depiction of what he would look like now?'

'I guess so.' Hannah seemed uncertain where Albert was taking this.

'And I saw him too. But I have only ever seen his image on the cardboard covers that his records were sold in. These pictures were taken decades ago. Therefore, I would not have any idea what his modern day appearance would be.' He looked at Hannah, who said nothing, and so quickly carried on. 'Eleanor declares she has never seen him. Even if that wasn't true, and she just didn't wish to admit she had, she would have never seen him before in her life and so would have no reason to doubt that the man she met would be anyone other than her new employer.'

'I see what you're saying, but what about Misty?' Albert raised his hand, as if she had just stumbled on something worth noting.

'You're quite correct. Stefan would undoubtedly recognise the swap from the genuine Andreas to the fake Andreas, is that not true?' Hannah nodded.

'However, is it also not true that Stefan is an old man, whose faculties are failing him? We know his eyesight is worsening by the day, which would explain him not noticing the change. It would also seem that his hearing is following in the same way as his sight. This would also account for him not picking up on the change in tone of the two voices that he would have heard.'

'I had no idea he had become so elderly.'

'It's what happens a lot when you, as a young child, meet someone much older than yourself. They always stick in your mind as someone who never ages and usually it becomes a great shock when the realisation of them getting older eventually hits you.'

'So basically, we all saw who we thought to be my grandfather, so temporarily we were not suspicious. That would have given whoever is responsible, the time they needed to carry on forming their plan – whatever that plan may be.' Albert nodded.

'Yes. We were all happy with the fact that we'd seen Andreas, but the only people that were allowed to see him, or whoever was supposedly meant to be him, were people who would not decisively be able to say that he wasn't who we thought he was. Quite clever really, when you think about it.'

'I hate myself for what I am about to say.' Albert looked at her.

'Go on.'

'What if Misty was only faking his ailments?'

'You mean he could be in on the whole thing?'

'I don't know.'

'But that is what you are suggesting?' She hesitated.

'Yes.' Albert let out a hefty sigh. It was never nice to have to agree with something that would likely disappoint somebody.

'Unfortunately, that suggestion is more plausible than your previous one about the police officer.' Hannah seemed slightly dismayed; it was probably better that the suggestion had come from her rather than Albert breaking it to her.

'I hope it's not true. But as you said, we have to look everywhere for our answers, and he does seem to be cropping up everywhere.'

'I know what you mean. He found the body in the garden. He happened to be in the locksmiths. And apart from me, I think he was the last person to see Andreas, sorry, the fake Andreas alive.' There was an awkward pause while both people contemplated Stefan's involvement. 'Do you know where he is now?'

'I'm afraid I don't.'

'Then we must find him.'

'What else should we be doing?' Albert thought for a moment.

'There's something not quite right about Andreas' finances. If he lost his fortune, most likely from his investments in the mining corporation, why was he still able to pay salaries to a housekeeper and a gardener?'

'Unless he didn't invest all his money? He may have kept enough aside so that he knew he would be financially stable regardless of what happened with the diamond venture.'

'Certainly that's true, but as we are now led to believe, Andreas has not been here for a long time. Therefore, who has been paying the wages for his staff? Take Stefan for instance. Assuming he is not involved in any way, his senses may be failing him but he would still be well aware if his money was not in his bank account. And as for Eleanor, whether Andreas paid her directly or she received her money from the agency, I can't imagine her remaining silent if she received no remuneration for her services.'

'No, neither can I. But isn't it easy just to set up a standing order from one account to pay their accounts every month.'

'Yes, but where is the money coming from? If Andreas was effectively penniless then his impersonator must have been involved in some way, otherwise why else would he embark on this whole charade? Usually these things are all about money. It certainly doesn't seem that there is any love interest or jealousy involved, or indeed any hatred for your grandfather, therefore money is pretty much the only bait for any of this. It could be that whoever acted as Andreas was using his own money to pay the staff for the time being, so that nobody became suspicious, because he was aware of a lump sum of money that would eventually come his way.'

'Isn't all this speculation?' Albert didn't seem too impressed by her question, but thinking about it, it was a perfectly eligible point.

'Yes it is; I can't deny it. However, when you have no idea where to start on such an involved case such as this, sometimes you need to just take a chance and run with it. We're at a loss as it is, and don't forget, your whole reason for coming to Germany was merely on a theory that you believed in.' He paused. 'That's not saying that you weren't right, because you were, but if you've ever heard of the phrase "speculate to accumulate", then you'll see that's exactly the position we're in.'

'I think we'd better go and see if we can find Stefan.'

'You're going to have much more luck with that then I am. All I'd be able to do is try and drag him back here, as he wouldn't be able to understand anything I said. Why don't you try and find him and do your best to get any information out of him that you can? I'll go and dig deeper on the financial side of things.' Hannah got up off the bed.

'That sounds like the best way to go.' Albert got up too as she walked over to the door. Then she turned back to speak to him. 'You know we said we're not totally convinced about the identity confusion between my grandfather and the man who was imitating him?' Albert nodded. 'Well I guess it actually makes perfect sense.'

'How come?'

'I don't know if you noticed but I didn't think his skin seemed as pale as it should be for someone so deficient of sunlight. Whoever it was clearly had not been in isolation for that long.'

'Do you know something; I didn't notice that at all. But yes you're right. Now you come to mention it, his skin colour was actually relatively standard.'

'I retract what I said about the Police Sergeant being involved. That was a rather silly thing to say.'

'In matters like these, nothing is silly. Absolutely everything is a possibility. Don't be afraid to mention anything for fear of it sounding absurd because it just might be the breakthrough we need to wrap up the case. If you think of it, then in some way your mind found a logical pathway that led you to it. If I'd have said to you at the very start that the man in the music room probably isn't your grandfather and is in fact just someone pretending to be him, you would have thought I'd gone completely bonkers – but now look at what we're dealing with; exactly that.'

'I take your point.' She took her coat off the hook on the back of the bedroom door, and put it on, ready to go and locate the absent gardener. 'Are we setting a time to reconvene back here? Half five? If we get back for dinner, and then we can chat about our findings after we've eaten?'

'Agreed. Good luck.' She smiled.

'You too.' Without another word, she left, leaving him alone. Where he was meant to go, he didn't quite know, but one thing was for certain, it was looking less and less likely that Stefan was the kind old man that Hannah had always looked up to.

Albert had left the house in a leisurely manner and was intrigued to find the milk float parked outside.

'Hello there, Albert!' Albert looked all around him and couldn't find the location of the voice no matter how hard he tried. 'Up here!' Albert stared upwards at the roof of the house, and was amazed to find Thomas perched on top of it. 'Would you believe I'm fixing a tile now? Stefan is too old to get up here, bless his soul.'

'Well you just mind you don't fall! I want my milk fresh in the morning!' Albert tipped his hat to Thomas, who raised a hammer, as a sort of salute for his return friendly greeting. Albert heard the hammering for a while, as he walked away from the property.

He found himself walking down one of the streets in Presberg and decided he had to pick up the pace. He had to delve deeper into the complex puzzle that was Andreas' finances. He was headed for the library for the second time, and was not looking forward to it. Even though the librarian had been relatively kindly, he had felt like he was five years old. It was only the language that he struggled with, not the actual turning on of the computer. Also, after his last visit, he had left with a ringing in his ears, and would have sworn he was almost deaf, as she had decided to shout at him in German in that way that foreigners always raise their voices, as if that would make what they were saying more understandable. He remembered thinking how unfitting it was for her to be shouting at him, helpful or otherwise, in the middle of a library. Still, at least this time he would be able to get on with his task quietly seeing as he was now knowledgeable of how to access the Internet, as well as which sections he should be looking in for the journals or old newspapers that he required.

He walked up to the automatic door at the front of the library and waited for it to open. It took its time; as if the door had fallen asleep out of boredom, but eventually it slid in jolted stages to the left and opened for him to enter. He walked in and was nearly trampled to the floor when what seemed like a stampede of wildebeest, erupted from the doorway. Slightly dazed, he heard an apology directed towards him. Strangely, it was in English, but was more astonished when he found that the stampede included no wildebeest, and was in fact just Eleanor who was now helping him to his feet.

'I apologise. I'm very sorry – I was in a rush.' Albert dusted himself down, as Eleanor next fetched his hat and cane from off the floor.

'In a rush from what exactly? Has somebody just pulled the pin from a grenade in there?'

'No Mr. Murtland, and do not be facetious, it is not a very appealing quality.'

'Neither is flattening one of your household guests, which you seemed to accomplish with the proficiency of an amateur wrestler.'

'Do not over-exaggerate what happened here Mr. Murtland. I merely came out of the doorway in a bit of a hurry, and it just so happened you were standing in the way. It was unavoidable and I have already apologised.'

'I might have known it would be my fault.' He reformed the crease in the crown of his trilby with his hand, before returning it to his head.

'It was nobody's fault; it was just an unfortunate occurrence, for which, once again I am sorry.'

'Then I accept your apology, and may there be no bad feelings between us.' He had calmed down slightly, ever since the shock of performing a lumbering gymnastics display has passed. 'Are you an avid reader of books Miss. Frankwell?'

'Occasionally I dabble in literature Mr. Murtland, but I usually find that I don't have much time for such leisure activities.'

'One must always find time to relax Miss. Frankwell.'

'One should also mind one's own business, Mr. Murtland.' Albert wondered whether he had tumbled backwards all the way into a Jane Austen novel, seeing as they were both suddenly acting very formal and genteel. 'I must go now Mr. Murtland. I have things to do, and recent events at the house do not make it any easier. It seems that a man that does not actually exist, and was in fact dead when he supposedly hired me, has employed me. Therefore, with all this commotion in the air, that's the reason I have made this special trip to give back my books. I do not wish to obtain a fine for returning them late.' She nodded her head slightly towards him and then turned to leave. Quickly, Albert stopped her from going:

'Just a moment! Can I ask you a question or two about what's happening back at the house?' She sighed and was not impressed with his request.

'If you make it very quick.'

'I will. Do you have any idea who might have been the impostor who was standing in for Andreas Krause?'

'What makes you think I would know anything about it?'

'It is just a general question that I will be asking everybody.'

'As much as I always associate with the sorts of people that do away with famous musicians and then hire somebody to impersonate them to cover up the fact that they are actually dead, I'm afraid I draw a blank as to who I think may have been the stand-in for that particular role. Does that make it clear to you?' Albert smiled, rather smarmily, which was the effect he was hoping to achieve.

'Perfectly. Now can you just tell me, if it's not too much trouble, why it is that even though you have been hired by the agency to take the post as housekeeper, there is no record with them to suggest the job had ever been assigned to you, and what's more, your contract with them had been terminated over nine months ago?' Eleanor was silent, for a while anyway.

'Don't be ridiculous. I'm an upstanding woman I'll have you know and I do not expect to be downtrodden by the likes of you.' Albert couldn't help thinking he had in fact been standing up until she had trodden him down. He silently praised himself on his play on words, as he was secretly quite proud of it but did not think it a good idea to reveal his cleverness to her. Using his own advice that he had given to Hannah, he had only speculated to accumulate with regards to his question anyway, but Eleanor's response was more than intriguing.

'Even so, Miss. Frankwell, unless of course that's an alias, I am only informing you of what I have been able to find out.'

'Then I suggest you check your sources, as they clearly are not reputable. I am not willing to answer anymore of your unfounded questions.'

'That's your choice, of course. But believe me, it is not the wisest option available to you. Why don't you have a think about things; sleep on it, and come and find me in the morning. I am not an ogre, but I do fight for what I believe is right. That is something I have always believed in.' She looked scornfully at him.

'Dinner will be served at six. Should you wish to dine with us then do not be late. Unless of course you fear I may poison you with it, as clearly you are so adamant that you know me so well and consider me to be unlawful.'

'I was merely asking questions; it is not my job to form an opinion. Well, not at such an early stage anyway.' She said nothing else to him. Her livid face said it all. She turned, and practically marched away from him. He watched her walk away for a few moments until she was out of sight. He figured that she probably turned down the nearest side street that she came across just so she could remove herself from his viewpoint. Albert braced himself slightly, in case another excitable library fanatic decided to sprint out of the door. Nobody did, and so he entered, removing his hat as he did so. What he couldn't help wondering, however, was why Eleanor had so insistently been present at the time Stefan had dug up the body in the garden. He had said how she had watched him from a distance with a keen eye. In light of the recent revelation about its newly confirmed identity, he couldn't refrain from believing that she wasn't as innocent and upstanding as she made herself out to be.

13

It was difficult for Albert to get his translation across to the librarian, but eventually he managed it and was able to borrow the books that Eleanor had returned. Of course, he wasn't permitted to take them out like she had done, because he wasn't signed up as a member of the library. But, he was allowed to read at his leisure within the four walls. When he sat down, he became annoyed with himself, as for some reason he had expected the books to be in English, mainly because Eleanor always spoke his own language to him. He felt such a fool within himself for his horrendous oversight and took the books to the computers so that he could attempt to translate them online. He tried to make himself feel better by reassuring his pride that not every person his age was capable of using the technology that he could.

There were two books that Eleanor had borrowed from the library. Neither of them was particularly thick or heavy, and they looked to be more like textbooks rather than fiction novels. Albert held up the first book in front of him to look at the title of the book, which he would then type into the Internet search engine. He had absolutely no idea what "Leben In Indigenen Asien" could possibly mean. He waited while the translation website loaded the information he was seeking. When it showed up on his screen, the meaning of the book's title baffled him - "Life In Indigenous Asia". It was a strange choice of book for a British woman working in Germany, who acted so unbelievably refined; it was improbable to think there was anything indigenous about her. Why on earth would she have any interest in such content? He put the book back down on the computer desk, and picked up the next. "Hauswirtschafts Wesentliche". Once again, he found himself unable to decipher the title of his own accord and so relied on the technology at his disposal to carry out the work for him. Yet again, when he viewed the translation, he was dumbfounded as to the choice of reading that Eleanor had selected – "Housekeeping Essentials". Admittedly, it was more relevant than the first book he had looked into, but it was like the two books went from one extreme to the other. On the one hand, the book about Asia was so different to her personality and so why should she wish to read it? But conversely, he would have thought she was already fully knowledgeable about the subject matter of the housekeeping guide, and so the same question hit him again: why would she wish to read it?

Albert wasn't really sure what he should do next. He knew he had to find out more about Andreas' money problems and his investment in the diamond mine, which was the reason he had gone to the library in the first place. But what he had discovered in relation to Eleanor had sort of taken over. He was always attracted to the parts that seemed the most suspicious because usually, if he could pick at them and probe further into them, it normally threw up a new lead, which in turn would lead to the killer. Still, whoever killed Andreas, and subsequently the man who had pretended to be him, it was better to find the motive. Once the motive was unearthed, then the reasoning would fall into place a lot easier. If Andreas was virtually penniless, then the motive could not be personal, monetary gain. If it wasn't that, then what was it? As Andreas was a successful and famous musician, could someone have believed him to still be incredibly wealthy if they hadn't heard of his financial misfortune? It was certainly a possibility.

He decided to keep hold of the books but put them to one side for the time being. He was determined to find out something about Andreas before he left. He had just started typing when a small commotion filled the library. It wasn't an outrageous din, but it was enough to cause everyone to look up, as it disobeyed the general rule of keeping quiet for the comfort of everybody present. The source of the uproar centred on a torn and tattered tramp that had wandered into the library, seemingly to get a plastic cup of free water from their dispensing machine. By all accounts, it looked as if the main librarian was doing her utmost to shoo the man out. Seeing as the library was a public service, Albert didn't view it as a very fair act. In fact, he considered it rather heartless. Several people were now gathered around him, some didn't even work there, and yet they were all trying to get him to leave; nobody wanted to give him the time of day. The tramp didn't seem overly offended by the spurn he received, and even though he did give a short outburst in retaliation, he essentially left calmly, and in all honesty, the better example to the human race. Still, Albert thought it was grossly unfair treatment. The man, vagrant or not, had entered quietly for a mere drink, and was not making a nuisance of himself in the slightest. In Albert's eyes, there was nothing wrong with that. He got up, and left his computer with the books lying next to the keyboard. He wandered over to the water dispenser and poured himself a cup. Nobody was interested in what he was doing, probably because he was dressed more to public acceptance, but he gave a quick look around him anyway, as he didn't wish to attract any bother. He had been unobserved in his task and so left the library with the cup of water in his hand.

It took Albert a few minutes to find the tramp. He saw him pottering around a bus stop talking to travellers and passers-by. They didn't hang about long and most didn't even reply. At most, the more polite people shook their head but that was about it. The tramp was holding out his hand as he spoke, and Albert could only assume that he was begging people for money. He didn't seem to be having a lot of joy.

Albert began mingling in the crowd and eventually found himself a seat on the plastic bench within the bus shelter. He heard the question that the tramp was asking everyone: "Entschuldigen Sie bitte, könnten Sie ersparen zehn Cent für Lebensmittel?" Albert was clueless as to its meaning, but nobody placed anything in the man's hand; even so he did not become disheartened and just moved on to the next person. It wasn't long before he found his way to the bench where Albert was sitting. The man was just an inch shorter than Albert, but he was a lot plumper, although that could be to do with the many layers of clothes he appeared to be wearing. He was unshaven and wore a thick, light-blue fleece and dark-blue jogging bottoms, which were held up by a piece of rope. He nodded to Albert, who reciprocated the action. Before long, the tramp asked Albert the same question he'd asked everyone else. Albert, always one step ahead when it came to being shrewd, replied with the one phrase he had made sure he'd learnt before his arrival in Germany:

'Ich bin Englander.' It meant he was English, and more often than not, it usually worked by sending on their way whoever had asked him a question. Logically, if he proclaimed he couldn't speak the language, it wouldn't be worth the Germans wasting their time by carrying on with the conversation. However, the tramp seemed wise to the trick and outfoxed Albert completely:

'That's okay; I speak English as well.' Now Albert was stuck to listen to the question and respond to him accordingly, although the question wasn't repeated. The tramp now had a drink. He had an old juice bottle, from which he drank a diluted blackcurrant cordial. Albert now felt a bit of fool sitting at the bus stop holding a small cup of water.

'I actually brought you this from the library seeing as the rest of them weren't feeling very charitable.' The tramp smiled.

'That's very kind. Thank you. I would pour it in here but I don't want to water this down.'

'Isn't that just a juice drink?' The tramp held up the bottle and laughed.

'No, it's red wine.' He pointed to a police officer ambling past. 'But it looks like juice and that's the main thing. Wine warms me up; it can get very cold on the streets.' Albert held out his hand.

'My name's Albert.' The tramp obliged the handshake.

'William.' He paused. 'So Albert, how come you find yourself in Germany?'

'I'm here helping a friend out with a slight family problem. And yourself?'

'I'm a hobo. I travel around.' His admittance of his status was not reluctantly offered. Not that it was said with pride, but he was comfortable with what he was, and didn't seem to care who knew it. He seemed to be happy enough with the hand that life had dealt him, and to be happy within oneself surely is the most important aspect of a fulfilled existence. Albert didn't find it strange that most people steered clear from vagrants and tramps, or indeed hobos, as was the chosen title by William, and yet, he felt an undeniable warmth emitting from him, almost the warmth of a fatherly figure if the miniscule age gap between the two men could be overlooked.

'So how is it you speak English so well?'

'I can speak a lot of languages.' He began rattling off various sentences in a variety of languages. Albert recognised French but there were some he didn't know. The man may have been a hobo, but it was clear he had a brain.

'If you don't mind me asking, how have you ended up as a hobo?' William let out a pondering sigh.

'I guess I chose the life I lead. There's just something in my head that tells me not to take orders. I have had jobs, but if I get unfairly treated or shouted at by the boss, then I lose my temper.' Albert nodded.

'I see.'

'I don't suppose you have ten cents that I could get some food with?' Albert felt completely at ease with him. He rummaged about in his pocket and pulled out a five Euro note, which he handed to William.

'That's far too much.' Albert held up his hand in protest, so William pocketed the money. 'Thank you.' Then, he got up, and Albert couldn't help thinking that now he'd got the money, he was fleeing in search of his next victim. However, he was wrong, he had simply gone to urinate behind the bus shelter. Albert couldn't help but smile at the evident rebellion against society that he had within him. He soon returned, which made Albert feel rather guilty of his previous thought.

'How do you survive on ten cents?'

'When a few people give me that small bit of change, I have enough for a loaf of bread and a carton of wine; that's enough for me. I can survive on that.'

'Well now you can buy a few slices of ham and make yourself a sandwich.' William winked at him.

'That's not a bad idea; you know I might just do that.'

The two men sat at the bus stop and talked for over an hour. At the back of Albert's mind was the niggling torment that none of this was benefiting his enquiries about Andreas. Yet, he found it difficult to move from his spot. William kept talking, and the conversation soon became very interesting, even reducing the guilt that Albert felt for temporarily abandoning his research. It all started with a simple question from William:

'Where are you staying my friend?'

'Not far from here.' Albert pointed behind them, and began directing him through the streets by moving his hand around. 'Just back down this street and past the church; the house that stands back from the rest of the village. Do you know where I mean?'

'I know exactly where you mean. Which one is your friend that you're helping? The hermit, the whore, or the idiot?'

'I beg your pardon?'

'That Krause fellow lives like a hermit and the housekeeper there, Rebecca I think her name is, gets about the village like a fly at a dung convention. And as for that idiot gardener, well, he's just an idiot.'

'It sounds as if you harbour animosity towards that household?'

'Is it that obvious? They think they can all do what they like and nobody will get hurt; well that's just not how life works.'

'What is it that you know?'

'I'm sorry, there's no need to be bothering you with it.' Albert jumped in quickly with his response:

'On the contrary, it's exactly the reason why I'm here.'

'How do you mean?'

'Have you not heard about the recent events there?'

'Can't say as I have. I used to roam around these parts many years ago, but only recently have my travels brought me back around.'

'You may be surprised to hear that the hermit has been murdered, and the whore has been reported missing.' William took a few moments to ingest the news.

'You certainly seem to miss a lot when you aren't around for a while.'

'Is that all you have to say?'

'Why is it exactly that you are here?'

'If you must know I am assisting Andreas Krause's granddaughter with finding out some information about her grandmother.'

'I can tell you now you won't find anything out about Imelda. They buried that secret long ago.' Albert was shocked he even knew her name, let alone be able to recall it so easily. 'Don't look at me like that; it's an unusual name. It's a pretty name. I don't know anybody else who has it.'

'It still rolled off your tongue a bit too quickly for someone who hasn't been around for ages.'

'I haven't been around for years that's true, but then again neither has Imelda. Perhaps I was around when she was.'

'Are you saying you were around when she was?' William cleared his throat.

'Perhaps.'

'I'd appreciate any information you could give me.' It took a while for William to speak again, as he appeared to carefully contemplate his answer. Eventually, however, he did so:

'Imelda was a sweet lady. She was beautiful, and her eyes sparkled with interest and excitement at everything she did or said.'

'You knew her well?'

'I knew her.' Albert got the impression he didn't like being interrupted. 'I used to work at that house, a great many years ago now. I was their mechanic for a few months. They paid me reasonably well for what I did for them. This was at a time you understand, when that pigheaded composer didn't live like an outsider. They had a fleet of posh cars, and I polished them all, and cleaned them inside and out. When they went off to a social occasion, I would be issued with a luxury suit and a top hat, and I chauffeured them to and from the event. So you see, officially I was the mechanic, but I was actually a lot, lot more.' He paused. It was more than likely to allow Albert a chance to interject, but he decided not to at that moment. 'Imelda treated me with respect. We became friends, or rather as close to being friends, as our two very differing social statuses would allow us to become. She always felt rather awkward knowing it would not be deemed a respectable act to form a friendship with the hired help. This was mainly down to her husband's reputation. She couldn't make him the laughing stock of the musical world. It was her duty to act suitably in light of her husband's vast fame. If he lost his illustrious reputation, both him and his career would have been reduced to nothing. It's ironic actually, to think that's how he ended up anyway. Although, I gather he is still highly thought of in the musical world – at least he was spared that humiliation.'

'You say that as though you are implying he suffered an alternative humiliation.'

'Not much gets past you does it? You are quite correct; he did indeed endure a bout of shame and embarrassment.'

'Do I take it this involved Imelda?'

'Yes. She was the cause.'

'Are you able to tell me about it?'

'I'm one of the only people who is able to tell you about it.'

'Is the bus stop the best place for that?'

'Well tonight it is my home, so I fail to see why not.'

Albert listened to William tell his story, or rather the side of a story that William told; there was a big difference. More often than not, when stories are passed from person to person, the details get altered considerably. Things were left out, and extra parts were created and included, usually to make the tale a bit juicier. However, Albert had no alternative but to listen; it was the best chance he had received so far to find out something worthwhile from a source that had been close at hand. He seemed a pleasant, honourable-enough chap, and certainly wasn't the stereotypical hobo. Yet, Albert had learnt through life not to take things told to him at face value. He should remember the information given and then find out for himself, which parts are the most near the truth, and which were just plain gossip.

'And so you see, it turned out Imelda was having an affair. She was fed up of being stuck at home all day, not being able to go anywhere or do her own thing. She was limited to being the wife of a musician, to hang onto his arm at events, and laugh at his jokes when in public view. She appreciated the gifts he lavished her with, and yet she craved the one thing that she didn't have. True love. She knew it wasn't his fault; it was the way his life had become, owing to the talent he possessed. I reckon she had no idea what a life in the limelight would entail until she was so involved with him that it became too late to turn back.' William took a swig of his masqueraded juice. He shivered as it travelled down his body inside him. 'Of course, it had to come out at some point; affairs always do in the end. I heard he threw her out, and she left without a second thought. They had a young boy at the time, I can't recall his name, but it will come back to me.'

'Jürgen.'

'That's it!' Albert now sat there feeling smug. 'Mind you, I don't know where he is now.'

'Do you know who she had the affair with?'

'That's the one bit I can't help you with unfortunately. Everyone thinks it was Hans Goldmann, but I can tell you now it wasn't him.'

'How can you be so sure?'

'No reason.' Albert had to think of his next question. He still wasn't really getting any information that would give him some sort of breakthrough in the investigation.

'What happened when she left? Did she not die at the house?'

'She left after a violent argument with Andreas. I was still there at the time, and I heard everything. I saw it too, well most of it. They were shouting and hurling insults at each other. It was terrible. We had a maid here then as well, and she'd taken Jürgen out for the evening, on the orders of Andreas. He'd told her he didn't wish their son to be around for what was going to happen.'

'What did happen?'

'You have to understand that it was difficult for me to hold down a job at the time. Well, I say at the time, what I mean is all the time! What he did was terrible, but he gave me a large sum of money to ignore it. Back then I had a family to feed, and I couldn't risk losing the job I had and so I had to take the money and run.'

'I am not judging you.'

'There's no need, I judge myself.'

'What did you see?'

'At the end of their argument, he swung out and pushed her down the stairs. I watched as she tumbled all the way down from the top to the bottom. Her head crunched against the wooden steps as she fell, and then in a flash it was over.' His eyes turned the colour of steel, as he pictured the image in his head, as vivid as the day it had happened. 'There she lay. Lifeless. Blood trickled from her skull into a small puddle beside her. Her blood had splattered along the wall and the stairs in the pattern of the motion in which she had fallen. And then as I looked up from her motionless body, I saw him staring down at me. His eyes met mine. They weren't full of anger anymore, but more of shock and fear. Whether that was because he hadn't figured on someone witnessing his act of violence I don't know, but instantly he offered me the prosperous opportunity to leave, so long as I never returned.' He paused. 'I'm ashamed to say that's what I did. Imelda had been my friend, but since her affair started, which I disagreed with from the off, we hadn't had any contact, and I knew I was likely to lose my job in the near future. I know I should have helped, but she was already dead.' Albert kept his professional demeanour afloat.

'What happened next?'

'After I left, I moved my family to Neumarkt, which is the name of a railway junction in central Cologne. Months passed, but then the police began to sniff around. They were tracking me down, as I was an employee of the Krause's. By this point, my marriage was falling apart, admittedly it was probably due to the strain I carried around with me. So, I left my wife with the money I had been given, and that's when I took to the streets. However, I did contact the police anonymously, to tell them everything I knew about the whole ordeal. They weren't interested as they had no intention of spoiling the great name of Andreas Krause, and so soon enough it was all brushed under the carpet, and life went on.'

'Not for Imelda it didn't.'

'I regret my actions, I really do. The only thing I have to console myself to a minor extent is the reluctance of the police to do anything about it once I eventually came forward. They didn't even do so much as fill out a report, or knock on his door to ask him a few questions. They weren't bothered then, so they wouldn't have been bothered at the time either.'

'Unfortunately I know this style of policing to be true. Sometimes it isn't what is right that people want to hear. If the truth will cause an uproar, or disgrace, in this instance to an entire country, then usually if possible, it is hushed up. That's not to say you aren't blameless, because for whatever reason you give, your actions were indeed despicable.'

'I know that. Ever since it all happened, my life's ambition has been to make amends; one way or another.' Albert looked at him, and couldn't help staring with a rather suspicious expression on his face.

'Are you going to be around here for a while?'

'In light of the recent events you've told to me then yes, the least I can do is stay and help you.'

'Thank you. I can see if a room can be made up for you back at the house.' This startled William:

'No! I'm not going back there.'

'A bed and breakfast then?'

'I am fine living as I do. It's what I have known for a long time now.'

'Very well then. It's getting late and everything will be shutting up soon. I need to work out a way of getting some books out from the library. I doubt sending you in for them will achieve much.' Albert drummed his fingers up and down on his thigh, trying to think of how to get them. 'I need to go and get my friend; she'll be able to get them for me. Do you mind telling me what time the library shuts? It's written on that sign over there. My eyes are no good at the best of times, let alone from all the way over here.'

'I'm afraid I can't even see the sign!'

'Then why don't you wear glasses?'

'I used to, but I always get into fights with other people like me. They get broken.' Albert sighed.

'Come on.'

It was rather entertaining to witness the expressions on the snooty salespeople in the opticians. They were horrified that a hobo was trying on all their spectacles. However, they didn't say anything to him, as Albert, who was smartly dressed, was clearly with him, and they likely felt they couldn't. It was Albert's opinion that they shouldn't say anything anyway, as a person should be judged on who they are and not how they are dressed. It didn't take long for William to find the right strength of lens that he needed and so Albert purchased the glasses for him. He again received polite thanks, but seeing as they only cost eight Euros, Albert was not exactly out of pocket. For the money, they were actually quite smart: all black apart from two red sections on both rims. When they had returned back to the library, there was only ten minutes of opening time left. William rummaged around in his pocket and pulled out a little card, which he inspected with his new glasses.

'You've shown me a great deal of kindness today, which I do not deserve. Even by merely speaking to me is much more than the majority of other people do. Here.' He handed Albert the card. 'It's old, but it should still be valid.' Albert took the library card and thanked him. They shook hands. Albert went into the library and left William standing on the kerb.

Shortly after a successful spell of book borrowing, Albert emerged once again onto the streets. He had noticed the full name that was written on the library card, and was astounded at what he had read. He thought it unlikely that he would ever see the hobo again. With nothing else to accomplish in town, he walked back to the house with the two books tucked under his arm. He did look around once or twice on his short journey, but it was clear that William Reinwald had already gone.

14

Learning about indigenous Asia was actually quite interesting. Albert had rushed his dinner, which was eaten at a table of glum people, all of whom sat in silence for the duration. Leaving it a specific amount of time so that he would not be thought of as totally rude, he had excused himself and hurried off to his bedroom.

He quickly flicked through the book with his fingers. The edges of the pages had turned a beige colour, yet the pages themselves when he opened the book were still white. There was little point reading the entire textbook. If he was searching for a specific indication of Eleanor's reason for borrowing the book, he would not get it by simply reading it through from cover to cover. Instead, he picked it up and held it so the front cover was in front of him, but then he gave it a quarter-turn to the left so that the thin edge of the pages were facing him. He slotted his monocle in front of his eye and stared closely at the top part of the book. He was looking for a "dog ear". It wasn't long before he found what he wanted. One of the pages had been bent over in a triangular shape that resembled a dog's ear. Because the amateurish attempt at futile origami increased the thickness of the page, it caused a slight gap between it and the page before. Albert had hoped he would find something like it. There was no evidence, as of yet, to suggest that Eleanor had turned the corner of the page over, but she was as likely as any of the previous borrowers to have done so. What the dog-ear symbolised was a page of interest, which somebody had marked by folding the corner over so that they could easily find it again without having to trawl through the whole book. He flipped open the book to the page in question.

Of course, he had no idea what any of the words meant, but he could certainly understand the pictures. Afterall, a picture was supposedly worth a thousand words, but more importantly they were not language specific.

There were various pictures that Albert found himself staring at. Clearly, the chapter he had turned to was about hunting in the wild. This was evident from the first picture he saw, which was of an old, dark-skinned man, with long, black, scraggily hair, and a similar beard to match it. He also had large holes in his earlobes, although they weren't plugged with anything. All he wore was a red loincloth around his waist, and was unmistakably a native of the country. He sat on a large rock, holding a small bag, or a pouch, which looked as if it was made out of some kind of animal skin, likely from a deer. He was barefoot and had a large machete resting beside him. Albert couldn't decipher the caption under the picture; he would have to wait for Hannah to join him so she could translate it. He could, however, pick out the odd word such as "Penan", which he recognised as the name given to the tribe of nomadic hunter-gatherers that resided in the Malaysian state of Sarawak in Borneo. As interesting as the picture was, it was the next one that attracted his attention the most. A younger tribal man knelt beside a wild boar, which he had killed. He wore a tan-coloured beaded necklace, complete with various teeth tied into it at regular intervals, which were obviously from an animal of some sort, which had become victim to his hunting skills. He rested one hand upon the dead animal, as he leant upon it, but in his other hand, he grasped a large blowpipe. Another picture further down the page, zoomed into the blowpipe. The weapon was very long indeed, probably even up to six feet. It was made of wood and had a hole in the centre that spanned from end to end. At the end of the blowpipe, was a metal spearhead, which was probably used for finishing off wounded animals after they had been darted. Suddenly, Albert jumped as he heard a knock on the door, which opened soon after. Hannah walked in.

'You left the dinner table quickly tonight didn't you? Is everything okay?'

'Everything is just fine. I've found something that may be significant here.' Hannah moved across the room and sat beside him.

'What's the book about?'

'Indigenous Asia: I got it from the library.' Hannah look puzzled.

'That's a strange choice of book isn't it?'

'Incredibly. But would you think it even stranger if I told you that it was the book Eleanor had borrowed before me?'

'What on earth would she want with a book like this?' Albert removed his monocle.

'Exactly.' They sat in silence for a few seconds, both trying to come up with an answer. 'Now you're here, you could translate some passages for me if you would.'

'Of course; what would you like to know?' He turned the book slightly so that she could view the text a bit better.

'This is the page where I found a mark in the book. We can't be completely sure that Eleanor was looking at them but it is highly likely that she was.' Hannah looked over the pages briefly and almost immediately, something sprung to her memory:

'She must have been.'

'I beg your pardon?'

'Again, we can't say for certain that it was her, but a dart that is used with these pipes was found in the shop after Herbert was killed.'

'Are you sure?'

'I'm positive.'

'Then that supports my thoughts on her borrowing this book, and if we can just...' He stopped. Hannah looked at him.

'If we can just what?'

'When we were outside the locksmiths – that time we bumped into Stefan, didn't you tell me that when he was planting the tree, something flew past his ear?'

'Yes, that's right. That's what he told me anyway.'

'Tell me again who was standing at the other end of the garden, watching him.' At first Hannah looked confused, but then realisation set into her face.

'Eleanor.'

'Precisely. Could that thing that flew past him, have been another dart?'

'Quite possibly! Should we look in the garden for it?'

'Perhaps. But it would be very difficult to find out there, that's if it hasn't been removed. We might be safer working under the assumption that it was a dart, seeing as this book, and the dart at the locksmiths, both support our theory already. Tell me what these things mean, and we'll see what we want to do after that.'

'Okay. Which bit do you want me to translate first?' He pointed to the picture that he had seen of the man wearing the red loincloth.

'What does it say about this picture?' Hannah read:

'An elder from the Penan tribe of South East Asia. Wearing a traditional Chawat, only two hundred people adopting the nomadic lifestyle remain.' Albert nodded.

'What about this one?' He pointed to the young man next to the boar he had slain. Again, Hannah read out the caption of the photograph to him:

'A young Penan with a Bornean bearded pig. An expert kill from a blowpipe, known as a Kaliput.'

'Okay, and what about this one?' He pointed to the picture of the enlarged blowpipe.

'The Kaliput is made out of one solid piece of wood from the Belian Tree. A long metal bar is turned through the wood to make the hole through the centre. A piece of rattan secures the spearhead in place. This is the main hunting tool used by the Penan people.' Albert pondered the information for a moment.

'It's not exactly the revelation I was hoping for.'

'Then what about this?' Hannah had turned over the page and was looking at the next bunch of pictures. A string of diagrams were overleaf, and showed how to make a blowpipe and the darts to use with it. 'It seems somebody was interested in making their own pipe.'

'What does it say about it? Just give me a summary.' She skimmed her eyes over the page, reading the bits she thought were most relevant:

'The Dahad (the dart) is made from Sago palm, or cut from a tin can for a metal tip. The bark of the Tajem tree is cut to extract its latex, which is then warmed over a fire to produce the white poison. The tips of the darts are dipped in the poison and blown from the pipe, penetrating through the skin of its intended victim. Tajem disrupts the functioning of the heart, which results in fatal irregular heartbeats, possibly killing a human within minutes.'

'It would seem that whoever has read this book is now completely knowledgeable about making their own lethal weapon.'

'And what's more, it's a silent way of killing whoever they want to get rid of.'

'Hannah, what do we actually know about Eleanor?'
Hannah thought about it, but not for long.

'Pretty much nothing.'

'She might not even be a housekeeper for all we know, which would explain her borrowing a book about the profession she is supposed to be an expert in.'

'Do you think it would be possible that she could be responsible for such things?'

'Like I said, we don't know her.'

'That's what I'm afraid of.' Neither of them knew what to say next. Both were thinking of the likelihood of the uptight housekeeper, Eleanor Frankwell, being a murderer.

'Albert, the only other thing that may be of some relevance in this book is here, at the end of the last paragraph. Apparently there are several antidotes available for the Tajem poison, but it must be administered without delay.' Albert nodded to show he'd understood what she had said.

'I have one further question for you in relation to that book.'

'Is there something else you want me to translate?' He shook his head.

'No. Turn to the very front of the book if you please.' She did so.

'What now? What am I looking for?'

'What is the date that the book was taken out of the library? It will be the stamp before the very last one, which was when I took it out for loan.' He waited while she found the information.

'She took it out nine days ago. Is that significant?'

'If I then told you that was one week before Stefan felt something shoot past his ear, would you say it was significant?' Hannah closed the book.

'We're finally getting somewhere aren't we?'

'I believe so, yes.'

'What do we do now?'

'We need to be refreshed so we're ready for the morning. Our workload is only going to increase from now on. We still only have an incredibly vague idea of what is going on, but it's important to remember we're one step closer to the truth.'

'So what do you suggest?'

'We get some sleep.'

The fact was, Albert couldn't sleep. There was still nothing that suggested anybody was responsible for the string of deaths that had taken place. It was as if somebody had planned the perfect crime. Whoever the culprit was had clearly worked on their plan for a long time. They had managed to con everybody into believing everything was normal, but had in fact bumped off the famous composer weeks, or possibly months before their impostor suffered the same fate. Surely the man who had been hired to pretend to be Andreas would not have known his life was also on the line otherwise he wouldn't have agreed to be involved? Unless whoever was overseeing the plot, realised that the man had spoken to Hannah and seemed prepared to give her a pointer as to where she ought to be looking to find out about her grandmother, Imelda. Drifting in and out of sleep, Albert knew his thoughts were all merely speculation. He just had nothing to go on.

He lay in bed, staring up at the ceiling through the faded light. There was surely only one thing that connected everything together: the room. The music room where both the real and the fake Andreas had lived had been a mystery from start to finish. There must be something in the room that would point him in the right direction. He was aware the police had taped it off, but Albert knew he had to get inside.

He tied his dressing gown around him and tiptoed down the stairs. He had always acted on impulse, and it was beyond his level of patience to wait until the morning. Besides, he needed to get inside when nobody else was about. None of the officers would allow him access to snoop around, although, he was unsure how he was going to be able to enter the room by himself. Undoubtedly it would be locked.

He stood outside the door. He would just about be able to bend himself around the strips of tape that sealed off the door, but how he was actually going to enter, he didn't know. When he looked closer at the door, however, strangely it was already open. He shuddered to think of the state of the modern police force. To leave a crime scene unlocked and unattended was simply shoddy workmanship. It was about as ludicrous as a burglar robbing a bank and then dropping his curriculum vitae when fleeing the scene. With an unlocked door, it could be accessed and tampered with by anybody. Evidence that had perhaps been overlooked in the first instance could be removed, and such occurrences would make the investigation much more difficult, and perhaps even wholly unsuccessful. Secretly though, he was pleased it was open. It meant he didn't have to break into it, owing to the constraints he was under; he certainly wouldn't have been able to make any noise, in case he woke up the rest of the household and so kicking the door down would have been out of the question. He could have perhaps tried picking the lock, but without the proper tools, it would have been an arduous task.

The door was just slightly ajar. It must have clicked open as the police left. Albert placed his hand upon the handle and slowly pushed it inwards. It creaked, and even though it was faint it still made Albert wince. He was conscious of the fact he had to be as quiet as he possibly could, therefore, if he could manage the job in hand without making a single sound, it would be all for the better. He pushed the door all the way open. The room was dark. It wasn't particularly light during the daytime for that matter, as the windows were always covered over. Albert didn't wish to put the light on, for fear of attracting the unwanted attention of somebody who may be walking across the landing for a quick trip to the bathroom. He had his torch with him and so switched that on instead.

He shone the torchlight over the grand piano. It stood there so magnificently, probably wondering why it was no longer being played. The last piece of music that Andreas would have played was still present on the music rest. Actually, when he recapped over his observation, he realised that was probably not the case. Even Albert himself, was getting confused with the identity of each Andreas. He lit up the sheets of music with his torch and looked at what was essentially a collection of horizontal lines, spanning from one side of the page to the other, adorned with little black dots at various points. Some had little squiggles underneath whereas some had dots. A few of them weren't even black, but instead had a black outline, which formed a white circle on the inside. At the end of the page, a large line ran off the sheet. It was clear that this was a composition, likely the most recent piece of music to have been written by the musical genius. Albert figured that all the dots and squiggles would have meant a lot more to Andreas than it did to him and so turned his attention to the record player in the corner of the room; it seemed an apt place to start searching. The pile of records was still there, gathering dust it would now seem. It seemed ironic that the records were used when the composer had been thought to be alive, and now he was dead, they were not used at all. If only he had paid more attention to the records when he had seen them before, he may have been able to form some sort of link together that indicated they were being played rather than the piano. He walked back over to the piano, and shone his light over the ivory keys. These were not dusty, as he had expected they would be. Clearly the killer was clever enough even to the finest details, to clean the piano, possibly even daily, to give out the impression that it was frequently used. Of course, with the music blaring out of the record player, it had to look as if it was being used otherwise suspicions would have been raised earlier than they would have wanted.

While still shining his torch onto the piano keys, he then noticed the dried bloodstains that were apparent on a group of them. He couldn't clearly make out the colours in the dim light, but he could see the noticeable colour difference where the blood has tarnished the ivory and had been left to dry for a period of time. It was impossible for him to ascertain, again due to the lighting, whether or not the black keys were also stained, as well as the white ones; however, quite frankly he felt that was immaterial. What Albert did find peculiar was why the man, whoever he really was, did not shout out as the knife was plunged into him. He hadn't even considered it before. Whereas most people would release some sound of pain if they cut their finger on a knife when chopping vegetables or even just stubbed their toe; this man hadn't so much as winced when being stabbed. Albert's mind began turning over the possible solutions that would explain the man's silence: on the one hand, it would not be implausible for the culprit to have killed him beforehand, and then have him stand in to imitate the genuine deceased. Albert had witnessed this on a previous case back when he was employed at Scotland Yard; somebody had been sitting in a chair, considered to be sleeping by the rest of the family, only to discover the next day that they were in the same position and had in fact been dead the whole time. The difference was, however, the fake Andreas had been very much alive just hours before, and when he was found, he was well and truly dead. On the other hand, he could quite easily have been gagged so that it was impossible for him to shout out for help. Then again, on the other hand…he stopped, before chuckling quietly to himself that he had just created somebody with three hands. No matter what level the severity of the situation was at, he always managed to get sidetracked from time to time with the odd bit of humour. Luckily, he was also used to pulling himself together and getting back on track. It was also possible that the man resisted the urge to cry out. The reason for this Albert could only guess; perhaps he was also of ill health and thought of death as an easy escape from the pain he was suffering. Whatever the reason was, however, did not alter the fact that it was another life lost, and an important one to lose at that in terms of potential witnesses they needed for interrogation. If Albert was forced to pick an explanation for the man's silence, he felt most strongly about him being gagged before the knife pierced through his skin and deep into his body.

Albert spent several hours poking around in the room that Andreas had spent a great deal of his life in. His meagre possessions that were dotted around did not represent the fame he had achieved. Probably the best thing he had owned was the watch that had been surrendered to Hannah for goodness knows what reason; yet another mystery with no clue of how to research it further. He shone his light onto his own watch. It was still the early hours of the morning and he still hadn't made any significant breakthrough. He still believed the lack of shout when the man had been killed, was a noteworthy point. It could have been that the walls were soundproof, but seeing as the piano, or rather the record player, was constantly heard during the daytime, that was not going to be the case.

He slowly moved back over to the pile of records. He sat at the bottom of the bed and took a deep breath. Had he really become so out of the loop that he couldn't figure out anymore who was responsible for committing a crime? Maybe he should subject himself to the fact that he was getting older and older, and he was not going to be able to keep up with the demands of an investigation. Admittedly, he had retired because he'd wanted to, but these situations he found himself in once every so often were almost welcome, if that was an acceptable thing to say owing to it being due to somebody else's misfortune. If he had the choice, without a moment's hesitation he would choose to live in a crime-free world, but sadly that was never going to be the case.

Once again, he picked up the top record from the pile; the one he had looked at when he had visited who he had believed to be Andreas. He stared at it, and raised his eyebrows in mild confusion. He tried to pretend he was seeing things, but despite the fact that everyone would no doubt claim they were sane, he knew, without any misgivings, that he was not senile. He couldn't have imagined what he was noticing now. A clue: at last. He took the record out of its cardboard sleeve and ran his fingers over its smooth surface. Suddenly he heard some movement outside the room. Quickly, he turned off the torch. He heard the familiar creak of the door, as it opened from the other side. Albert sat there in the darkness. His heart beat at a tremendous rate; he was certain it would be heard by whoever was entering the room. A silhouette of a figure loomed in the doorway. The light was still dark outside the room, just as it was in. The outline of the person was only visible due to the soft moonlight that pierced through the window in the hallway. Albert couldn't detect whether the body belonged to a male or a female. He just sat there, holding his breath as much as possible, while tensing his muscles so that he could not move. The figure raised its arm, and Albert saw the contours of a small pipe held in the body's menacing palm. The old detective felt his heart stop. Then it jumped, and pounded within him, crashing against his rib cage, which ordinarily shielded it from injury. He felt pain soaring through him. He wanted to clutch his heart, but feared to move. Hopefully, whoever brandished the pipe was unaware of his presence and only carried the weapon for their own protection. However, he knew that it was more likely they had detected him from his torchlight. All he could do was wait; his fate was in their hands.

Albert saw their arm elevate until it was parallel to the floor. The pipe that was gripped in their hand was brought up to their mouth and pointed right at him. Albert sat like a sitting duck, and felt like a small rabbit charging through the meadow, trying to prevent the imminent strike of a hungry falcon. Only Albert wasn't running, and the falcon that stood in the doorway didn't budge. Suddenly, he heard a large intake of breath in the darkness. Then, a pain seared through his upper thigh, which made him bolt upwards. Albert dropped the cardboard sleeve, and it fell to the floor silently. Albert staggered backwards briefly. He was sweating profusely. He felt faint and he was frightened. Gradually he dropped down to his knees. He landed on the floor with a light thud and swayed briefly in the kneeling position. The attacker took a step into the room. Albert couldn't keep his remaining energy for much longer. As the figure edged further and further towards him, he felt his body uncontrollably fall forwards and he crashed to the ground with a thump. He managed to keep his eyes open momentarily, but his energy had dwindled from him, and he was now too weak to even hold open his eyelids. His last waking moments were of a pair of feet around him, although he could feel their eyes analysing him as their latest victim. The feet walked around the body before quickly turning and exiting the room. They left Albert in a heap, motionless, and fighting for his life.

15

The cause of death was poisoning of the blood. Or it would have been, had the dart been laced with Tajem. Whoever had fired it obviously meant it as a warning to Albert rather than removing him from the equation altogether. The wounded ex-detective sat up in a hospital bed, in pretty much the same condition as he usually was, only this time with a sore leg. He had been taken to hospital as a precaution, just in case it had contained the toxin, although when he had been found, hours later, he would certainly have been dead if the poison was present.

Despite Eleanor being the first person to arise in the morning, she had completely walked passed the music room door. Even though the door was essentially right at the bottom of the stairs, she had waltzed straight into the kitchen to begin breakfast preparations. It had actually been Thomas who had found him. He had knocked on the front door to deliver the milk as he usually did and had been invited in by the housekeeper for a morning drink. His attention to detail was evidently a lot sharper than hers, as on entering the kitchen, he noticed a section of the police tape hanging off the doorframe where it had been pinned after the body of the mysterious pianist had been found. He had sauntered over to attach it back in place, which is when he noticed the door was open. On entering, he had found the fallen Albert, lying down with the dart sticking out of his leg, and had called an ambulance for him immediately. Albert had been weak when Thomas found him, but probably more out of shock than from the injury. He had lost minimal blood, and just required a checking over to ensure no life-threatening damage had occurred.

Hannah sat with him in the hospital. He didn't like hospital beds, but then again he didn't like hospitals all that much. However, he had to admit that the German hospital, or rather the "Krankenhaus", seemed to run quite efficiently. Albert and Hannah had plenty of time to talk while they waited for Albert to be discharged.

'What were you even doing in that room on your own?'

'There was nobody else around at such an ungodly hour.'

'You know what I mean! It's dangerous around here at the moment. I would have thought you'd have known that.'

'I've spent the most part of my life in situations like these – I think I've managed so far, don't you?'

'You could have been killed.'

'But I wasn't. I'm here and I'm fine.'

'This is the third dart that's come into this investigation you know.'

'I know it is. But I found something when I was in that room. The sooner we get out of here the better.'

'What did you find?' Albert hesitated.

'A clue.'

'Well I know you must have found a clue! But what is it?'

'You'll find out when we get back. We need those records that are on the floor.' Hannah became puzzled.

'What records?'

'There's a pile of records in the room, near the end of the bed. I was even holding one when I was shot.'

'Even so…there's nothing there now. I believe you if you say there were records there, but they've been removed if that's the case.' Albert looked irately at the ceiling.

'Damn it.'

'All we have to do is prove it! We know it's Eleanor!'

'How do we?'

'Because she borrowed the book, which showed her how to make the blowpipe and the darts! Misty was almost shot with one, and then there was Herbert's death, and now you've been shot at.'

'Hannah, you have an awful lot to learn. You are right to be headstrong with these matters, but you must also be sensible and rational at the same time. Don't forget we are only assuming that Stefan was shot at with a dart. We don't actually know for sure. It could have been a twig blown in the wind, a flying insect, or even a bird; we just don't know. As for the murder of Herbert Lorenz, you are correct that a dart was present at the scene of the crime, but he was not killed by that method. Just because the dart was there, it does not mean it had anything to do with his death. And as for me – I know I was shot with a dart, believe me I do, but don't forget it was dark – the culprit may not have known it was Albert Murtland, specifically, who was in that room. And whether they knew or not it was me who was in there, they only fired it as a deterrent to stop me meddling in their business. They had no intention of killing me, just to warn me. So you see, we can't conclude anything just yet.'

'But what about the opportunity for someone to take that shot at you? I mean, the only people in the house at the time were you and I, which we know didn't do it; my father who I know wouldn't have done it, and Eleanor. She's the only logical explanation.'

'The only logical explanation apart from the fact Stefan has a key to the house himself; absolutely anybody can burgle a house if they wish, and I found out while at the library that during the time of your father's compulsory conscription in the military, he had spent some time in Indonesia and Malaysia, which puts him in the frame just as much as anybody else.'

'You've been researching my father? You didn't say.'

'Some things are better left untold, until the time is right for them to be disclosed.'

'But why research him? He's my father; I know he's not capable of anything like this.'

'Perhaps. But that is something that you believe to be true, whereas I do not know your father at all. It is my responsibility to find out for myself what anybody connected with the case is capable of.'

'But he's my father – I know him.'

'You already told me at some point that you haven't seen your parents for a good while. How do you know people don't change, even in the slightest?'

'You know your own parents!'

'Let me tell you something. About six years into my role as a Detective Inspector, I was assigned to a case concerning the rape and murder of a twelve-year-old girl. She was found beaten and bruised with multiple cuts and wounds to her body. Tests showed she had been penetrated many times and their was a variety of different semen present inside her. The culprit turned out to be her own father, who had charged a group of his friends fifty pounds each to molest and rape his daughter. He himself also joined in. They took her down to the river and drowned her afterwards. It turned out her father owed a lot of money for drugs he had used, and he thought it would be a quick, although immoral way of gaining money. If it wasn't bad enough that he hired her out in forced prostitution, his reasoning for killing her was that he couldn't bear to see her face anymore as it was a constant reminder of the wickedness he had set upon her and ultimately the rest of his family, should they ever have found out. So you see, anybody is capable of terrible deeds; anybody and everybody.' Hannah stayed silent. It was a dreadful story to hear, but it really hammered home the truth about the position that Albert was in. Whether it was secretive or not, he had to research everybody he could to get the best possible perspective on everything and everyone. He didn't know her father from the next guy that walked along the street, and so she couldn't really be angry with him for doing what was his natural instinct to do in matters such as the one they were facing. It took her a while before she spoke, as she still mulled over the story he had told her, but eventually she did restart the conversation, and with such an adult view to the situation, even Albert was taken slightly aback.

'You should research my father more.'

'I beg your pardon.'

'He's my father and I love him, but even though I am unaware of anything he may have done that is wrong in the eyes of the law, that doesn't mean he is innocent of absolutely everything. He's always appeared a rather shady character, and if I can detect that as his own daughter, then goodness knows what just anybody else would perceive of him.'

'I'm glad I have your understanding.'

'The only thing I do ask is that you inform me of anything that you may find. I won't mention anything to him but I would rather be in the loop than oblivious on the outside. I'm growing up fast and I need to learn. Anything you can tell me will be kept between us. I promise.'

'I'll see how I get on. If it's relevant I shall let you know.' She smiled. A nurse popped her head around the door.

'Herr Murtland ist frei, jetzt gehen.' She soon disappeared after she had delivered her message. Hannah did her duty as translator:

'She said you're free to go now.' Albert swung his legs around instantly and hung them off the side of the bed.

He stood up and put on his jacket. Placing his hat on his head as best he could without a mirror, he satisfied himself with its position and picked up his walking cane.

'Come along then; we must get back to the music room.' He briskly walked out of the ward with a somewhat anxious Hannah following him.

It seemed that the German police officers had given up trying to get Albert to conform to their rules about unauthorised persons attending the crime scene. He didn't consider himself unauthorised; he believed himself to be an integral member of the investigation team. While he had been lying down in hospital, he had telephoned his former Police Chief, Martin Knight, back in England. They kept in touch from time to time and Albert thought he might wish to hear about the predicament he found himself in. Astonishingly, all he had done was laugh down the phone at him. It appeared he found it incredibly amusing that his old comrade had been darted by a tribal blowpipe, usually meant for such creatures as warthogs. Had the matter been much more serious, Albert hoped the Chief would have acted with slightly more concern than rapturous guffawing. Even so, a lot of good came of their chance phone call. Albert had explained the situation to him, about the circumstances of the case regarding Imelda and Andreas, as well as the rest of the unfortunate ones who had fallen victim to the loose murderer. He then went on to moan about the German Sergeant who, whether understandably or not, was blocking Albert from making his enquiries. The Police Chief unfortunately sided with the German Sergeant, and deep down Albert also knew he was in the right – it was just frustrating for him that he was restricted in what he could do. However, it turned out, after their phone call, his former Police Chief had dialled through to an acquaintance of his in Germany, and had managed, through the use of their friendship, to get a message to the German Sergeant instructing him to allow Albert free access to wherever he needed to go. When back at the house, he was greeted by the sullen Sergeant whose moroseness had spiralled since their last meeting. Even so, Albert had what he wanted and so couldn't care less about the evil glares he felt darting into him as he ambled past.

The music room was essentially untouched. Hannah had been quite correct – the records were not there; they had vanished. Albert wondered why his attacker would have wanted them so badly. They had clearly detected him poking around the room, and decided to act quickly. Once he had fallen to the floor, they had gathered the records up and left, leaving no trace they were ever there. But why would they not have just killed him? If they believed him to be on the right track with uncovering their identity, why not just claim another life to their killing spree? At least they would know he wouldn't be coming back, whereas now he was fully recovered and back with less restriction to do his investigating than he had before.

Hannah stood in the doorway watching Albert scour the room for more clues. He still seemed intrigued with the record player, which stood in the corner of the room. It was incredibly dusty and Albert looked over it closely. He peered at every edge and examined the handles and the side panels. Then, he raised the needle and inspected the arm that it was attached to. He didn't say anything; he just bumbled along looking at anything and everything, most of which Hannah believed to be insignificant. Then, he followed the cable from the record player all the way down towards the socket in the wall. He found the plug and inserted it into the power point.

He turned on the switch. Nothing sounded from the record player. He looked over it once again, and found the power button on the machine itself. Then, he switched it on. Still nothing came out of the speakers. He didn't expect to hear any music, because naturally there was no record for the needle to attach itself to. However, he expected to hear some crackling or any other sound, but nothing emitted from the system. The platter wasn't even turning, which was strange, as his turntable at home automatically began turning once the device was switched on, ready for a record to be placed onto the spindle. It didn't seem to be working at all. He pondered it for a short while longer before switching it all off again. Suddenly, he straightened himself up and walked over to one of the roller blinds that kept the room in darkness, and had done so for quite some time.

'It's time these came up. Hannah help me with these please.' She pushed herself away from the doorframe she had been leaning on and obeyed his instruction. Together, they lifted the three blinds that forbade the entrance of light. They creaked as they pulled on the mechanism to raise them up. Truly, they hadn't been opened for many, many years. When the task was completed, they both looked around the room. The light showed how vibrant the room had become. Neither of them had ever seen it with natural lighting, only with the dim glow of a light bulb that hung inside a tatty lampshade on the ceiling. The piano still looked magnificent and elegant; nothing could ever take that away from it, but the rest of the room clearly benefited from the new addition that shone through the windows. Albert looked out and saw the glorious steeple of the Church. It was practically central within the middle window of the room. The large cross that perched on top glistened in the midday sun.

'What do we do now Albert?' He held up his hand as a signal to stay quiet. Hannah stopped talking and looked at him, wondering what had struck him now. He moved to the window that was on the most left of the room and quietly opened it. The sound of voices travelled through the new hole in the wall. Albert beckoned his young assistant over, as she was needed to interpret what was being said. She put her ear as far out of the window as she possibly could, which was a rather difficult task, standing on tiptoes, eavesdropping, and maintaining her concealment from whoever the voices belonged to. Albert, albeit uselessly, also listened intently.

'Es ist besser, es jetzt zu kaufen, weil die Preise etwas im Winter zu erhöhen.'

'Lassen Sie mich nur den Schlüssel zum Schuppen finden.' Albert looked at Hannah. She whispered her thoughts to him:

'The second voice is Misty, I think. It's hard to tell exactly from where we are.'

'Who's the other one?'

'I don't know.'

'What are they saying?'

'The first one said it's better to buy it now because the prices will increase slightly in the winter. And Misty said he has to find the key to the shed.'

'What's better to buy now?'

'I have no idea.' She turned her head back to the window and leant out again, as far as she dared to. She wasn't exactly sure at what point she could be seen. They both listened into the conversation once again.

'Ich nehme nicht an, Sie können mir helfen überhaupt; es ist viel auf meinen eigenen zu bewegen? Es ist eine ganze Tonne.'

'Ich fürchte, ich kann dir nicht helfen, nicht in meinem Alter. Aber der Milchmann hat gerade gewesen, ich kann sehen, ob er wird Ihnen helfen, es in zu bringen.'

'Ich würde es zu schätzen wissen, wenn Sie könnten.' One set of footsteps walked away and became fainter until they could no longer be heard. Hannah brought her head back into the room.

'I still don't know who the other person is, but whoever they are, they want help with bringing something in. And whatever is it, there's a tonne of it.' Albert clicked his fingers.

'It must be coal! The only shed outside, or near enough to where we are anyway, is the coal shed. You tend to be able to buy the coal earlier in the year at summer prices, which are cheaper than in winter. I know we're in late autumn now, but maybe there's still a price difference.'

'That would make sense because Misty said he can't help bring it in as he's too old, but Thomas has just delivered the milk, so he's just gone to ask him if he wouldn't mind giving the coalman a hand with it. Thomas obviously had to come back because he wouldn't have had chance to leave the milk this morning after he'd sorted out your ambulance and accompanied you to the hospital to make sure you were okay.'

'Why would the coalman be asking for help to bring in the coal? It's his job afterall.'

'I haven't got a clue; perhaps they're short-staffed this week. I don't know anything about it if I'm honest.'

'Wasn't it the coal shed that Stefan got a key cut for?'

'Yes. He told us when we bumped into him in town. It was before Herr Lorenz was murdered.'

'Indeed it was.' Hannah wasn't sure whether or not Albert wished to say anything else, but she interjected all the same:

'Somebody's coming back; be quiet!' The sound of footsteps travelled through the open window.

'Guten Tag. Stefan sagt mir, Sie brauchen Hilfe, um etwas Kohle zu bewegen. Zum Glück hatte ich einige Ersatzkleidung in meinem LKW, so dass wir sofort, wenn Sir beginnen können?'

'Vielen Dank. Es sollte nur zehn bis fünfzehn Minuten. Ich schätze es.' The owners of the two voices walked off. Hannah instinctively translated the conversation for Albert without being asked; she knew he would have asked her to anyway.

'That was Thomas. He said he has some spare clothes in his truck and so he can help him move the coal straight away. The coalman just thanked him and told him it should only take ten to fifteen minutes.' It wasn't long before they heard the two men struggling along the drive, presumably carrying bags of coal. Albert had told Hannah that when he had lived in the country for a short while, he had needed to make a similar purchase every year. There was nothing like an open fireplace, filled with newspaper, kindling, logs and coal, to warm the room. Sometimes on Bonfire Night or even a cold winter's night, he would sit cross-legged on the rug that lay in front of the hearth and toast marshmallows or roast some chestnuts, the smell of which filled the air and was adorable and mouth-watering. The coal that he used to have delivered was weighed out in twenty-five-kilogram bags. Therefore, he felt for the two men outside, as he knew they would have forty bags to move between them. Where he had lived, the coal wagon was able to reverse right up the drive and park outside the barn where it was kept. The German coalman had no such luck – it was understandable why he had asked for help.

Hannah was enjoying hearing Albert narrate his story of country living, even if he had to tell her using a dull whisper. Unfortunately, nearing the end of the two men's trips, an irate voice sounded outside. It was instantly recognisable to whom the voice belonged; Eleanor was clearly not happy to see the coal delivery.

'Warum hat das alles Kohle bestellt? Niemand hat mir davon erzählt! Du solltest besser nicht im Haus danach kommt – ich will nicht, dass Sie stapfen schwarzen Staub auf der ganzen Teppiche. Ich habe gerade erst meine Putz fertig für den Tag!' The coalman stayed silent, but Thomas found his tongue to answer her:

'Wir gehen nicht zu kommen. Wir haben nur noch eine Reise noch zu tun, und dann wir beide verlassen. Er hat mehr Kohle habe an anderer Stelle liefern, und ich muss wieder an die Molkerei zu bekommen.'

'So stellen Sie sicher, dass Sie nicht kommen. Habe ich schon aus diesem Gärtner mit seinen dreckigen Stiefeln auf gejagt.' She let out an exasperated groan before Albert and Hannah heard her hurry away from the shed. The coalman spoke:

'Ist sie immer so?'

'Ich habe solche Angst.' They both left to fetch their final bags from off the truck. Albert raised his eyes towards Hannah, indicating a translation.

'She's annoyed nobody told her about the coal being ordered, and told them to steer clear of the house when they've finished. It seems she's fed up of cleaning up after everybody and hasn't even let Misty in because of his dirty boots. Thomas just said they weren't going to go in the house and they only have one more trip to do. Then the coalman asked if she was always like that, and Thomas essentially just said yes.' Albert let out a short noise as he contemplated the scenario that had just occurred.

'Why would Eleanor need to be informed of the coal being ordered?'

'I'm as confused about that as you are I'm afraid. It doesn't make sense.'

'Unless of course it's not the coal she is concerned about.'

'What do you mean?'

'Think about it. When Stefan was digging up the garden and he felt something fly by his ear, where did he say Eleanor was standing?'

'Behind the coal shed wasn't it?'

'Exactly. What if she has some sort of interest, not in the coal, but in the shed itself?'

'But what?'

'I wish I could tell you.'

'You may be right though.'

'Possibly. It's just another theory. Anyway, keep quiet, they're coming back.' They heard the two men trudge along the pathway and reach the coal shed. The door clattered against the side as they entered.

'Vielen Dank für Ihre Hilfe.'

'Erwähnen Sie es nicht. Wir alle brauchen Hilfe, an einem gewissen Punkt.'

'Auch so habe ich es zu schätzen wissen. Mein Lehrling ist im Urlaub in dieser Woche, so dass wir kämpfen, etwas zu bekommen die Lieferungen erfolgt.'

'Geben Sie den Schlüssel wieder an Stefan, wenn Sie hier fertig sind, es sei denn, Sie woollen vor allem die Haushälterin zu sehen!' The coalman laughed.

'Nicht wirklich!'

'Nun, ich fürchte, ich würde besser wieder an die Molkerei zu bekommen.'

'Was machst du?'

'Gleichen alten Sachen – Ich werde vor allem die Herstellung von Käse und Joghurt werden heute.' The door flung back open as Thomas left. 'Haben Sie einen guten Tag!'

Soon enough, his footsteps disappeared out of earshot. Albert whispered to Hannah:

'What was all that about?' She whispered back:

'The coalman just thanked Thomas for his help and said his apprentice is on holiday this week, which is why they are struggling. Thomas told him to give the key back to Misty when he's finished unless he particularly wanted to see Eleanor – the coalman wasn't overly enthusiastic with his reply!'

'Was that it?'

'Pretty much! After that, Thomas just said he's going to go back to the dairy. The coalman asked him what he was doing, and Thomas just said he'd be making cheese and yoghurts. Then as he left, he said have a good day. That's it.'

'That's a strange end to the conversation.'

'Why do you say that?'

'It just seems a bit odd that's all; probably just me being cynical – it happens after you've been investigating murders most of your life.' Albert and Hannah had to stay quiet for one final time, as they heard the coal shed door close onto its latch and the padlock lock into place. His footsteps sounded along the gravel path until they could no longer hear them, but they did just about manage to pick up the sound of his truck being started up, as he drove away. Albert shut the window. 'Now please tell me you noticed something strange about that.' Hannah looked at him. She was confused again, as he always seemed to go off on a tangent and bring up points that she didn't, and probably would never, consider.

'What was strange?'

'Well I'm not being cynical this time.'

'About what?'

'The coalman has just left.'

'Yes….'

'Why has he taken the shed key with him?'

16

The golden weathervane that stood on top of the steeple attached to the house, reflected the sunlight brilliantly. The cat ran after the mouse in the direction of the East, although the wind was not especially that strong. It was quite warm for the time of year, and the local vineyards would be enjoying a good harvest of their crop. Nevertheless, daydreaming about juicy grapes being made into a medium-dry white wine was not going to help Albert solve the case. He felt things were slowly coming together but he still had to investigate a couple more areas to make sure of his facts. Unfortunately, however, he was still at a loss with regards to Imelda. Her death was still a complete mystery, and he feared it always would be. But then something struck him. It was a notion that dawned on him stronger than any before. He had been concentrating on Imelda's death too much. True, she had fallen down the stairs and died during a ferocious argument with her husband, but this was believed by hardly anybody. What he thought was ludicrous, but he couldn't think of what direction to take to solve her death, and that problem threw up an interesting question: what if she hadn't died? He had travelled to Germany on Hannah's belief that she had died. Admittedly, Johann and Stefan, and a whole host of other people, also believed she had died, because why wouldn't they? But, none of them actually knew whether she had in fact passed away. Someone had told him that her body had just disappeared. One minute she was there, and the next she was gone. Apart from Andreas himself, who was confirmed to be dead, nobody was able to answer the simple question: did Imelda die? The more he thought about it, the more he believed she could be very much alive. The only other point that involved itself with his theory was quite simply, why? This was a brainwave he had needed. It was predominantly unrelated to Andreas' murder, and all the others that were connected with it, but it was the main promise he had made to Hannah and he knew he had to get her the answers she so desperately sought. He decided not to tell her about his idea for the time being; it was better for her to believe Imelda to be dead and for that to be true, than to give her hope she is alive, and then find out that was not the case.

He had left the house in secret so he would not attract Hannah's attention to where he was going. Despite the language barrier, he was determined to do his utmost to rifle through the death records at the library, in the hope of finding Imelda Krause, or rather not to find her, as the case may be.

Johann was busy in the kitchen annoying Eleanor. He had entered the hallway after a walk down the garden, picked up and played with a couple of the ferrets, and had traipsed back in leaving a trail of mud behind him. He had wandered into the kitchen and been shot a filthy glare by the easily infuriated housekeeper, who soon after her deathly frown had chucked a dustpan and brush at him. Unluckily for Eleanor, Johann had picked it up and chucked it straight in the bin in an effort to irritate her further. It worked, and on retrieving it from the bin, had clobbered him around the head with it. Hannah, who had walked passed the room about halfway through the incident, decided to leave them arguing between themselves, as she had no desire to get involved herself. Instead, she decided to make her way into the music room to try and see exactly what Albert had been so intrigued with, regarding the record player. She had no idea where he was, but she was not worried, as she knew it was within his personality to take off by himself, especially if he considered himself to have stumbled upon some sort of breakthrough. He had instructed the police officers to allow her access if she wanted to do some digging for herself, and whereas the German Sergeant had almost burst a vein in his neck, his agreement was assumed by a snort and the way he stormed off, as he didn't wish to upset his superiors any further with regards to Albert and his independent investigation. She also wanted to accomplish a progression of her own while he was gone, so that she could present him with some findings of her own on his return, and show that she was useful to him and not just a piece of deadwood merely waiting for him to crack the case for her. She knew he was undoubtedly more experienced in these matters than she was but even so, she just wanted to help.

No matter how many times she tried, she too couldn't get the record player to work. She even resorted to bashing it with her fist in a hollow effort to jumpstart the electrics. That didn't work either; she had been successful using that method with such devices as her television remote or her DVD player, but the old gramophone was determined not to oblige. Feeling somewhat defeated, she gave up and admitted to herself that it was undeniably broken. However, it must have worked since her grandfather's death, which led her to believe that somebody, for some reason, had sabotaged the equipment. What difference would it make whether it was working now or not? It just didn't make sense. She stored her queries at the back of her mind while turning her attention to the grand piano. She walked all around it, becoming absorbed by the smooth texture of the shiny wooden body. The top board prop held up the lid sturdily in place, and she looked inside to see a complex structure full of strings, dampers and hammers that struck backwards and forwards to play the intended notes when the corresponding keys on the outside were pressed by the pianist. It was a complicated design, and she could only pretend to understand the true workings of it all.

She hesitated when she got to the piano stool. The soft leather cushion looked inviting and in excellent condition. She felt disobedient to a certain extent at the thought of sitting on it herself. Her grandfather wouldn't have wanted anybody else to sit on it except him, although that rule had already been broken several times by the impostor that had masqueraded as him for so long. The difference being, however, he wouldn't have cared in the slightest about his feelings, whereas she had, and still did. Nevertheless, after a few more moments of wavering, she lowered herself onto the spongy seat, and waited as it gently lowered itself into a position that conformed to her weight and the shape of her body. If only she could play the piano herself, she would have felt so honoured to play on the instrument her famous grandfather had played so many times over the course of his life. However, she was not a pianist and had no desire to purposely insult his memory by merely punching groups of random keys to make whatever tuneless sound erupted from her disorderly action. She had told Albert a couple of days ago about her feelings towards the piano and how she would never play it without her grandfather's permission. He had commended her devotion to him, but quickly followed it up by a witty comment from an old comedy show he had seen many years ago. The names had meant nothing to her but he had told the story with such a fondness in his voice that suggested the comedians involved were among his favourites. It was during a show of Morecambe and Wise, and the sketch in question was situated in a grand music hall with a vast orchestra led by the famous conductor André

Previn. The vivacious comic Eric Morecambe had sat down at the piano and knocked out a string of unconnected and dreadful combinations of notes. When criticised by the conductor about him playing all the wrong notes, he had been adamant in saying he was in fact playing all the right notes, just not necessarily in the correct order. Hannah had chuckled when she'd heard the story, but even so remained adamant that she would never play a note on her grandfather's piano without his permission or his presence.

She sat for a while on the stool, staring at the piano in front of her. It didn't seem natural that it hadn't been played for what had likely been several months, and yet the constant playing of records that had sounded from the room on a daily basis had fooled everybody. It was too late to dwell on that now, however, and Hannah instead stared at the sheet of music on the music rest that would have been the last piece her grandfather would have played. There would have been little point to the fake Andreas changing the music that was there, as hardly anybody would have seen it on there anyway, and anyone that did access the room would not have paid any attention to it at any rate. The piece of music that was present on the rest did not have a name, which obviously meant that to anyone other than her grandfather, the composition was unidentifiable. It was most likely to be his newest symphony that he had been working on. Hannah could only vaguely read music and the majority of the piece looked like a highly skilled creation. There were notes all over the place, with scribbles and crossings out – even one whole staff had a big line all the way through it, which was clearly a section he hadn't been happy with. At the end of the paper was a line that had been drawn on; only this line was different to the rest. It appeared to have been written with a shaky hand and looked as if the pen had started off writing music but then had gradually wriggled downwards off the page. She looked closely at where the ink had touched the paper, but couldn't see anything out of the ordinary. To be honest, it just looked as if the composer had slipped while writing on the notes.

She sat there for a while longer until coming to the conclusion she was kidding herself at trying to be an expert at detective work. She felt dejected at being so useless and not contributing anything to the investigation. Becoming increasingly downhearted with every second that passed, she got up from the stool and took a step to her right. Her plan was to leave the room and go and find Misty for some comfort, which he had always been successful at providing when she had visited as a young girl. However, the step she took while moving out of the gap between the piano and the stool was an awkward one as there was not a lot of space. She stumbled slightly and her foot ended up further under the piano than intended. Her taken step had ended with a slight crunch. She knelt down to inspect the damage she had caused and was a little intrigued to find the remains of a standard pen, with its plastic casing shattered and splintered owing to the impact of her foot pressing down on it. She picked it up, which she instantly thought was a bad move owing to the fact that it should be taken and dusted for fingerprints. It did occur to her though, why the police hadn't found the pen when they had searched the room after the stabbed body was found. Then again, the incompetence of at least one of the officers who had left the door unlocked the night Albert was darted, summed up the working practices of at least that individual from the team of crime scene investigators. Perhaps they had not bothered taking it because it was quite simply just a pen. Or maybe they had overlooked it as it had been pretty much hidden under the three pedals attached to the base of the piano. Of course, the alternative solution would be it was added at a later date; it was difficult to know how many nights the room had been left unlocked, although the addition of a pen seemed rather pointless. What struck Hannah the most was not what the object was, but in fact the position that she had luckily found it in. She looked around the room, and saw everything had its own place and it seemed as if the room had remained in the same way for quite some time. As she held the pen loosely in her hand and let it roll to and fro in her palm, it seemed highly unlikely that her grandfather, or indeed the person pretending to be him, would have been happy with the pen being out of its place. Everything else in the room was in order, even as far as the pillows on the bed standing on their corners, or the keys in the windows all turned to the same position. As she looked at the room in more detail, the pictures on the wall were identically parallel to one another; not a thing was out of place. It was the easiest human error to drop a pen, but her grandfather obviously had a neat and orderly trait, which his impersonator must have abided by to keep up the pretence. If the pen had been dropped, it would have been picked up and put back to its spot at once. So the fact that it hadn't been was surely a clue.

Albert was busy searching through the death records for Imelda Krause. He had the date of her death as thirtieth of December 1983 from remembering what Hannah had told him back when they were in England, walking in the park. He searched in the area of Rüdesheim am Rhein and she wasn't hard to find. It was an unusual name and there certainly wouldn't have been that many women named Imelda in the region, which narrowed down even further when Krause was added to it. In fact, she was the only one. The records showed: Imelda Krause (Bernstein), 45, Presberg, Rüdesheim, 30th Dezember 1983. It had to be her; she would have been about that age when the accident happened. That concluded that line of enquiry. She was dead. Perhaps her death was accidental afterall.

Albert held his head in his hands. He knew Imelda being alive was just a whim he had invented, but he had become so fixated with it being the truth that he now felt extremely disappointed on finding out she was dead. He glanced over the death record several more times before admitting defeat. There was an option for a burial date to be entered; this was not filled in. It puzzled Albert why it wouldn't have been completed. Her death was fairly recent as far as the keeping of records was concerned. They had been kept for hundreds of years and the death in question was only a few decades old. Surely, they would have known the date of her burial, especially with her being part of a famous family. It didn't make sense. Defeated once again, he gathered up his things and left the library. He stood outside and stared up at the sun that shone down upon him, and the rest of the village of Presberg.

'What's the matter?' A familiar voice sounded nearby. Albert turned to his left to see William leaning against the wall of the library, still wearing the red-rimmed glasses he had bought for him.

'Well if it isn't Stefan's brother – I didn't imagine I'd be seeing you again.'

'You noticed that then did you? Speaking of my brother, I haven't seen him for ages – I don't suppose you know his whereabouts?' Albert dug into his pocket and handed back the library card he had borrowed.

'Thank you for the use of this, it came in very handy. With regards to Stefan, I'm afraid I don't know exactly where he is, but he is around. Somewhere.'

'Do you not need this card again?'

'No thanks; I've got what I need from there. What I need to find out now doesn't require a library card.'

'What does it require?'

'I really shouldn't say.'

'Please yourself. I expect to be moving on soon; if I don't happen to see my brother before I go, just pass on that I said hello, if you wouldn't mind that is.' He pushed himself off the wall. 'Cheerio. And good luck with your search.' He swivelled around, and Albert saw his old juice bottle in his pocket with the red wine splashing around inside it, caused by his movement.

'Just a second.' William stopped and turned back to face Albert. He didn't say anything but just looked expectantly at Albert, waiting for him to speak again. 'You say you knew Imelda well?'

'Indeed I did.'

'When was the last time you saw her?'

'As I told you before, I watched her get pushed down the stairs.'

'And then you left employment at the house?'

'That's correct.'

'Where was she buried?'

'In a cemetery, I would imagine.' Albert felt angry inside on hearing the flippant comment, but managed to keep calm. Afterall, this man might be his only hope to find out anything more about the whole ordeal.

'Which one?'

'Have you looked at her death record?'

'Yes – literally five minutes ago.' William stayed silent. 'Can you add anything to it?'

'The last time I saw her was when she was pushed down the stairs.'

'I'm aware of that.'

'But that wasn't the last time I heard from her.' Albert's heart skipped a beat, which wasn't a pleasant experience, especially seeing as the surprises that he continued to find when he carried out his investigations always seemed to make that sensation occur.

'What do you mean?'

'When you worked as a detective, did you conduct all your enquiries by simply asking for answers, or did you actually find out anything for yourself?' Now Albert couldn't keep calm.

'This is a very difficult situation. I have been brought to a foreign country of which I do not know the language, to help a young girl find out about the death of her grandmother whom she has never met. I am continually obstructed by the police force here even though a select few of them seem to be about as competent as an aardvark driving a bus. I merely asked you for a piece of simple assistance, to put right a wrong that has been erroneous for over thirty years. If you cannot help with that then I have clearly made a mistake when I brought you out that drink from the library the first time we met. Perhaps I am going blind in my old age, and if so please return those glasses so that I can wear them!' William bit back, but not quite so hard.

'I told you everything you needed to know before. I told you what has happened throughout my life, and you should be able to work it out from that. The biggest clue I gave you was my library card, which you seem to have overlooked. Now I admire you Albert. I admire your generosity, and I admire what you stand for. I also marvel at just how far you have come in your investigation, although it baffles me that you don't realise it yourself. I haven't returned to Presberg for all these years for a good reason; a

223

reason so major that it meant I had to cut ties with my own brother because of it.'

'Then why return now?'

'Because circumstances have changed. Really, there's not a lot else I can say.' He started to walk away. Albert called after him:

'Wait! Is that all you can tell me?' William didn't look back as he spoke:

'You're so close Albert, and you have all the information you need. Solve this; solve it all, and reward yourself with the knowledge you seek.' No sooner had he uttered his last words, he had gone. Albert trotted around the corner but he truly was nowhere to be seen. What did his last words mean? He didn't have a clue. Only one thing was for certain – he was going to have to think very hard about every single aspect he knew of, and if he really was close to finding the answers, he had an inkling the murderer would also be aware of his imminent unearthing.

Hannah still occupied the music room. She was back on the stool, holding the pen and staring at the music on the stand. She was still plagued by the reasoning behind the inconsistent positioning of the pen and couldn't think of any rational argument that would have the pen stay on the floor. It was unlikely for it to have fallen there during the time her grandfather was in the room; therefore the fraudulent stand-in must have dropped it. Why would he have done so and not picked it up afterwards? He could have been distracted and then forgotten all about it, or perhaps he…she stopped her train of thought. Subconsciously she had thought of something, which possibly could give her the explanation she sought. She got up and walked over to the window. She looked out and saw the Church steeple looming over the rest of the village. It was taller than the steeple on top of her grandfather's house but that didn't take away any of the magnificence that the shorter one possessed. As she stared out at the St. Laurentius Parish Church, she brought her mind back round to thinking about the one reason most feasible for why he couldn't have picked it up. Clearly, he mustn't have physically been able to do so. That made perfect sense. As far as Hannah knew, the only point in time where he would have been incapable would be when he was dead. Her logic led her to another revelation. If he had dropped it while he was being murdered, it meant he was using the pen at the time. And what did anybody sitting at a piano use a pen for? To write music! She didn't get chance to turn around again, as she felt a dull thud strike her from behind at the base of her neck. She collapsed to the floor and that was the last she saw of the music room.

She awoke with an aching head in a dark room. The room was cold and smelt musty. She could hear some scuttling close by and assumed the sound to come from some lively rats going about their business. When she breathed in, the air did not taste clean – it was filled with particles of dust and it felt stale and rough as it travelled up her nose. She couldn't remember a lot about what happened. All she knew was she had been stood by the window in the music room, and then she thought she remembered a quick flash of green before being hit on the back of her head. Then, she woke up, which brought her to where she was now. She needed to see Albert so desperately but first needed to find a way to escape her makeshift prison cell, if there was even a way to do that.

After sitting there for a while, still trying to regain full consciousness, she began moving her hands around her to give her familiar hints as to where her location was. She was on a hard surface, which was cold through her clothing, and felt like concrete. The walls were close around her, and the texture and smell gave away the material as being made of wood. One of her hands that rummaged along the floor soon became colder, as it entered into a mildly damp area. It didn't feel anything like a puddle, but it was definitely different to just plain concrete. She could see a gap in one of the wooden walls, and so she clambered to her feet to go and see what it could give away. Despite treading slowly and carefully, she tripped over a large object that lay on the ground. She put out her hands to move it, but ended up dragging them back swiftly and covering her mouth. She didn't want to scream for fear of attracting her attacker's attention, but finding a dead body outstretched next to her, tested her powers of control to the extreme. Quickly, she moved so that she didn't block out the slim crack of light that entered the cramped building. Firstly, she could make out the outline of all the coal and so she knew it was the coal shed where she had been taken. The body on the floor, however, she didn't recognise. It was lying in a pool of blood that had largely dried. In fact, as she looked more closely, pretty much the entire concrete floor was stained red. The body had lost a lot of blood, although in the dim light, it was not possible for her to determine the cause of death. She turned around to face the door, hoping that she could break it down. All she needed was a crowbar or something similar to slip through and force off the lock. She looked to her right in case the shed housed something she could use, purposely in the opposite direction to the dead body. To her horror, she was greeted by the outline of another person, staring straight at her.

17

Hannah stumbled backwards. Her eyes were fixated by the gruesome figure. Her heart beat fast, and she began to perspire from the fear that had invaded her. She had hit the wall of the shed hard when she fell, and had banged her head on a horizontal beam that had been nailed on for extra structural support. The terrified girl didn't particularly want to pull herself up, but she knew she had to; she was more at danger cowering in the corner. She cried out:

'Who are you?' No answer came through the darkness. From her new position crouching on the floor, she now couldn't see what the thin ray of light that shone through the narrow slit exposed. However, she couldn't hear anything, so for the time being, the mysterious human hadn't moved, or at least, she hoped it hadn't. Slowly, although her knees trembled uncontrollably, she raised herself back to her feet and leant against the wall of the shed. The figure had returned to an outline that sat on the some of the lower bags of coal, which had been stored there. 'Who are you?' Her pathetic enquiry again fell on deaf ears.

It was a case of being bold or probably dying without trying. The chances of her escaping the shed alive were not high, and so she summoned the last speck of remaining courage from within her and took a step forward to her unwanted guest. Whoever it was still didn't speak. She steadied herself with her hands against the shed walls, and resisted screaming when feeling a large spider scurry over her fingers. It was also a matter of acting cautiously so she didn't, for a second time, trip over the dead body that she was already unfortunately keeping company with. The shadowy figure still sat on the coal, saying nothing, and merely waited for her to get closer. She tried again with her futile question:

'Who are you?' There was still no answer. There were not many more steps she could take before she would be sitting next to the sinister individual. After every step that was taken, the light showed more and more of who sat just a few feet away from her. With just a couple of paces left to go, she saw what sat inside the coal shed with her. The horror of such an image would leave her scarred for a long while. Nobody should have to see such an image. Hannah turned for a few minutes, simply to vomit onto the floor behind her. Unluckily for her, there was no escape to the situation, and all she could do was turn back to view the sickening sight.

The mutilated body of what was once a human being, sat on the coal, propped up against the wooden wall. Its clothes were missing, and its whole body was covered in scars from the torment and suffering it must have endured. The main part of the body Hannah couldn't help but focus upon was the area that used to be its face. It was bloodied and had clearly been pummelled and beaten until the skin and everything under it had been reduced to pulp. The pain its owner must have suffered surely would have been agonising, unbearable torture, leaving the victim wishing they would just hurry up and die. What was left of the face wasn't recognisable in the slightest. One eye was missing, and the other eye was bright red and cut, barely even intact. The ears were mashed and had been pulverised so much that they resembled two blood-spattered sponges, one on each side of the head, although one had been torn and was hanging on by only a quarter of its size. The nose was partially missing. Any hair that the victim had once possessed was now blood red. Its lips were both cut open and bore the soft tissue that had erupted out of the horrific wound. Even part of the person's jaw was dangling under the rest of the face. Hannah still stared in horror. It could have been a stranger sitting before her, or it could easily have been her best friend. All she knew was their face had been so badly battered and destroyed by the force of some heavy object, that the frenzied attack had not only taken their life, but also removed their identity. She had to escape; unless she wished to become the third carcass in the bloodbath she had landed in.

Albert struggled to think of exactly what William had meant. He had no idea how the unusual hobo had reached the assumption that he'd already divulged everything Albert needed to know. As far as the retired detective was concerned, he had barely disclosed any facts that were going to be of any use.

Since their brief encounter, Albert had returned to the library to mull over his thoughts. He didn't know how to explain it, but he felt time was greatly running out. Too many deaths had already occurred, and the climax for the whole scheme was surely imminent. He had to work fast if he was to bring the killer to justice and stop any more deaths from happening. It was helpful that the library was a quiet place to be, as he sat in a chair with his head held in his hands, desperately straining for a breakthrough. He started going over all the points he could remember from the first conversation he'd shared with William. It would seem that he'd had a good job before the terrible events forced him to leave. He had got to know Imelda very well; in fact, in his own words, they had become, as close to being friends, as their differing societies would allow. Now Albert's mind began to wander. Why had he specifically mentioned their different social classes? Surely that was only relevant for when they were seen out in public. Naturally, behind closed doors they could act how they pleased. They could watch television together, play cards, even hug…he paused his thought process…or perhaps more.

Quickly, he took to searching through the records again. Only this time it wasn't the death records that had his interest, it was the marriage ones. After several failed attempts, but not too many considering the difficulties he was facing, he soon found that a William Reinwald wed Imelda Bernstein on the 30th June 1984, exactly six months after her "death". She had used her maiden name during the ceremony, which was why she could not be traced, assuming that is, anybody had even tried to find her. If she were assumed dead, then nobody would have been looking to locate her, although if they were, they would most probably be searching for Imelda Krause. Acting as typically as Albert did, he immediately searched for Imelda Reinwald back in the death records. This time, there were no records that were a definite match; the chances were she was still alive. If that were to be the case, then Hannah would be overjoyed, as he imagined, would Johann. Despite that part of the investigation being able to be temporarily stored, he still had no clues on where to restart his hunt for Andreas' killer, as well as the killer for all the other victims, the likelihood being it would be the same culprit. He figured that the most success he'd had so far was to do with Imelda. Perhaps she, being the kindly old woman William had described, would be able to provide more insight into her ex-husband. She may have vital information that could help him locate the murderer quickly and easily. It would certainly be a lot more effortless than stabbing around in the dark for an attack of inspiration.

He stood outside the library. He knew he wasn't going to see William again; he had done his bit already and had made it quite clear he was not prepared to help anymore. Perhaps Imelda had sent him with the pieces of information he had passed on to Albert. Maybe she had heard of the recent deaths on the news and wished to help in some way. It was unlikely, but then again, nothing was impossible, especially in the cruel world of murder. Tracking her down could essentially just be a waste of time, but it was still the only lead that Albert had and so far, everything seemed to be connected in one way or another, no matter how remotely.

It wasn't overly difficult to escape the coal shed. The sides were rickety and most of the panels were rotting. It had stood in the garden for a number of years, and had been subjected to neglect since it was built. Originally it had been painted green but that had long since faded and deteriorated gradually into flaky remnants dotted over the almost bare wood. The shed had only received an annual coating of wood preservative, administered by Stefan, to protect it from the weather, but that soon faded after a few months went by.

Hannah smashed through the old door that hung on its rusty hinges. She had found a spade leaning against the coal bags, and it sufficiently acted as a battering ram for her to break out. After several attempts at bashing the door, the catch that held on the padlock broke off. The old screws that had held it in couldn't withstand the force she had applied and so she was able to run out, thankful to be free. She threw the spade to one side, and inhaled deep breaths of clean air, grateful that no particles of coal dust were mixed in with it. She was still frightened and knew that events had gone much further than she would ever have imagined. Her next task was to find Albert; she desperately needed to see him more than ever, as she hadn't a clue what she should do, or even, where she should go. She looked around before she took some steps in her chosen direction. It was an obvious thought to telephone the police, but her mobile phone had been taken, and she didn't relish the prospect of using the landline. The house seemed a daunting place to go; she didn't know where she was safe or which people she could trust. The only person she knew she could completely depend upon was Albert, and she sincerely hoped she had not put him in danger, as she had asked him to accompany her to Germany in the first place. It occurred to her he would be in the village, and as that would also be the obvious location for a phone box, she quickly decided it was the destination she had to go. She crept along the wall of the house, staying watchful of her surroundings as she went. The best route for her to take was around by her grandfather's room, as it was seldom used by anybody. In addition, that side of the house was also sheltered by hedges, which meant she wouldn't be seen from the road. Ensuring her footsteps made as minimal noise as possible, she made her way outside the windows that had remained covered for a very long time. She peered in through the first one she reached, and was shocked to see Eleanor rummaging around inside. It was difficult to not be seen but she hoped she'd managed it well enough. She only covered the window as much as she needed to get her eyes in view of the room. Eleanor was busy rooting through possessions that either belonged to her grandfather or his stooge. It looked as if she was hurrying through the things she came across, which gave Hannah the impression she was trying to find something in particular. Her observant eyes stayed focused on the housekeeper as she carried on poking around in the boxes under the bed, unaware she was being watched. Once everything had been put back, she stood up and walked over to the piano. It enraged Hannah to watch her sit on her grandfather's piano stool. Luckily, she didn't begin to play a few notes otherwise Hannah thought she might not have been able to stop herself and would actually have jumped through the window to deliver a verbal attack to her. However, all Eleanor seemed to do was stare at the music. Hannah wondered what intrigued her so much. She didn't think the woman was a musician; she had never let on about her musical interests or aspirations, but then again all she ever seemed to do what moan at people – she wasn't exactly the type of person that could easily have a general conversation.

Hannah watched her for a fair while, until realising that her time was probably better spent elsewhere, for example, contacting the police and finding Albert, which had been her original plan. She was about to turn to go when all of a sudden she couldn't breathe. A hand had reached over her shoulder and grabbed around her mouth. The strong arm pulled her close to the body it belonged to and dragged her out of sight of the window. She couldn't even scream, as the sound, if any escaped at all, just became muffled in the clammy hand that gripped her. Obviously its intention was to prevent her from making any noise, and it worked well. The skin around her lips became moist as the sweat from the hand leaked onto her. She felt sick and couldn't even turn to see who had tackled her. A voice sounded, taking the tone of a gruff whisper:

'Will you keep still until we're out of sight?' The voice certainly didn't sound threatening, but more protective. It was definitely male, although she couldn't identify who it belonged to owing to the whisper hiding its true sound. There wasn't really much else she could do but obey, and so she relaxed her muscles as much as she was able to and walked with the man to just around the corner of the house where he let her go. She spun around.

'Are you crazy?' She also adopted a whisper, but hers was a lot more hysterical than the calmer one he had used. Johann stood in front of her, however took a step back when he saw how angry she was.

'I'm sorry – what did I do wrong?'

'You grabbed me from behind! I thought I was being attacked!'

'I saw you there and I just had to get you away from that window that's all.'

'Have you not heard of tapping somebody on the shoulder?'

'I didn't want to startle you; you know what you're like, you'd have jumped and shouted out.'

'Why did I have to come away from the window?'

'Because careful as you thought you were being, you were making yourself pretty obvious as the world's worst spy.'

'She didn't see me!'

'No, but she would have done if I hadn't pulled you away. Nobody can fail to notice a big head bobbing up and down outside a window. And talking of your head, you've got a nasty bump on the back of it, how did you get that?' Hannah nervously avoided answering his question, and dodged it by asking one of her own:

'What would it matter if she saw me?'

'If you have to ask me that question then why is it you were spying on her?'

'Okay, then what were you doing so close to the window that you were able to see me looking at what she was doing?'

'I was spying on her! But the difference is; I was doing it from a suitable distance in a safe place. You were ruining the whole thing, and if she'd seen you then I wouldn't be able to carry on would I?'

'I suppose not. Why were you spying on her?'

'Because there's something very suspicious about her, and she needs careful watching. She has no reason to be in that room, so I'd like to know what she's up to. Where's Albert, surely he'd like to know this?' Hannah contemplated telling him about the bodies in the shed. Ordinarily, she would never have hesitated, but the simple fact was she really didn't have a clue who she was able to trust, and that unfortunately included her own father. Johann detected the worry on his daughter's face, however, which gave Hannah the lead in to divulging her troubles that she needed. If he hadn't mentioned anything, she probably wouldn't have told him. 'What's the matter? You have that face on you when you're bothered by something?' Hannah still paused before answering:

'How long have you been watching Eleanor?'

'Only about twenty minutes, how come?'

'I was in that room a while ago when somebody attacked me. I don't know who it was but it's how I got that bump on my head.'

'What! Are you okay?' Johann flew at her with a comforting hug; or at least, he believed it to be comforting, whereas Hannah felt smothered and the act, although kind in thought, made her feel trapped again because of her ordeal. She pushed his arms away from her.

'I'm fine Dad, now that I've calmed down again. But I need to find Albert so he can tell me what to do. And I need to ring the police.'

'Can't you confide in me?' Hannah began to answer but then kept her words in her mouth.

'The truth is', she paused, 'I don't know.'

'Now don't be ridiculous – I'm your father. You know I'm not going to harm you don't you?'

'Well I would hope not.'

'Come on, what is it you need help with?'

'It's around here; there's something I should show you.' Johann smiled.

'That's a good girl. You can trust me.'

Cologne was a charming place. Albert stepped out of the carriage and looked directly at the sign that read 'Neumarkt'. The junction was bustling with people, and there were many shops, banks and street traders ready to take their money in exchange for the goods or services they provided. Once he had taken a taxi to Rüdesheim, it had taken Albert just over two hours to travel to his chosen stop. The journey had been pleasant but now he had arrived, he feared any pleasantness would be difficult to find. The last satisfying view he allowed himself to take in was the sight of a beautiful Romanesque Church, which was just about visible from where he stood. The dark, vivid stone stood out clearly, and its two tall towers were easily seen from the ground, made all the more prominent against the light blue sky in the background. The church was seeped in detail, with pillars and grand windows dotted all over it; a true Roman design, just like many of their iconic buildings that were scattered around the world. Albert was truly captivated, but now, after one last glimpse at the Holy building, it was time for him to find Imelda.

The last address he could find for Imelda was on Sülzburgstrasse. After consulting a map and trying his best to understand the street names and the rail routes, he opted to hop onto a tram to make his journey. He greatly enjoyed walking, but time was of the essence, and he certainly didn't want to be responsible for holding up proceedings for the sake of a relaxing amble through the German streets.

The scenery whizzed by in one long blur, as he sat staring out of the window on the tram. He knew it wouldn't be long until he reached the area he greatly hoped she would still be. The tram soon pulled in at the junction and Albert quickly left. The street was quirky and full of activity, and he kept his eyes peeled for number twenty-one, which was supposedly her last place of residence. A little way into strolling along the street, he began to feel concerned, as the majority of the buildings seemed to be businesses rather than private dwellings. He passed a lovely little chocolate shop, with golden decorations covering the windows, making a mental note to pop in when he returned. He reached number nineteen, which by all accounts looked like a veterinary practice. It was not looking positive; he wondered just how long ago she had lived on the street and whether her home had been redeveloped into commercial premises. However, a small door appeared after the veterinary building. It had the number twenty-one stuck on it, made from brass, and a buzzer just to the right of the door with a strip of plastic bearing the wording "Reinwald". She had to be there. Albert took in a deep breath before pressing the buzzer. He waited a few moments but soon enough some crackling sounded through the speaker, followed by a lady's voice.

'Hallo.' Albert stuttered before he spoke, undecided whether he should attempt a bit of German in case she didn't speak English. The result ended up being a combination of both.

'Guten Tag! Ich am looking for Imelda Reinwald. Am ich at the richtig address? Vielen thanks.' A long pause lingered after Albert had spoken, so long in fact, that he thought she'd gone. He nearly jumped when the woman spoke again.

'Come up, Albert.' The buzzer sounded, and the astonished investigator pushed the door inwards and ascended the stairs to her apartment.

Albert sat in an armchair upholstered in a bright, floral cover, drinking tea with an older version of the lady Hannah had described to him from the picture she had once seen. She was still thin, but her curly blonde hair, although the same length, was now quite grey and was tied straight back behind her head.

'How did you know it was me?' Imelda put down her cup.

'Not everyone has the skill of languages that you possess, Mr. Murtland.' She smiled. He knew she was being sarcastic, but she meant no harm by it.

'I meant, how did you know my name?' He knew the answer, but he didn't like to presume.

'William told me.'

'You still keep in contact then?'

'Oh yes, of course we do. I love that man. Circumstances drove us apart, as I'm sure you know.' Albert squirmed slightly in his seat. He felt awkward. As far as he had known for a long while, the woman was dead.

'I am not dead, Mr. Murtland.' Had his face been so obvious?

'I can see that Mrs. Reinwald – I'm not senile quite yet.' He felt uncomfortable calling her by her first name, as she was clearly intent on keeping it formal. It was difficult because he had referred to her as Imelda throughout his whole time in Germany.

'Do you have any questions for me? I presume you are not here because I make good tea.' She smiled at him again. He couldn't help thinking that her tea reference was a cruel joke seeing as the cup she had given him was quite frankly rotten, and resembled a sample of canal water.

'You have a granddaughter, were you aware?' She lowered her glasses to the tip of her nose.

'No I was not. How old is she?'

'Nineteen.' Imelda began to weep and promptly began searching for a tissue. The ever-present gentleman that he was, Albert was quick to offer her his handkerchief to use. She threw him a look of gratitude as she took it and began dabbing her eyes.

'This life has been so cruel. I have missed my son growing up, and have been unable to keep track of his life since he moved to England. I haven't been there to hold him, or kiss him, or congratulate him for anything he may have achieved. And now I've missed out on my own granddaughter too.' Her crying was soft. Albert got the impression she was saving her tears for when he was gone. 'What's her name?'

'Her name is Hannah.'

'To think that all these years have been wasted.'

'Not completely wasted.' She looked at him, wondering what he meant.

'What do you mean?'

'Hannah was the only person who never gave up on you. Despite not being allowed to talk about you, and everybody saying that you had died, she always believed that not to be the case.'

'Is that true?'

'I have nothing to gain by lying. It was, in actual fact, one of the reasons we came to Germany. She had been told Andreas was not well and so she decided to come over to try and see him, but also to find out the truth about you.'

'I heard Andreas had been murdered; that was dreadful to hear.'

'Do you have any help you can give me, as to why someone might want to murder him? Whoever it was also went to the trouble of installing an impostor who carried on the pretence that he was still alive.'

'Are you being serious?' Albert began to wonder if he had inadvertently disguised himself as a clown, seeing as she kept thinking he was joking with everything he said.

'Yes. And not only that, the local locksmith has been murdered, which I believe to also be connected. Plus, the impostor I've just told you about – he's also been killed.'

'What on earth has been going on there?' Albert looked bewildered.

'I've just told you!'

'It was a figure of speech.' Now Albert felt like a fool. The whole situation had made him tense, and his mind was all over the place with queries, questions, problems and possible solutions. He knew it was only Imelda that could give him the answers he sought. 'Does Stefan still work there?'

'Indeed he does.'

'Kind, old Stefan.' She smiled, affectionately. 'He's William's brother; did you know that?'

'I did, yes. Listen, do you have any idea who might have done this?' She hesitated before she answered, and looked directly into his eyes when she spoke:

'I know exactly who has done this.'

18

Albert sat on the train back to Rüdesheim. He could think of nothing else except the person who Imelda had told him was responsible. Something just didn't add up; he couldn't quite make it all fit together in his head. The meagre evidence he had would have to be combined with a lot of logical thought if he was hoping to bring the killer to justice. Imelda's words had haunted him so much, especially seeing as everybody had recently spent so much time with the person in question. They had more opportunities than they had cared to use, which led Albert to believe there was a specific goal they had been after. It was abundantly clear, however, that although they had spared some lives, preventing a reckless killing spree, they were not going to let anybody get in the way of what they wanted. He carried on mulling things over, until he was interrupted by somebody's mobile phone ringing. It irritated him when phones rang, although he found himself even more annoyed when he realised it was his own phone that was making the noise.

'Hello?'

'Albert, it's Martin Knight here.'

'This must be important if you're paying for the call – and long-distance too. And to a mobile! Are you not feeling well?'

'Cut the cynicism Albert; I thought I'd got away from all that when you retired.'

'I'm sorry.' He didn't mean it, and Martin knew he didn't, but it was all good humour between friends. 'How can I help you?'

'I've got some information for you that may help you with your enquiries over in Deutschland.'

'Deutschland?' Martin's voice became very emotionless; he spoke slowly, as if he was explaining something to an infant.

'It's German, Albert, for Germany.' Gradually his usual tone returned to his speech. 'Listen, I had a call from my friend – the one who I contacted to give you a bit of breathing space over there. He asked me to pass a message onto you.'

'Well hurry up about it – the signal is quite bad here; I'm on a train and there's quite a few tunnels.'

'I could have told you in the time it took for you to say that.'

'Get on with it!'

'Right. Yes. Apparently, the cause of death for the body that was found in the music room was not due to the stabbing.'

'It wasn't?'

'No, it seems he was poisoned and was stabbed after he had already died.'

'Any idea what he was poisoned with?'

'Yes I wrote it down, as I've never heard of it myself. Tajem – is that how you say it?'

'Yes I think so, thank you for that. Have they managed to identify the body?'

'Unfortunately, they didn't say. If I'd known you were in the dark about that then I would have asked for you. The general feeling I got though, was it was just some random person, a down-and-out, or a tramp, paid to do a job, although they obviously weren't told they would lose their life in the process.'

'Unless of course, they were poisoned by mistake – that would certainly make sense, as I sincerely doubt the culprit would have wanted their own man to die. He was buying them a lot of time.'

'You know more about the case than I do Albert; I'm just passing the message onto you. Seems the police over there don't have a contact number for you. Mind you, I'm guessing you're not exactly flavour of the month with them!'

'When am I ever Martin? Look if that's everything then we'd better say goodbye. The signal is getting progressively worse, and I'd hate to just cut out on you altogether.'

'Pardon?' Albert raised his eyebrows, and then subsequently his voice.

'Thank you very much! Goodbye!'

'No problem Albert; good luck!' He rung off and Albert returned to his mundane journey. The journey was unexciting in the physical sense anyway, mentally it was incredibly challenging. He began thinking things over again, although not for long because as soon as he'd returned his phone to his pocket, it started to ring again.

'Good grief!' A snooty looking woman in the next set of seats also remarked on the nuisance he was making of himself:

'Mein Gott!' Albert could only imagine what it meant. Nevertheless, he had to answer it.

'Hello?'

'Hello Albert.'

'Hannah, is that you?'

'Yes, where are you?'

'I'm just on a train, I'll be back in a couple of hours.'

'There's been some things that have happened here Albert, I need to know what to do.'

'What kind of things? Probably best to try and tell me quickly in case the signal disappears.'

'There's a lot to tell.'

'Even so, I'll keep up. Go on.'

'This afternoon I was looking around the music room and I found a pen on the floor under the piano. I noticed how

243

everything else in the room was tidy and in order, and then the pen just seemed out of place. Whoever was at that piano was obviously using it when they were stabbed, and that's why they couldn't pick it up again. Just as I'd thought of that, I was struck on the back of the head with something heavy and a while later I woke up in the coal shed.'

'Are you okay now? That's the main thing!'

'Yes I'm fine now. But listen there's more. In the coal shed with me were two more dead bodies. One is definitely a man although I can't make out the other one, but I don't recognise either of them, and the one I can't make out is so disfigured with injuries that I doubt anybody would be able to recognise them. My father thinks one of them was the coalman. He said he looks familiar and has seen him delivering to other houses. His throat had been cut.'

'Where are you now?'

'I'm calling from a phone box in the village.'

'Phone the police, if you haven't already done so. Hopefully they'll get to the house before I do.'

'Do you know who has done all this?'

'Yes, but I need to put it all in a rational order before I can go accusing someone. They've been very, very clever indeed.'

'What shall I do after I've called the police?'

'Just stay in the village; go to a café or something until I come and get you. Whatever you do, don't go back to the house.'

'Okay, I won't.'

'Is anyone with you?'

'Yes, my Dad.' Albert paused.

'Right go back to the house.'

'But you just said…'

'Never mind what I just said. Go back to the house. It's dinner time anyway isn't it?'

'Yes. Okay I'll do as you say. Where have you been? Have you managed to find anything out about my grandmother's death?'

'Well actually, yes I have. Your grandmother was in fact…' Three short beeps sounded indicating that the call had ended. He looked at his phone and noticed the signal had disappeared. Of all the times it could have gone, it was probably the most annoying. However, it probably went at the least important point seeing as he could just tell her in person when he got back to Presberg, which in retrospect would probably be a better, more touching moment than over the phone.

Albert ignored the evil glare from the snooty woman as he put his phone back in his pocket for what he hoped was the last time. He couldn't think of anyone else that may ring him. The picture on the front of the newspaper she was reading showed a picture of an elderly couple. The headline read: "FEHLT: DÜSSELDORF PAAR NOCH NICHT GEFUNDEN". He recognised one of the words from his phrasebook, which he took from his pocket. He flicked through the pages quickly to the lost property section and saw the word "gefunden" translated to "found". He knew "fehlt" meant "missing" and so he could only guess that a missing couple had still not been found. He shook his head in disbelief; what a dreadful world it was where crimes happened continually through every waking moment. But he couldn't allow himself to be sidetracked by anything now. The clues, the identities, the movements, pretty much everything, were all muddled together in one big tangled mess inside his head. It had all been like a jigsaw puzzle of an all-black night sky. All the pieces were there but there was just no way of fitting them together, as each individual piece was just as indefinable as the next. He had, however, accumulated several substantial clues, which he considered to effectively be his corner pieces. Now he had them, he knew everything else would slot into place. He had a tough challenge ahead of him: two hours to sit and think of everything, absolutely every little thing that came to his mind. He started virtually oblivious, but it was imperative that he ended educated enough to catch the culprit. Two hours was a long time, but just like the train, he knew it would hurtle by.

Hannah sat with Johann in the lounge. They could hear Eleanor preparing the evening meal in the kitchen. Silence took over as neither could think of anything to say that wouldn't sound abnormal. Stefan walked passed the window. Hannah cried out:

'Misty!' He turned briefly and threw his arm up lackadaisically but carried on walking. He had certainly become increasingly downhearted following the news of his employer's death. The recent events hadn't exactly done anybody any good and morale was at an all time low. It was a terrible situation to be connected to; Andreas' death was from long ago and it was a difficult, slow process for the police to ascertain anything concrete in relation to his murder. The murder of the fake Andreas, although recent, made matters all the more complicated, as the police then had to search for the murderer of a man who had pretended to be another man who had already been found dead. Added to that the miscellaneous killing of the local cobbler, the unfortunate coalman, and a further unidentifiable body, it really was a confusing state of affairs. Everything seemed so unrelated but the fact was; that couldn't be possible.

It was like a giant waiting game. Hannah longed for Albert to return. She also wanted comfort from her father, or even from Stefan, whom she had also thought of as a father or grandfather figure. Johann had nipped out of the room momentarily. He had decided a visit to the toilet was in order before sitting down at the table to eat. Stefan walked by the window again. He seemed very busy seeing as it was so late. Still, he had a good work ethic, and if employed, he would strive to work until it was time for him to go home. Hannah didn't bother calling out to him when she saw him for the second time. She saw little point in wasting her breath, and besides, it would shortly be his finishing hour and so would likely be rushing to complete his last few tasks. She wondered if he'd seen the massacre in the coal shed. Two more people who were likely innocent, slaughtered because they were in the way or just in the wrong place at the wrong time. Hannah couldn't even begin to imagine the pain and horror they'd have felt when their lives were drawing to a close. She hoped Misty hadn't seen the carnage; the chances are he wouldn't because his job didn't concern anything to do with the coal. Perhaps it did during the winter months but that was just for a bucket or two every couple of nights, and the evenings were nowhere near cold enough at the time of year that it was; it was too mild. Knowing his bumbling personality, he probably hadn't even noticed the shed was open. Johann had closed the door and stopped it swinging open by placing a brick in front of it, so with any luck the two examples of amateur butchery would be shielded from view until the police arrived.

It seemed ages that Hannah was sat all alone and was engrossed in daydreaming when Eleanor marched in with a carving knife gripped in her fist. Hannah shuddered when Eleanor's presence disturbed her but did manage to refrain from letting out a little shriek. The knife presumably was for dinner, although Hannah would have been more than happy with a bowl of soup, under the circumstances. A lot less damage could be done to a person's flesh with a spoon. Eleanor didn't speak; she just brought in the food and waited for everybody else to get to the table.

The clock chimed seven. Johann returned to the room to find Eleanor and Hannah patiently waiting for his presence. It was one of the things Eleanor loathed; she thought it was only good manners to wait until everyone was at the table with their meal before anybody started eating. She was quite correct in her belief, however, she had so many things that niggled her, it made everybody do their best to annoy her at any opportunity they could find; hence, the reason why Hannah was already chewing on a carrot, purposely just before she heard Johann entering the room. It received a glare from Eleanor, which made Hannah thankful that the phrase "if looks could kill" was only an expression; otherwise she feared she would be dead right now.

All three of them sat down at the table. Finally, Eleanor spoke:

'Where is Albert?' Quite honestly, neither Hannah nor Johann knew the answer, as Albert hadn't divulged his whereabouts to them. Luckily, they didn't have to answer, as the dark blue beacons of police cars became visible from the window and seemed to be heading in the direction of the house. Eleanor stood up. 'What do they want?' Again, the two other occupants of the table remained silent. Soon there was a knock on the door, which Eleanor went to answer. The conversation could clearly be heard from where Hannah and Johann sat. They began whispering to each other.

'Dad, I'm scared. Once Albert gets back, I think all this will be sorted out.' Johann seemed hesitant to reply, but he did so all the same:

'I'm sure it will all come to a close, one way or another.'

'Eleanor doesn't seem very happy about the police being here. They've told her we all have to wait inside with an officer guarding us, while they search the grounds.'

'Well that makes sense I guess. Let's just hope she doesn't wait in here with us!' He chuckled.

'I doubt they'll allow us to all split up. If we all went in different rooms they'd have to get three people to watch us all.'

'We shouldn't be treated like prisoners. Isn't it meant to be innocent until proven guilty?'

'They haven't said we're guilty; they just need to keep track of the household while they search outside. At least we know why they're here – we called them!'

'Oh yes; I'd forgotten about that.' He paused. 'I wonder who that body belongs to, you know, the one with the smashed up face.' Hannah closed her eyes and now didn't feel like eating anything, not that she did before. But the reminder of the horrifying images in the coal shed really didn't help her hunger.

'I have no idea. Please stop talking about it, it makes me feel sick.'

'I'm sorry.' It felt awkward, as it now seemed like there was nothing else to talk about. That was the case until Eleanor stormed back in.

'This is outrageous! Locked up inside your own house!' Johann seemed slightly mystified by her remark.

'But it isn't your house.'

'You know what I mean.'

'Actually I have no idea. It isn't your house at all. You work here, that is all. Technically, provided my father has not left a will specifying otherwise, it is actually my house.'

'And I don't suppose you want a housekeeper when you take over do you?'

'Not a miserable one, no.'

'Well that's just charming; everything I do, every action I carry out, is for the good of the house and the benefit of the people in it. Don't you want a nice, clean house?'

'Yes, but the difference is, we want it with a smile. There's no need to be so uptight about everything? We want to live in a cosy, comfortable environment, not a prison where there are rules and regulations to abide by.'

'Well if that's how you feel, then I don't suppose you wish me to stay here a moment longer. I shall go and pack my bags at once, and leave as soon as I am able.' Eleanor turned her nose upwards and marched out of the room.

'Hannah, don't you think it's strange that she's opted for a quick departure out of here? I didn't think I said anything too harsh that would make her want to leave here immediately. She was ready to pack up and leave with not much persuasion; it was almost as if she was looking for an easy way out. Guilty conscience, perhaps?'

'Dad, don't you think you were just a bit hard on her?'

'No! I admit she is a good worker, but she needs to change her demeanour. I want this to be a happy house when it's mine.'

'Provided she isn't a mass-murdering maniac, if you want a housekeeper then I would suggest retaining her. I'm sure she can mellow a bit in time. Don't forget she hasn't exactly had the best employment here. She was called upon at short notice to work at a house for a man that she never met. The only other person she had for company was Misty who she didn't really get on with. It's not surprising she acts how she does.' Johann thought about his daughter's reasoned argument.

'I suppose. I'll talk to her when tonight's over with. It shouldn't be long now; Albert should be back within the hour.'

'I hope so. I really do.'

The police had sectioned off the scene surrounding the coal shed. The two bodies were in the process of being removed. The coalman's clothes that covered his torso were soaked in blood. The stained trickles of blood that had oozed out resembled a waterfall that had poured down his chest when he had suffered the attack. His neck had a wide semi-circle slit travelling from one side all the way to the other. The back wall of the shed showed the results of a tremendous explosion of escaping blood from when the attack would have happened. The blood-spatter pattern covered the wooden panels of wood, as well as the coal bags that were in the same direction. Blood had also erupted from his mouth, as it had clearly flowed out of the body with so much pressure that it found the nearest exits it could to surge from. The other victim had been viciously assaulted by use of a heavy instrument, such as a shovel or a baseball bat. They had been continuously bludgeoned until every part of life had been beaten out of them. Once that had happened, the attacker had sadistically continued the violence by disfiguring and mutilating the face of the other lifeless person until that too had essentially been removed. What the police officers found was a body that was relatively intact, but with only a structure of a head, as its face was missing. It wasn't as if the face was just bruised, it was bloodied and just consisted of flesh and everything that should ordinarily remain under the skin. The parts of the face that would have been present before the attack had likely burst upon every strike that they had received. The severed jaw, the detached ear, the absent eye, were all injuries so horrifying that it was hard to believe they had once been an unblemished face attached to a living human being.

Stefan watched from a distance as the police carried out their duty. He was careful not to be seen, but he was just intrigued in watching what the officers were finding. He observed them bringing the bodies out to transport them away to wherever they would be taken; he assumed a laboratory for further tests, as well as samples of DNA to be taken, which would undoubtedly help with the identification process. It was time, however, for him to return home. He had no wish to be caught, and if seen, it would be considered unusual for him to still be present at the house, even more so outside, looking at the murder scene. He sloped off around the back of the house, unaware that somebody else had been watching him and had now set off in pursuit of the shifty gardener. Two red tints tracked the gardener's movements, as Stefan made his way around the back of the house to cut across to the village without being detected by the police. He found himself in a greatly shaded area, which was almost in darkness owing to the fading evening light and the trees that sheltered that particular section of the grounds even further. He found himself alone, yet unknowingly followed, in a lonely, darkened area, which might possibly be the worst mistake he'd ever made.

Albert got out of his taxi once they had reached Presberg. For some reason, he didn't wish to be dropped off right outside the house. He knew the police would now be on the scene, and figured that nobody was in any real danger for the time being. He also didn't wish to alarm the culprit by arriving in full throttle. If he wasn't present, he hoped the perpetrator would just consider the police presence as routine and not suspect that their whole operation was about to be uncovered.

Albert positioned his hat into the most comfortable spot on his head. After all the years he had spent wearing it, he felt he had invisible grooves embedded around the circumference of his head, and the hat just slotted into place like the correct key for a corresponding lock. He silently praised himself on the apt analogy he had thought of. The taxi drove off and Albert looked at the street in front of him, which would take him back to the house. He tapped the tarmac with his walking cane as he walked along and admired the sights as he went. This beautiful, scenic village had been the unfortunate location for such brutality. Albert wondered how this picturesque area made up of ornate stone buildings and surrounded by vineyards whilst absorbed in tranquillity, should be subjected to the trauma and violence that somebody had decided to bring to it. Life would not be the same for a long while. The happy community that was present just days ago would take years to recover the harmony that had been lost during the short period of terror that had taken place. He had already decided to wait until the morning to let everyone know of his fulfilment of solving the crimes. Everyone was a lot fresher after a good sleep, whereas trying to explain the complexities of every transgression that had occurred would indubitably be a lot more tiresome late in the evening. During the train journey, he had just about managed to piece together every snippet of the clues he knew of, and it was just possible, literally only narrowly feasible that he had reached the solution.

He reached the Church of St. Laurentius and once again admired it from top to bottom. The grand steeple that rose high up towards the sky glowed with pride in the moonlight.

He saw flashes of blue lights from behind the place of worship and knew they were from the police cars outside the house. Albert stepped out from behind the church and saw the house just a short distance away. The steeple on that also stuck out as the masterpiece of the construction, with the golden weathervane shimmering brightly. A ladder had been put up against the side of the house, although it wasn't an unlikely sight; in fact, Albert was happy his instructions were being followed. He returned his gaze back to his normal eye level and began walking the few more steps required to reach where he needed to be. Every step was a step closer to the truth. He reached the house and stared up at the door. He had no intention of stopping off to see the police at work. He wouldn't exactly be able to talk with them anyway, but he knew what he needed to know from the scene without even observing it. With regards to the dead body with the maimed face, regrettably he knew exactly who it was. Too many people had lost their lives, as was usually the situation with many of the cases he had been assigned to over the years.

Eventually he placed his hand on the doorknob and turned it to open the door. With one last look at the charming village behind him, he knew it wasn't possible to put it off any longer; it was time to go inside and act normal. A decent sleep was what he needed, and then after sunrise, everything would all become clear for everyone. He stopped off at the music room before he retired to bed. He took the sheet of music from the piano and stared at the very thing Hannah had mentioned to him on the phone. It stood out now like a grizzly bear in a funeral parade. How could he have been so blind? Whether he was annoyed at himself or not, it comforted him to know that the killer was safe for now; but in the morning, it would be a different situation altogether.

19

Everybody watched as Albert entered the lounge. He had asked them all to congregate after breakfast, simply on the preface that he had something to tell them. Nobody had anything else to do seeing as the house was still infested with police officers and so they had all agreed to his request. Johann and Hannah sat together on the sofa, while Eleanor sat on an armchair away from them. Stefan was not yet present, although it hadn't yet reached his starting time for work so nobody was particularly worried. Besides, nobody expected him to attend anyway, as it was likely a family matter more than anything else. Eleanor was under the assumption it was family business anyway; that was, until Albert started speaking. He began pacing in his usual fashion, across the room and back.

'This has been a challenging task. A series of events so complex that I often wondered whether they would even be solved.' He paused, to add a bit of drama to the occasion, which captivated his small audience while they waited for him to continue. 'This was a tale of greed. A plan was formulated from events that occurred around thirty years ago. Yet despite the lives that have been unfortunately lost; the climax, the result that the killer had chased through all of their immoral actions, was never reached.

'Are we to assume, Mr. Murtland, that you know who the killer is?'

'Miss. Frankwell, please be patient – everything I have found out will be disclosed to you. But in answer to your question; yes, I know who is guilty.' Eleanor didn't respond, and instead, for once, allowed him to carry on.

'Where is Misty?'

'I'm sure he will be along soon, Hannah.' She nodded. 'Now let us go back all the way to when the real Andreas was dug up. Who was present at that time?' He gazed at the crowd over his spectacles. Nobody spoke. 'Well we know Andreas was present, but he was of course dead, and had been for a long time by that point. Who else was there? Stefan dug him up whilst in the process of planting a tree. So Andreas had no choice but to be there, and Stefan was there for innocent reasons. However, there was one other person present at that particular time.' He stared at Eleanor. 'You were also there, weren't you Miss. Frankwell?' Eleanor looked intently at Albert with a blank expression.

'I have never made any secret of the fact that I was there. But I had gone back inside the house before the body had been dug up.'

'You had gone back inside the house before the body had been dug up, that is quite correct, but you had not gone back inside before a wooden dart had been fired at Stefan while he was kneeling down next to the rockery.'

'I haven't got the slightest clue what you are talking about.' Albert's eyes flared up.

'When Albert Murtland says he knows, then believe me he knows!'

'Well you don't know very much about what happened at that particular point in time. I was merely standing by the coal shed, watching him do his work, basically making sure he had no intentions of entering the house with his dirty boots covered in soil.'

'And so you have no idea about the dart that was fired at Stefan while he worked?'

'I have no such knowledge of anything of the sort. You're barking up the wrong tree, I'm afraid.'

'Then how is it you borrowed a book from the library with a title that translated to Life In Indigenous Asia?' Eleanor said nothing. 'This book contains information on the darts that the natives of the country use to hunt. It shows you how to make your own, and describes what poison is used to effectively kill the animals that they shoot.' Eleanor still remained silent. 'Am I still barking up the wrong tree now?' She looked at the floor, now unable to meet his eyes with hers.

'It just looked like an interesting book to have a look at. I don't do a lot in my spare time, but I do like to read and learn about unusual cultures and ways of living. If it's a crime to educate oneself then yes, I am guilty.'

'It's coincidental though, is it not, that you borrowed a book, which contained the information needed to make poison darts, and ever since these tiny weapons have been found around the vicinity on multiple occasions?'

'Yes it is a coincidence! I've had nothing to do with it.'

'And as for your borrowing of a housekeeping textbook – do we really know who you are at all?'

'I had a difficult stain to remove from my eiderdown, and I wanted some expert advice so I didn't ruin it when I tried to remove it.'

'Still seems a bit fishy though, wouldn't you say?' Johann couldn't keep silent anymore, especially when it meant he could further inflame the situation concerning Eleanor:

'You're good Albert. Keep it going!' Albert turned to face Andreas' son.

'And what makes you so vocal when you are another who should be quivering in your shoes? During your conscription in the army, were you not based for some time in parts of Asia, giving you the necessary knowledge and skills required to make and use the darts and blowpipes that we are talking about?' Eleanor found it easy not to look at the floor any longer.

'That's exactly the reason why I had that book! When I heard that a dart had been found at the locksmiths and then saw on the news that he'd been arrested in connection with the cobbler's murder, I borrowed the book because I wanted to know exactly where the darts originated from. Just like yourself, Albert, it was easy to find out about Johann's history, as being the son of a celebrated composer, his life, at least for the time he was in Germany, was forever in the public eye.'

'I was released without charge over any connection I had to Herbert Lorenz's murder. It all amounted to nothing, I was just in the area at the time, and the hour was very late, so they just wanted to question me in case I saw anything unusual, that's all.'

'Even so, you were still arrested.' Albert interjected:

'There really is little point in arguing over this. Might I suggest, Eleanor, you start thinking of your own defence rather than the prosecution of somebody else. The police had no evidence against Johann; they only arrested him because of the time of night that he had chosen to pass through Rüdesheim. I knew about it because I too, saw it on the news. Now please, let me continue explaining.' He looked up to give all three people a chance to oppose his request, but nobody did. 'Somebody had clearly wanted rid of Andreas, but it would seem not so much that they didn't at least want his presence to disappear from the household. Andreas was murdered and was buried in the garden. But how were they able to give the impression that the famous composer was still around? The answer was simple: by installing a record player in the music room that would continuously play all the records that he was renowned for. When I was granted permission to see Andreas, or rather the bogus stand-in, I saw the pile of records stacked at the bottom of his bed. I didn't think anything of it at first, as I believed they may just be keepsakes, sort of special editions of his achievements that he had chosen to accumulate over the years. Only when things started taking a more deadly turn, and the impostor was stabbed, did I begin to notice things a bit more clearly.' He paused; it wasn't easy to continually be speaking, and with all the details that he had to include, it made the task even more arduous. 'The record player in the room was completely covered in dust. The dust was untouched; no fingerprints were present that illustrated anyone had opened the cabinet it was in, for a long time. Either the record player hadn't been used for a good while because it had broken, which is why the plan of installing somebody to pretend to be Andreas came about; or, it had never been used at all. This was an interesting fact to stumble upon. Perhaps the record player was installed in the first instance because it was the easiest way of proving Andreas was still alive. But what happened when it came to simple things like taking and eating meals, hearing the toilet flush, or any laundry that would need seeing to?' He looked to his listeners for an answer, but before anyone could speak there was a knock at the front door. Albert smiled. 'Excuse me.' He left and the remaining people stayed silent, listening to the voices that sounded from the hall. Thomas' familiar voice could be heard when the door opened:

'Hello Albert, and how are you today?'

'I'm very well thank you. I'm afraid we're having a bit of a meeting in the lounge at the moment regarding Andreas and all the other unfortunate people that have recently lost their lives. Can I be cheeky and ask you to take the milk through to the kitchen and make us all a quick drink?'

'I'm a bit tight for time today, if I'm honest.'

'It really will just take you a few minutes – I wouldn't ask if I could avoid it.' There was a brief silence, while Thomas thought about it.

'Very well; I suppose it will only take a minute or two.'

'Thank you very much. Bring them through when they're done, if you would be so good.' The door closed and Albert returned to the lounge. Hannah asked him a question:

'Shouldn't Stefan be here by now?' Everyone glanced at the clock that faintly ticked away in the room. Eleanor gave a sharp retort:

'Yes; he's late.'

'Nevertheless, I shall continue with my explanation.' He took in a deep breath before carrying on. 'Somebody had left a note under Hannah's pillow for her to find on her arrival at the house. The note had Hannah's name written on it, and there was also a key with it. Obviously the note just meant that the key was for Hannah's attention. Or did it? Our murderer was the one who left this note and the key. The only reason they would leave the key is so Hannah would be another pair of eyes on the lookout for the box that it fitted. If she found it, then I'm afraid she would have become another victim of this crime. Hannah's name was just concealing the real reason for the note being there. It had been a torn piece of paper from a notepad, and contained the indent from the page before it. Perhaps the murderer had been careless with their choice of writing materials; or perhaps not.' He took his own notebook from his pocket. 'This indentation read: It is somewhere; I know it is. He isn't a problem anymore. One part of the plan is complete. Just one to go, then I will be gone. I'll make him pay. Johann will never know.' Albert lowered his glasses and looked at each individual in turn. 'What does that mean? What were they

260

looking for? What plan? What will Johann never know? So many questions, and such simple, simple answers. Obviously Johann's name has crept into the investigation again; it's not looking good for you is it Johann?' He stared deep into Johann's eyes. Johann said nothing. Thomas could still be heard clattering about with cups and saucers, as he placed them on the kitchen worktop whilst waiting for the kettle to boil. 'Andreas, as you all know, was virtually penniless. Penniless, yes; possession-deficient, no. Let us analyse the note broken up into smaller parts.' He glanced at his notebook while reading each section. 'Here we go. "It is somewhere; I know it is". What is somewhere? We'll assume a valuable possession. "He isn't a problem anymore". Who isn't? We'll assume Andreas. "One part of the plan is complete". That's likely the murder of Andreas, which ties in to the part before. "Just one to go, then I will be gone". Possibly, that's to do with finding the valuables. I can't imagine it relates to any of the other murders, as they seem to have only occurred when the plan was looking to be uncovered. "I'll make him pay. Johann will never know". This sounds like revenge towards Andreas for a wrongdoing he had committed in the past. However, perhaps Johann is able to explain better than I can what exactly he will never know.' Albert held out his arm and outstretched his arm, signalling Johann to give an explanation. It took a while for him to speak, but what he said didn't add anything of significance.

'I haven't got the faintest idea what you're talking about.' Albert smiled.

'Of course you don't. Why would you? You see; I believe that final line to be a red herring; a decoy to throw us off track and take us down the wrong path, which in turn provides the culprit with more time to carry out their plans. Out of the whole passage that I've just read out to you, that final sentence is the only one that doesn't fit in with the rest. Therefore, I don't believe it to be true and I discounted it from my investigation altogether.' The door opened and Thomas walked in carrying a tray of drinks. He didn't speak, but placed them down on the coffee table. 'Thank you Thomas.' The milkman nodded and turned to leave. 'Oh don't go yet.' Albert smiled at him; a warm smile, yet somewhat smarmy all the same. 'Sit down with us for a while, and listen to what I have to say.' Thomas really didn't know what to do. He didn't feel like he could leave; instead, he felt trapped, and the only way of escaping was to join them and pay attention to Albert's narration. He sat down next to Eleanor, but on a separate chair. She looked at him, and he shot her a confused expression. 'All will become clear Thomas, just bear with me.' Albert continued his story, pleased with himself at cleverly securing another listener. 'Now the key that was found with the note fits some sort of box, which led us to the shop in the centre of Rüdesheim, which at that point was being run by Herbert Lorenz – the son of the shop's actual owner. Herbert's father had been attacked one night after he had closed his business for the day, and yet nothing was stolen from the shop. This is highly unusual – if someone plucks up the courage to break into a shop and harass the shopkeeper, then surely their reward would be the money from the cash register or even just some luxury item that they cannot afford to buy. The only logical explanation is for some reason, the owner needed to be out of the way. That could be because whoever had ordered the box we are looking for, perhaps didn't want to go into the shop at a later date and be recognised and so by making it so the old man couldn't work, removed him from the shop. Or, perhaps the intruder who broke his leg was looking for the book that the sales records were kept in, and again didn't wish to be recognised at a later date and so put him out of action for a while. When Herbert came to take over while his father recovered, he was a completely new face and so wouldn't recognise anyone. However, our culprit picked the wrong shop to have as their supplier of boxes, because they wouldn't have known Herbert was a languages expert and lectured on the subject at Heidelberg University. He even noticed a difference in Stefan's voice after just the second time he had met him. Therefore, it just goes to show you just how good his memory was when it came to detecting dialects that different people used. And that's probably the most important point I've made so far: different people.

'I really need to get going.' Thomas stood up.

'You sit right back down. Need I even say that you've implicated yourself enough during this whole sequence of events? Was it not you who saw Hannah and Stefan entering the locksmiths on the same day that Herbert Lorenz was killed? If I were you, I'd cooperate. And if you don't then I shall have you arrested.' It took Thomas a while to remove his glare from Albert's direction, before sitting back down without saying another word. 'The dart that was left in the locksmiths next to Herbert's body, I believe to have been planted there. Whether it was left to frame Eleanor owing to her fascination with them, or Johann because he knew all about them, is anybody's guess. Although, it wouldn't be overly strange for it to frame Thomas either.'

'Why me!'

'Because you have clearly spent a lot of time in Asia, which is where, I believe, you met your wife. Do correct me if I am wrong.' Thomas was speechless. 'You see, I am an old man, I am more than aware of that, but the Internet, or indeed marriage records are not out of reach for anybody.'

'So what if I have an Asian wife; it's not like I dragged her from the depths of the jungle is it?'

'So you are knowledgeable of the fact that it is within the dense jungle that the poison darts are used? Please, do carry on and incriminate yourself even further.' Thomas stopped talking at once, whereas Albert became quite intense. 'Perhaps one of the darts fell from your pocket, as you hurriedly left the shop after murdering Herbert Lorenz?'

'Don't be ridiculous!' Albert reduced the anger in his voice.

'Well, we shall see won't we? The fact of the matter is that you are too busy constantly driving your milk float all over the town to even have time to be involved in such things. I know how busy the milk business is, as my father-in-law was also a milkman. Only then, they carried around milk churns on the back of a horse and cart.'

'I should be busy, but instead I'm stuck here listening to you and your tale of glory.'

'There's nothing magnificent about the story I am telling. In fact, it is not even a story – it is a monologue of facts, filled with ultimate sadness. So, as it is not you who is to blame, and Hannah is of course innocent; it leaves just Johann and Eleanor to accuse does it not?' Johann piped up:

'And Stefan! Don't forget him; he's been around here longer than I have!'

'Which is simply why I can also rule you out Johann, so you can sit back and relax. I was told only yesterday, by a very dear, elderly yet sorrowful lady, who the culprit was likely to be. And I have to say I agree with her implicitly.' Silence filled the room. Everybody almost suffocated from the instant dread that leaked in through every crack in the wall and under the door. The next few words that Albert would utter would change someone's life forever, and indeed, all the others that would have to deal with the revelation of the culprit's identity. Everyone just waited for Albert to open his mouth. He wet his lips with his tongue, as he teased them over the moment that he would choose to speak. Nobody stirred; they all sat still in their seats simply awaiting the most crucial words they would ever hear him say. Finally, he opened his mouth. 'The words that I was told are as follows, and I quote: "The person you should be arresting, and will be guilty of all the murders that have taken place is…Andreas Krause's housekeeper".' Eleanor jumped out of her seat, shouting as if her life depended on it – which it did.

'How on earth do you come to that conclusion?'

'It was a clever little trick wasn't it to pretend to hate Stefan so much, but instead you both worked together on this dreadful series of events?'

'What are you talking about?' Albert hammered on the door behind him, and two police officers charged in, handcuffed her and removed her from the room at once. Hannah had tears falling down her face, relieved that the mystery was finally over. Johann tried to comfort her by placing his arm around her shoulders. It was only Thomas who spoke:

'I must say, most likely on behalf of Presberg, a heartfelt thank you for bringing this awful ordeal to an end. But how did you do it? How on earth did you get to that conclusion? She may have been an old battleaxe, but never would anybody have thought she was capable of such things.'

'It is always the ones you least suspect though, isn't it Thomas? But seeing as you have asked, and I for one, would love to explain it all in elaborate detail, I'm afraid we all have a two-and-a-half hour journey ahead of us before that explanation can take place.' Hannah stopped snivelling.

'What do you mean?'

'If you would all accompany me outside to one of the unmarked police cars, we are heading off to a place where I will be able to enlighten you of all the details much clearer than I could ever do so here. It is where we will find Stefan.'

'I can't go with you; all my milk will go sour.'

'Quite frankly, I couldn't care less. This is far more important. Now come along.' Albert left the room, and a police officer stepped inside in his place to make sure that the three perplexed individuals obeyed and followed him.

The drive was boredom at its best. Nobody spoke, as none of them really knew what to say. They knew Albert wouldn't give any details to them until they reached their unknown destination. Everyone was still in shock that Eleanor had masterminded the whole plan and recruited Stefan into assisting her. The car they were in eventually pulled up outside an ordinary-looking house in Düsseldorf. On Albert's confirmation that they had arrived, everybody got out of the car. The German Sergeant, who had been against Albert for his entire stay in the country, was dressed in regular clothes, and walked over to greet him.

'He's in. His green coat is hung up in the hallway. My officers are going to gain access through the back door. If he tries to escape this way, we'll all be here.'

'Excellent.' It wasn't long before shouting was heard, and the men stormed into the house. Everybody outside looked at each other in amazement at what was going on. Hannah could barely look, as her dear friend, who she thought she knew, was being captured. Before long, one of the officers came out of the front door.

'Wir haben ihn.' The Sergeant nodded.

'They've got him.' Albert replied; bearing a smile that said he knew he was about to disclose everything he had worked out.

'In we go then.' He walked off and everybody followed.

Albert restarted his pacing, this time with a new, fuller audience. Hannah, still in tears, sat together with Johann, as they had done before. Eleanor was on the far side of the room, detained in handcuffs with policemen on either side of her. Thomas sat next to the German Sergeant, who was also keen to hear how Albert had uncovered the details that led to the arrests. An elderly couple, which nobody knew, sat on a sofa in the corner of the room next to an old upright piano, and looked greatly shaken up by the whole ordeal. Stefan had not yet been brought in the room, but there was still plenty of time for him to be paraded in front of those he had hurt and betrayed. Albert looked at his listeners, and then proceeded to speak:

'What a difficult case this was.' He paced up and down a little longer. 'When I was told by my trustworthy source that the housekeeper was to blame, I couldn't believe my ears. Sure, Eleanor was tetchy, she had her little mannerisms, she was annoying and strict, but I just couldn't bring myself to believe that she was a murderer. But now here we are, and she is handcuffed ready to be thrown into prison.' Eleanor opened her mouth to object, but Albert silenced her at once by raising his hand into the air. 'Sergeant, please tell your men to take off her handcuffs.'

'But you said she is a murderer?'

'I am aware of what I said.'

'You said you agreed implicitly with what your source had told you.'

'I do. Please tell your men to take the handcuffs off.' The Sergeant scowled, but obeyed the order nonetheless.

'Nehmst du die Handschellen ab.' He didn't seem pleased in telling them to do it and the officers looked as confused as everyone else, but also did as they were told.

'You see, when I was told that the housekeeper was to blame, I was also sceptical, as the person who told me was actually Mrs. Reinwald who had lived at the house years ago and was able to tell me exactly what she was like.' Hannah shouted out, she couldn't seem to help it:

'Misty was married?'

'Hannah, please keep quiet. I'll reveal everything in time.' He waited for Hannah to calm down and lean back in her seat before continuing. 'But how could she possibly have known Eleanor Frankwell, as she was instated as the housekeeper only a few weeks ago?' He turned his head directly to the German Sergeant. 'If you could have Stefan Reinwald brought in now please.' The Sergeant shouted to his men outside the room:

'Bringst du ihn in!' Two more officers brought Stefan into the room. 'He had been crafty when they'd caught him; he'd managed to get his coat on ready to make a run for it.'

'That's not a problem thank you. This man is responsible for the death of Andreas, whom he buried in his own garden; the murder of Herbert Lorenz, whom he had wished to silence for fear of being found out; the poisoning of the man who impersonated Andreas, by doping his tea every time he went in to visit him, and the murder of the coalman and another unknown individual. It hit me when I realised of course, that my source had only used the generic term "housekeeper". It didn't necessarily mean, Eleanor.' He turned to look at Stefan. 'I was always told it was rude to wear a coat inside the house – and let's face it, you're not going anywhere so you might as well take it off. Sergeant, if you could give the order please.'

'Nehmst du den Mantel ab.' The two officers that accompanied Stefan, removed his coat, his hat and glasses, and unpinned his hair that had been tied in place on top of his head.' Albert looked at him, and then at his audience.

'Doesn't he look like a completely different person without that horrible green coat on?' Hannah stood up this time:

'Rebecca?' Rebecca Sharp stood before them, defiant in her stance, with evil trapped in her eyes. The elderly couple that had sat silently in the corner, burst into tears. Albert reverted back to his explaining:

'Yes, Rebecca was the housekeeper that was accused by my source; she was obviously unaware that Rebecca no longer worked there, and saw no reason to state her name, as in her understanding, it could only have been Rebecca that was the housekeeper. All this time, she has been masquerading as our friendly gardener. It was simply a ploy to put the blame onto him, while giving her a disguise that would allow her access to pretty much anywhere in the house and grounds. As long as she wore Stefan's famous green coat, everyone would be oblivious to the fact that it wasn't actually him.' Hannah, with tears rolling down her face, managed to ask another question:

'So where is Misty then, if she has his coat?'

'Hannah, I'm afraid it isn't good news.'

'He's dead isn't he?'

'Yes, I'm sorry. Unfortunately, he was the other body in the coal shed; the one which was severely beaten.'

'You bitch!' Rebecca just smirked, and displayed a loud, uncouth sniff, which made the people in the room hear her phlegm travel up her nose and into the back of her mouth, which she then swallowed. 'He was a lovely man!' Johann pulled her back into her seat, and smothered her with a massive hug. Albert carried on:

'And he didn't have a cold!' He glared at Rebecca. 'It was necessary for him to be disfigured so badly because if his body was found then her disguise would be found out. He needed to be unrecognisable, as it bought her time to carry out the terrible deeds she had been doing.' Rebecca stared coldly, just in front of her but not at anybody in particular. Hannah still wept for her friend into her father's shoulder. Albert took from his pocket, the wristwatch that had belonged to Imelda. He held it up in the air for everybody to see. 'This watch had a diamond encrusted within it. It was clearly an addition after it had been made, which led me to believe Andreas had commissioned a jeweller to do the job. But where would he get such fine jewels? The answer to that question is easy, as we all know he invested heavily in a mining corporation during the eighties. Why he did that I have no idea. It is a risky business, and he had already made his money. Ironically, the venture he had involved himself in to make him more money eventually ended up costing him his fortune. He was penniless, in the monetary sense, which I touched on before, but he had possessions that were worth a fortune. This disreputable woman found out about his stash of diamonds, which he had recovered from the only find the mining corporation achieved. It was then she decided on her quest to find out where he had hidden them, so that she could take them for herself and be made for life.' He walked over to Rebecca. 'It would have meant no more running about after everyone else; no more employment; no more being somebody's servant and cleaning somebody else's house for a wage. You wanted his diamonds and you killed in order to get them. You made the coal shed your hideout while you carried out your attacks around the house and only vacated it once you had filled it with bodies.'

'You think you're so clever don't you?' She sneered at him, in fact Albert backed away slightly, as he thought she was getting ready to spit at him.

'I am certainly cleverer than you are, as I am not the one who has been arrested, and am in fact standing here a free man.' She pulled a face that represented her blasé attitude towards the whole thing. 'I put it to you that you murdered Andreas Krause to get him out of the way so you could do your digging around. And speaking of digging around, when Stefan was uncovering his body, you fired a dart at him through a gap in the coal-shed wall where you were hiding. You missed, but you couldn't risk another shot while Eleanor was stood so close to you. The cause of Andreas' death I do not know, as I have not been told, however, whether you physically attacked him or just poisoned him, the results would be the same. It would evidently look like murder, which of course it was but you didn't want anybody to find that out. Therefore, you decided to hide his body in the dead of night, by digging a hole in the garden and burying him. You knew if you dug it deep enough, in a place where it was already dug over, the addition of the body wouldn't show and nobody would suspect anything. Also, by hiding his body in the garden, it was the first step you took to making it appear as if Stefan was responsible – who else knew their way around the garden as much as the gardener himself did?' Albert paused to give his moustache a quick twirl. 'Only now you had the problem filling the gap you had made. It wasn't viable that you could make out he had gone out and not come back, as why would a recluse who lived his life inside one room, suddenly decide to leave and either purposefully disappear or unintentionally go missing? Additionally, how could you keep up the pretence he was still in the room by continually feeding dinners through the ridiculous cat flap that had been installed on the door. It would be too risky to find times throughout the day to try and collect the multiple dishes that would still have been full of food, and that said nothing of the fact that Stefan used to go in and see Andreas on a regular basis. He would soon notice that his friend was no longer there. Your next alternative I imagine would have been to pretend Andreas was sick and was not eating, as well as not being well enough for visitors. However, it would appear strange that no doctors ever called to see the ill man. Therefore, your only option was to pretend he was still alive. You knew he had some old records of his symphonies that he had kept as mementos of his career and decided to put them to good use. It is immaterial whether or not you had to buy a record player or if there was one already at the house, but either way, you had one installed in his room, and put the records on a continuous loop, which gave off a very realistic impression that he was alive and well. I presume that idea lasted a short while, but at some point the record player stopped working.' Rebecca yawned, and exaggerated it to enhance the point she was growing increasingly more bored with each detail Albert unfolded. Albert, and the rest of the crowd, simply ignored her. 'Now you had a dilemma. What could you do? There was only one other option available to you. It was Hannah who had remarked to me after we had seen the fake Andreas, about his skin having a healthy colour, and not the pale appearance that it should have had for somebody who had been enclosed and out of sunlight for years on end. It was a remarkable observation, and it really set my mind to work. Anybody who had gone in to seem him would not have been any the wiser as to his true identity, or indeed just that it wasn't actually Andreas Krause. Hannah hadn't seen him for years, and her only image of him would have been created from the image stored away from when she was a small child. She would not have necessarily known that it wasn't her grandfather. The same would be true for Johann, if he had been to see him. Eleanor, to this day, still hasn't seen him, and I had never seen him before, and so would be none the wiser as to whether it was the real Andreas or not – it was a point that would not even come into question. Why would you doubt that it wasn't him? The only guest Andreas always had on a regular basis was Stefan, but with his sight and hearing failing him in his elder years, the impostor was safe in the knowledge that nobody in this household would doubt who he was, should any of them see him. And so, it kept up the pretence to allow visitors on an infrequent basis. It was after Hannah had told me what she noticed, I began thinking of the point I had noticed myself about the stooge in the room. I noticed it when I had spoken to him, but I only really thought about it on the night I was shot in the leg by the aforementioned darts. Luckily mine was not laced in poison, and so was only a deterrent for me to keep my nose out. Unfortunately, I am not built that way. I digress. The man, who pretended to be Andreas, had terrible teeth. They were teeth that had discoloured and rotted due to excessive smoking; it was clear that was the cause. The appalling condition of the man's nails also indicated he was a heavy smoker. On the cover of one of the records, my favourite Goldmann and Krause symphony nonetheless, was a picture of the two composers, smiling for the camera while their picture was taken. One of them sat at the piano, arms outstretched, as if about to play it, whereas the other stood behind him, grinning and holding a cigar in his hand. Now, if we revisit the scenario of the broken record player, how else was the impression of constant piano playing supposed to be portrayed?' He looked at his almost stunned audience.

Nobody spoke; everybody listened intently. 'By the actual playing of the piano! Somebody was needed who could play the piano just as skilfully as Andreas. There was only one other person alive who could live up to that task, and that's if he was even still alive himself: Hans Goldmann. Who else knew the famous symphonies back to back? Who wouldn't be recognised after a considerable number of years out of the public eye? Who had terrible teeth?' He paused again, while he stared at everyone in the room directly. 'Hans Goldmann was the man in the room. He had been hired to impersonate Andreas Krause.' Several gasps echoed throughout the room, as everyone, including Albert, looked at Rebecca. She remained still with a blank expression. 'However, you didn't wish to cut him in on the deal, and so at the earliest opportunity you had, you killed him. I found it peculiar how a man who had been stabbed did not make any noise while the steel blade was penetrating through his skin. I had been so stupid, because of course the only reason there could be is if he was already dead before he was stabbed.'

'But how would he have already been dead?'

'A good question Johann, to which I have the answer right here, in my pocket.' Albert delved into his inside blazer pocket and removed a blowpipe and a dart. 'You will no doubt recognise these two items, but I shall describe them to you.' He held up each item in turn. 'This is a hunting blowpipe used by the natives in certain tribes of Asia, and this is a dart that they fire using the pipe, to kill the animals they wish to eat. It kills them by being laced in poison. Allow me to demonstrate.' Albert held the pipe and dart in one hand, while he rummaged in another pocket for a new item. He pulled out a small bottle, which contained a white liquid. 'Tajem is the poison used to kill the prey.' He opened the bottle and dipped in the dart. He left it sitting in the poison while he carried on with his explanation. 'The dart gets laced in poison and then placed into the blowpipe. Usually the pipes are very long, but they do not look out of place in the jungle. Using a long pipe of several feet would of course be too noticeable here in Presberg, which is therefore why I have a shorter one. The dart is then fired at its intended victim and the poison instantly gets to work, killing the victim in minutes.' He placed the dart inside the pipe. 'In my opinion, it's a life for a life. Death is too good for a murderer, but is at least an equivalent fate.' He raised the pipe up to his lips, and pointed it at Rebecca. 'You shot me, it's only fair I shoot you too.' She squinted slightly, cowering at the thought of being shot with the poisoned dart. Albert took in a deep breath, turned away from Rebecca, and fired the dart in another direction.

'Have you gone mad?' The German Sergeant jumped out of his seat and rushed over to aid the person whom Albert had shot.

'Help me! Help me! The antidote isn't here; it's at the dairy!' The dart had pierced through into his shoulder. Thomas had torn it out and was acting hysterically, as he contemplated his imminent death. The rest of the crowd were flabbergasted at the physical display they were watching; it had been unexpected and quite out of character for Albert. He was the calmest of them all, as he firmly spoke:

'You can relax Thomas. You're not going to die; there was no poison on the dart.' Gradually, unsure whether to believe Albert or not, Thomas calmed down. He probably felt he could only truly believe he would survive after the few crucial minutes had passed. Albert resumed his speech to the small throng before him. 'I do a lot of research when it comes to solving crimes, because it is essential to be in the know. You begin clueless and must work out the majority of facts by yourself; everybody is capable of research but only a select few embark on it. When I researched the Tajem poison, it was described as a milky substance. Therefore, does the penny drop for you all listening to me now? How better to disguise a milky substance than in milk itself? Who better to rely on for milk, than of course, the local milkman?' Silence. 'Thomas poisoned the milk, in the bottle with the specifically coloured top, and Rebecca, disguised as Stefan, took it in for Hans Goldmann to consume it. Again, making it look like Stefan was poisoning the milk, as he was the one who always collected it.'

'You mean Rebecca and Thomas were in on it together?'

'Indeed they were Hannah. You see, from Thomas' day-to-day deliveries around the village, he got to know Rebecca quite well, but more importantly, she got to know him. After she had located and installed Hans Goldmann, she desperately sought a way to get rid of him; her greed had overtaken her. When Thomas innocently told her about his Asian wife; Asian customs crept into the discussions and after time conversations deepen, and in their case they darkened too. It was only a matter of time before the topics cropped up regarding Rebecca's plan, and the idea to use Tajem in the milk. It was from there that they became linked by murderous thoughts, and in time led to the actual murders themselves. Their plan was always to frame Stefan. But one man was too clever for both of them: Herbert Lorenz. He had picked up on Stefan's distinctive accent of north-eastern Germany, however when Rebecca, disguised as Stefan visited the shop, although doing a good impression of Stefan's tone, Herbert noticed the dialect difference. Thomas, who had seen Hannah enter the shop with Stefan, decided to go back after hours and end the innocent locksmith's life. Thomas also came in handy on another occasion when unfortunately for them, the coalman made a delivery. Hannah and myself were fortunate to hear the conversation through the open window in Andreas' room. It all seemed harmless enough at the time, but panic stations must have been alarming when the coalman needed access to the coal shed – the place where Stefan's mutilated body was being stored. When Thomas went with the coalman to collect the first bags, Rebecca, disguised as Stefan, must have entered the coal shed to hide Stefan's body so that the coalman was none the wiser. However, just to be sure nothing could come back and interfere with their plans, Thomas decided to end all doubt by slitting the friendly coalman's throat. This is why we were confused at the end part of the conversation. Thomas had said he was going back to the dairy. Then the coalman had asked him what he was doing? This must have been when Thomas raised his hands to around the coalman's neck, and while he innocently answered his question, sunk a blade into his skin and cut his throat deeply, making him unable to shout for help, and knowing he would soon die from the loss of blood that had showered over the insides of the coal shed. This is also why the coalman didn't hand the key to the shed back to Stefan. There was no need. Instead, the footsteps we heard walking away were Rebecca's, who had gone to drive, and likely dump, the coal wagon somewhere.' Thomas had since quietened down and was not squirming around quite as much.

'This is all very fascinating, but it is all merely speculation. You actually need proof and hard evidence in order to obtain a conviction.'

'Thank you Thomas for those words of wisdom; obviously, after all my years on the force, I wouldn't have realised that. But by proof, do you mean the fact that Rebecca is wearing Stefan's clothing, and the antidote to the Tajem, which you have already cried out, is currently at your dairy?' Thomas, yet again, fell silent. Rebecca, however, became more vocal:

'You need more evidence than me in my gardening clothes.'

'They are not your gardening clothes; they belong to Stefan. Do you remember him? He was the one who you brutally murdered. Well, one of the ones who was brutally murdered anyway.'

'I don't know what you're talking about.'

'You can play it the hard way if you like Miss. Sharp, but I'm sure your parents who are sitting over there won't mind testifying against you. You made them believe you were missing, even to as far as waiting for them to issue a statement to the media. Once they had, you locked them away in the attic of this house so that you had a cosy little hideout while you completed your shady business. If it weren't for the fact that I recognised your parent's faces from the television, we wouldn't even be here now. I glimpsed at a headline on a newspaper yesterday on my return train journey from Cologne. It said something about a couple from Düsseldorf who were still missing. Their picture was printed, and that's when things started to really add up. Plus, I had somebody I'd met follow who he thought was Stefan and he contacted me to tell me where he, or rather Rebecca, had gone.'

'If you knew it was them two all along, then why did you have me arrested and put me through that awful ordeal?' Eleanor was angry. She had held her tongue long enough, and now she wanted her answer, the only answer she was due.' Albert turned to her. His face was apologetic; he felt dreadful that he'd had to put her through the stress he had done, but it had been necessary.

'I am deeply sorry Eleanor. At the time, I was so fixated on the word "housekeeper". If the housekeeper was responsible, for a while I obviously did believe that you could be guilty. That's also why I initially told Hannah to wait in the village, but when I realised she was with Johann, I knew she would be safe enough to go back to the house. Also, I didn't wish you to find it suspicious that everyone had vacated the house at the same time, as that would be an unusual occurrence. When I realised that the housekeeper in question was in fact Rebecca, I couldn't divulge that information because there would have been no chance of getting Thomas to come with us. That's also why I waited until the morning to begin my explanation to you all; I knew he would be delivering the milk unaware of what was about to happen. If he saw you had been arrested, he would no doubt have assumed that luckily for him I'd made an awful mistake in my accusations, and he was in the clear. He would gladly come with us knowing he was safe. It was a necessary trick to play on him, and I am truly sorry that I had to involve you in it, especially as you yourself did not know the truth about your false arrest.' She seemed to understand, and Albert hoped that her swift head movement away from him with her nose upturned, meant there were no particularly hard feelings over the situation. The main thing was she wasn't going to be incarcerated for crimes that she didn't commit. Albert turned back to Rebecca. 'And as for more pieces of evidence; I wondered why Stefan stopped shaken my hand, which had become his greeting to me, as we couldn't understandably converse with each other; it was because you had taken his place and didn't know of his little habit. Also, when you took his place after killing him, you began wearing mittens, which I found very strange, as Stefan never had done, but I realise now it was because they disguised your small, delicate, female hands, as opposed to his thick, scratchy, rough ones.'

'It's hardly evidence that will stand up in court is it?'

'No. But perhaps this is. Hannah would you mind?' Hannah got up and walked over to Albert. She took out of her bag, a long sheet of paper and unfolded it for Albert's perusal. 'Have you ever heard of the phrase "to be stabbed in the back", Miss. Sharp?' He chuckled quietly to himself. Rebecca just looked annoyed. 'Of course you do, as you stabbed Hans Goldmann in the back by hiring him and then killing him off before giving him his share of the fortune you hoped to obtain. Goldmann will have known he had been poisoned, as I imagine the effects of the Tajem are not very nice, and that's putting it mildly. However, he will not have known that you were planning to also physically stab him in the back as well, to make it look like it was the knife that killed him. However, he has stabbed you in the back in return.' He held up the long strip of paper for everyone to see. 'This piece of paper was found on the piano. It is the final piece of music that was played by Hans Goldmann, and seems to be a new composition. As the man struggled for his life, while the effects of the poison took their toll on him, he completed the piece of music in a rather bizarre fashion.' He directed his next question to his audience. 'Who here can play the piano?' There was a brief silence until Johann reluctantly put his hand up.

'But not very well; it's been years, and I mean many years, since my father taught me.' Albert smiled.

'I'm sure your skills will be adequate enough for the task I have for you. Please, accompany me over to that piano.' Johann followed Albert. The composer's son sat on the stool, while the retired detective stood up and leant against the large instrument. Albert positioned the music on the music rest. 'Play it.'

'What, all of it?'

'Of course; we need to get a feel for it.' Johann played. He played like he owed it to his father. It hadn't been the best relationship, but they had spared a special bond for the first few years of his childhood. The composition was almost idyllic; the people in the room nearly forgot that they were coming to the end of a murder investigation. The chords that sounded from the keyboard were played at an allegretto tempo, and encompassed notes from a variety of different octaves. The listeners engaged with the beautiful sound that Johann was producing, until he got to the end. As he played the final melodic arpeggios, he ended by prodding five individual staccatos with one finger. They sounded out of tune and out of place. Why had Goldmann ended such a marvellous piece of music with such an infantile, lazy, tuneless finale? It certainly didn't send a shiver down the spine like all great, iconic music should. Johann looked up at Albert once he had finished.

'That's it.'

'Just play those last few notes again, if you wouldn't mind.' Johann turned back to the piano and prodded the same unsystematic five notes that had been randomly included in the music. 'You see everybody, the scruffy conclusion to this composition stuck out most astonishingly to Hannah. This was before she was attacked and imprisoned in the coal shed. There is a line on the page, where the pen had fallen out of Hans Goldmann's hand while he was still writing, or what was more likely; his hand had fallen away from the page, as that was the moment that signified his death. In a hurry, he had grabbed his pen and written in these indiscriminate notes. The pen on the floor contained the same colour ink that was written on the paper. Johann – you can read music. What notes are they?' Johann stared at the sheet of music and read them out one by one:

'B, E, C, C, A.'

'And what is that hash symbol that is attached to the last letter?'

'It's called a sharp. It's where you play the black note next to the letter A, which raises the pitch of the note by a semitone.'

'Read out the notes again please, including the hash symbol.' Johann obliged.

'B, E, C, C, A-sharp.' He paused. 'Becca Sharp.' He paused again. 'Rebecca Sharp.' Albert smiled.

'Precisely.' He looked around the room at the astonished faces that stared back at him. 'He couldn't simply write her name, as she would likely have found it and done away with the evidence, so nobody would be any the wiser. By incorporating her name into his music, he was able to leave a vital clue that would enable us to identify his killer.' The German Sergeant, who had remained quiet for the majority of the explaining, had a question of his own:

'Where is the stash of diamonds that you say this pair were after?'

'A good question Sergeant; I'm glad you've woken back up.' Albert took a key from his trouser pocket. 'This key will lead us to the box that stores the diamonds.'

'And where is this box?' Johann took from his own pocket a black box, which he handed to Albert.

'It's here.'

'Thank you Johann.' He addressed the gathering once again. 'There were many clues to the location of this box, but none that stood out as completely obvious. You could look high and low for it, but unless you were looking high, you would have no chance of success. When I was churning over all the little things that people had said to me, perhaps innocently, perhaps not; I came to organise each thing in my head, and soon enough they began to form an order. Hans Goldmann had said to me a sentence that was very crucial. He told me that for a lot of things we wish to know in life, people usually find they are waiting in vain.' He looked around the room. 'He couldn't have been more precise with what he said. However, whereas my mind naturally recognised the phrase "waiting in vain", he had meant it another way. He had actually meant waiting in vane, as in weathervane. And that's when it hit me: the golden weathervane on the top of the house was the newest addition to the property; I had noticed that pretty much as soon as I arrived there. Owing to the fact that a long time ago, Andreas had worked as a steeplejack, it did not take long to put two and two together and realise that his fortune was at the top of his custom-made steeple, in an inconspicuous black box, which his beloved weathervane perched upon. I had already seen Thomas on the roof of the house, supposedly mending a tile, although I did wonder why he was the only milkman I knew that got about as much as he did. He delivered the milk, made foodstuffs at the dairy, drove constantly around the village and the neighbouring towns, helped carry the coal bags around the back of the house, and he also helped to repair broken tiles. He was doing no such thing; the only job he had in hand, was finding the box with diamonds in, and he was on the right track. I got the police to fetch this down for me only yesterday.' Albert put the key into the box and turned it. The lid clicked open and Albert lifted it all the way over. Inside it was a small, red, woollen bag with green twine tied together to form the handles. He pulled on one of the strands and the top of the bag easily came open. The people in the room straightened their backs and stuck out their necks to try and get the first look at the contents. The German Sergeant decided to handcuff Thomas to the radiator and left his prisoner to get a closer look for himself. Albert tipped the bag upside down and a small cluster of bright, sparkling diamonds tumbled into the palm of his hand. They clinked together as they fell and glittered in the light that was available. Everybody gasped. Nobody could quite believe they even existed; they would be worth a fortune. 'These, I suspect, are the reason that the Goldmann and Krause partnership broke up. I imagine Andreas became very greedy, and decided to keep them for his self. With no idea where to look for them, Goldmann would have become very bitter over his loss, or if he didn't actually know they'd had a valuable find, the partnership may have broken down because Goldmann just couldn't believe his expensive investment had amounted to nothing.' Rebecca had a stony expression, whereas Thomas looked defeated. Rebecca's parents still huddled together, and Albert wasn't entirely sure whether they had even understood a word he had said. Hannah still wept for her grandfather, but more so for Stefan, whom she felt particularly aggrieved about. Johann had since returned to hug his daughter, whereas Eleanor sat alone, although no longer angry at her part she had been forced to play in the capturing of the criminals. Rebecca and Thomas were both led out of the room and bundled into the police cars to take them to prison.

The German Sergeant slapped Albert on the back, and nodded acceptingly towards him.

'Not bad.' Albert smiled at him.

'Not bad for an English worm, you mean?' For the first time since they had met, Albert saw the Sergeant smile too, which he secretly chortled to himself, was likely a greater breakthrough than the finding of the diamonds.

20

The following day, Albert and Hannah made the trip to Cologne. She still had no idea that Imelda was in fact still alive. He had conned her into accompanying him by saying that he'd always wished to visit that part of Germany. As he'd had essentially no time to appreciate it when he saw it two days ago, it would likely be his only other chance to see it before he returned back to England. The two friends sat on the train, now talking, but merely enjoying each other's company. They had grown very close to one another in such a short space of time and under horrendous circumstances; yet, the bond that they had formed they knew would never die. The train soon pulled in at the junction they required, and Albert steered Hannah in the direction of Sülzburgstrasse. They passed the decorative chocolate shop on the way, and seeing as Albert had forgotten to pop in for a purchase, he made a point of stocking his pockets full with various chocolate treats. Scoffing a chocolate-covered marzipan each, they left the shop.

'Albert?'

'Yes Hannah?' She looked up at him.

'Why did Hans Goldmann give me the diary and the watch? He would have known it would help me.'

'The only reason I can think of is that he wanted to get even with Andreas over the whole diamond situation, but when he saw you, probably upset, and desperate to find out the truth, it's likely his conscience got the better of him.'

'There must have been another reason why he ended up dead; was it to do with him helping me? It can't just have been about Rebecca's greed.'

'I remember that when I was in the room with Hans, although at the time I believed him to be Andreas; Stefan came in the room, which must have been Rebecca in disguise.' Albert paused to steady his head; it was so confusing for him to keep up with all the different names. 'Unfortunately, I think I carried on our conversation slightly too soon. Rebecca was still in the room but because I thought it was Stefan, I didn't think he would understand what I was saying. I asked Hans how he had killed Imelda, and that was probably when Rebecca knew it was time for him to die.' Hannah paused before speaking again:

'Thank you for doing everything you've done here; it means a lot. I honestly can't thank you enough.'

'It's not a problem. We still have some time left you know.'

'What I mean to say is; I know it was difficult to find out about my grandmother. But I know you've tried your best and I'm not annoyed that we didn't manage to find out for definite.'

'As I said, we still have some time left.' Hannah laughed.

'I hardly think a gourmet chocolate shop is going to provide us with any answers!'

'It provided me with one; I love German chocolate. The creations they have are unique and it tastes delicious!'

'What else do you want to see before we go back to the airport?'

'The only thing I want to do is see a private art gallery. It's not far from here – actually it's number twenty-one on this street.' Hannah looked around at the door numbers and saw the building that displayed the word "Tierarztpraxis".

'Well we're nearly there. That veterinary practice is number nineteen.' Albert looked to where she had pointed.

'So it is! It's a good job you're here with me otherwise I'd be walking around in circles for hours!' They reached the number of the place they were searching for and Albert purposely stood in front of the buzzer where Imelda's name was displayed. 'Before we go in, seeing as you just mentioned your grandmother, what would have been the news you'd hoped to hear about her?'

'I've always hoped that she'd died peacefully. Just in her sleep or something like that. I'd rather she'd died of natural causes instead of being murdered.' Albert smiled.

'I actually wasn't honest with you before because I didn't want to upset you, but I did find out something about her death.' He pressed the button, which sounded loudly.

'Well I'd like to know if it's all the same to you.'

'I'm afraid she didn't die of natural causes.' Hannah's face dropped, as she stared at the ground.

'I guess that was the most likely outcome anyway. How did you find out?'

'I asked somebody who would know, that's all. But don't be too downhearted because your grandmother wasn't murdered either.'

'Did she kill herself?'

'No! Stop jumping to conclusions.' Hannah's face perked up slightly.

'Really? Well that's better news! So how did she die? And who did you ask?'

'The same person you're going to ask. That's why we're really here. There's no private art gallery up these stairs; we're here so you can find out everything you want to know about your grandmother.'

'But who would know so much about her?' The chain on the door rattled from inside.

'The very kind lady behind this door; she'll be happy to see you. If there's anything she doesn't know about your grandmother, I'd be very surprised.'

'Why do you say that?' The door opened, and the elderly woman that was Imelda, stood before them. In a kind, welcoming tone, she spoke:

'Hello.' Her smile was kindly, and a tear rolled down her face.

'Hannah, this is Mrs. Reinwald.'

'Oh, are you Misty's sister?'

'No, my darling, I'm not.'

'Hannah, this is Mrs. Imelda Reinwald – your grandmother.' Hannah took a step backwards.

'I beg your pardon?' More tears rolled down Imelda's cheek. She was too happy to speak; she just smiled and cried. She couldn't even bring herself to wipe her tears away.

'She didn't die Hannah; she's here, alive and well, and can't wait to meet her granddaughter.' Hannah looked at the woman standing in the hallway. She was sceptical, but she didn't disbelieve Albert. She knew he would be sure about it otherwise he wouldn't have gone to these lengths.

'Oma?' Imelda couldn't stop her tears, as she nodded slowly and then frantically, in answer to Hannah's query. She snivelled and fought her tears to speak:

'I've waited a long time to hear that word.' The old woman felt broken, as the pain of all the nineteen missed years came flooding back to her. How hard it had been to discover she had a granddaughter only forty-eight hours ago, and now the beautiful young girl stood before her. She raised her arms, and Hannah needed no more indication. She flew at her grandmother, whom she had loved since the very first moment she had learnt how to, and melted into her outstretched arms. They hugged each other tightly, pressing hard against one another, making sure that neither of them was encountering a cruel hallucination. In fact, after several minutes, it was Albert who had to push them both inside so he could shut the door on the outside world.

Albert sat in an armchair with his glass of water, having carefully remembered not to accept a cup of tea. There was a traditional German delicacy on the coffee table, which he had been told was "Handkäse mit Musik", although he didn't partake, as he had been warned the taste of the sour milk cheese together with the chopped onions was pretty ghastly. Hannah and Imelda sat arm in arm on the sofa, hardly able to take their eyes of each other.

'For nineteen years I thought you were dead.'

'For nineteen years I didn't even know you existed.'

'It was Hannah who set herself the goal of finding out the truth about your death, or not, as it has turned out to be.'

'Albert, I really can't thank you enough.'

'The joy you are both bringing each other is the only thing I need to see to make it all worthwhile. I'm just happy I could make this happen, but as I said, without Hannah's determination, it probably wouldn't have done.'

'Well I'm just so glad I have my granddaughter now. I'll be indebted to you forever, Mr. Murtland.'

'But what about my grandfather's diary; it says he killed you?'

'No, my darling, you have misunderstood the diary entry completely.'

'But he cheated on you too!' Imelda shook her head.

'No. The affair he referred to was his business affair – the mining corporation. After it went bankrupt, the financial strain it put on us, greatly affected our relationship. When he said I was his rock, he meant none of the diamonds meant anything to him compared to what I did. But it was too late by then, you see, I was the one who had an affair. I ended up marrying him – a man called William; he was Stefan's brother.' Albert chirped in:

'And the man who followed Rebecca, disguised as Stefan, on that night I got back late to the house.' Hannah tried to work things out in her head:

'So I suppose the hands of time that will haunt him forever, would be your watch that he kept and had a small diamond encrusted into it?' Imelda nodded.

'Exactly. When he wrote he'd killed his wife; he wasn't lying. He had killed his wife, because he had driven me away and I left him, but he hadn't actually killed me, as a person.' The two women, who were generations apart from each other, sat staring at each other once again. Albert got up from his seat.

'I'm afraid I must be making my move. My flight is in a few hours and I'll need to make my way back to the airport.' Hannah jumped up.

'I forgot about that! I'll come with you.' Albert smiled. It was his warm, kindly smile, which wasn't easy for just anybody to bring out of him.

'No. You two have lost enough time already. I'm quite sure I can find my way back to the airport by myself.' Hannah threw her arms around the great man, in much the same way as she had greeted Imelda. It was clear that even after such a short space of time, she loved him so dearly. What he stood for were all the attributes that were now rare to find amongst her younger generation. He was humble and kind; humorous and a gentleman; caring, determined, and honourable. She hoped she would see him again; she wanted that more than anything. But if the recent experiences had taught her anything, she knew that life was unpredictable, although nothing would stop her from hoping. Afterall, without hope, a person had nothing. Hannah kissed her friend tenderly on the cheek, and then backed away from their embrace. Albert shook hand s with Imelda, who gripped his hand tightly, the tremendous force with which she squeezed, symbolised the appreciation that she had for him. He walked to the door, and with one last look and another kindly smile, he placed his hat on his head, tipped it towards them, and left.

The retired detective approached Neumarkt for the final time. He walked into the shelter next to the tram stop and patiently waited for his train. He had to return to the house to collect his bags, say farewell to both Johann and Eleanor, and then travel to the airport for his flight home. He wished he could see William one final time just to thank him for all his help, but being a hobo, he could quite literally be anywhere. He glanced around at his surroundings. The people that bustled back and to in crowds carried on with their everyday lives, unaware of the traumas that some people had to endure on a daily basis. As he looked around, two flashes of red light gently dazzled him. He was amazed how he hadn't seen it on entering the tram shelter. A package rested on the other end of the long bench that Albert sat on. It was long and thin, and was wrapped up in brown paper. Positioned on top of the parcel, was a familiar pair of glasses, black, with two red rims, one above each lens. Albert was confused. He sidled over to the two items and picked the glasses up. They were definitely the spectacles he had bought for William; it was too coincidental for them not to be. He got up and took a closer look around. He called out:

'William? William?' There was no reply, and the man he shouted for did not materialise from anywhere. He felt downhearted, but he saw his mode of transport arriving in the distance, and so he picked up the brown package and waited to get on board.

The tram was comparatively empty, and so he picked a window seat, which looked out onto the row of shops opposite the shelter. As the tram pulled away from the junction, Albert looked out of the window. A familiar tattered man, wearing blue clothing, stood a few windows down, right next to the tramline. Albert waved, but a conductor asked to see his ticket. When he looked back, William had gone.

The only hand luggage Albert had taken onto the plane was the package left for him at the tram shelter. When they had taken off and were steadily on their way, he decided to open it. The concealed item felt hard and thin, and he was bemused, as to what the parcel may contain. He peeled off the paper and held the contents on his lap. It was part of a number plate from an old vehicle. It had been cracked at the end and was covered in scuffs and small splits all over. Because of the complete break at the far right part of the plate, it meant the whole registration number wasn't visible, but the most part was. Albert looked at it: "N946 PK". He wondered why the number plate was significant that William had wanted him to have it. Perhaps it was just another one of his little quirks like when he had declared Johann's name to be Jürgen, which can only have been because he didn't wish to be tested to make sure he was telling the truth. Albert chuckled to himself, and tucked the number plate in the holder on the back of the seat in front of him. He closed his eyes to have "forty-winks". It wasn't long however, before his eyes shot back open, and his mind was working overtime. He thought back through all the years of number plates that had gone by. An "N-registration" would have been manufactured in the year 1995. That was nineteen years ago. It was also the year that Hannah would have been born. But, more prominently than that, it was the year that his wife Elizabeth had been killed. What was going on? Was this, after all these years, however it had come about, finally a clue towards solving his wife's murder? He greatly hoped so. His life's ambition was to solve that one crime, which was so personal to his heart. He felt warm and sick; he was angry, and yet hopeful. No longer calm, but with a newfound optimism that he would one day achieve his goal, he pulled the number plate out of the holder and grasped it with both hands. It seemed he was experiencing a crescendo of his own.

THE-END

Lightning Source UK Ltd.
Milton Keynes UK
UKOW04f2328110116

266228UK00001B/12/P